PRAISE FOR THE DCI RYAN MYSTERIES

What newspapers say

"She keeps company with the best mystery writers" – *The Times*

"LJ Ross is the queen of Kindle" – *Sunday Telegraph*

"*Holy Island* is a blockbuster" – *Daily Express*

"A literary phenomenon" – *Evening Chronicle*

"A pacey, enthralling read" – *Independent*

What readers say

"I couldn't put it down. I think the full series will cause a divorce, but it will be worth it."

"I gave this book 5 stars because there's no option for 100."

"Thank you, LJ Ross, for the best two hours of my life."

"This book has more twists than a demented corkscrew."

"Another masterpiece in the series. The DCI Ryan mysteries are superb, with very realistic characters and wonderful plots. They are a joy to read!"

Also by LJ Ross

THE DCI RYAN MYSTERIES

1. Holy Island
2. Sycamore Gap
3. Heavenfield
4. Angel
5. High Force
6. Cragside
7. Dark Skies
8. Seven Bridges
9. The Hermitage
10. Longstone
11. The Infirmary (Prequel)
12. The Moor
13. Penshaw
14. Borderlands
15. Ryan's Christmas
16. The Shrine
17. Cuthbert's Way
18. The Rock
19. Bamburgh
20. Lady's Well
21. Death Rocks
22. Poison Garden
23. Belsay
24. Berwick

THE ALEXANDER GREGORY THRILLERS

1. Impostor
2. Hysteria
3. Bedlam
4. Mania
5. Panic
6. Amnesia
7. Obsession

THE SUMMER SUSPENSE MYSTERIES

1. The Cove
2. The Creek
3. The Bay
4. The Haven

THE ROCK

A DCI RYAN MYSTERY

THE ROCK

A DCI RYAN MYSTERY

LJ ROSS

PENGUIN BOOKS

PENGUIN BOOKS

UK | USA | Canada | Ireland | Australia
India | New Zealand | South Africa

Penguin Books is part of the Penguin Random House group of companies
whose addresses can be found at global.penguinrandomhouse.com

Penguin Random House UK,
One Embassy Gardens, 8 Viaduct Gardens, London SW11 7BW

penguin.co.uk

First published by LJ Ross 2021
Published in Penguin Books 2026
001

Copyright © LJ Ross, 2021

The moral right of the author has been asserted

Penguin Random House values and supports copyright. Copyright fuels creativity, encourages diverse voices, promotes freedom of expression and supports a vibrant culture. Thank you for purchasing an authorised edition of this book and for respecting intellectual property laws by not reproducing, scanning or distributing any part of it by any means without permission. You are supporting authors and enabling Penguin Random House to continue to publish books for everyone. No part of this book may be used or reproduced in any manner for the purpose of training artificial intelligence technologies or systems. In accordance with Article 4(3) of the DSM Directive 2019/790, Penguin Random House expressly reserves this work from the text and data mining exception.

Cover artwork and map by Andrew Davidson
Cover layout by Riverside Publishing Solutions Limited

Set in 12.25/16.5pt Minion Pro
Typeset by Riverside Publishing Solutions Limited

Printed and bound in Great Britain by Clays Ltd, Elcograf S.p.A.

The authorised representative in the EEA is Penguin Random House Ireland,
Morrison Chambers, 32 Nassau Street, Dublin D02 YH68

A CIP catalogue record for this book is available from the British Library

ISBN: 978–1–804–96032–5

Penguin Random House is committed to a sustainable future
for our business, our readers and our planet. This book is made
from Forest Stewardship Council® certified paper.

This book contains some hard, but important, themes.
It is therefore dedicated to all who have the bravery
to question themselves and the world around them.

To all the 'Ryans' and 'MacKenzies' out there:
it is thanks to you that we strive for better.

"There is something in the human spirit that will survive and prevail; there is a tiny and brilliant light burning in the heart of man that will not go out, no matter how dark the world becomes."

—Leo Tolstoy

CHAPTER 1

Saturday 13th February
The North Sea, 03:17hrs

Mick Donnelly could think of better ways to spend his time.

After a plate of steak and chips down at Billy's Chophouse, he might've lined up a couple of pretty lasses and spent a few pleasurable hours letting them tend to his every need—for a price, of course.

Nothing in this world came for free.

Then, after a suitable interval, he might've treated himself to a few beers and a few lines of coke with the lads—although, he was trying to cut back on the snow, after that last nosebleed. Weakness wasn't a good look, in his line of work, and it could give people the wrong impression. They might start to *think*, and they weren't getting paid to think.

That was his job.

Fixer. Courier. Postman. Whatever they wanted to call him, so long as they paid him half up-front, and half on delivery.

The fishing vessel lurched ominously to one side as another wave crashed against its bow, and Mick's hands gripped the boat's wheel tightly as he fought to regain control. His square, weather-beaten jaw was set into hard lines as he steered the boat resolutely through treacherous North Sea waters, determined to reach the drop-off point before sunrise.

"*Mick!*"

The cabin door flew open to reveal a young man of twenty or so, his shaven head slick with water which ran in rivulets down his pasty skin, dripping into eyes that were wild with fear.

"Mick!"

"Shut the bloody door!" he roared, over the sound of the wind and sea which howled like a banshee around their heads.

"Why aren't you lookin' after the cargo?" Mick demanded.

The man they called 'Noddy' shoved the door closed, then shivered and dripped his way into the small cabin. Outside, there was a fathomless expanse of ice-cold water from which he would never survive, if anything was to happen while they completed the last leg of their journey, and the enormity of it all weighed heavily on his skinny, pimpled shoulders.

"Well? Howay, man! Spit it out!"

Mick narrowed his eyes against the torrent, watching all the time for the first, tiny lights that would signal they were drawing near to land.

"It's not good," Noddy said, shifting from one foot to the other, feeling his stomach roll as the boat tipped back and forth. "Gaz says we're takin' on too much water—"

Mick spun around at that.

"*What*? What the bloody hell d'you mean? How *much* water?"

"I—I dunno, but it's a lot! Gaz is workin' the pump, but he can't shift it fast enough!"

Mick turned back to the wheel, thinking fast. If the boat was taking on that much water, it wouldn't last much longer in a storm like this one—especially without the benefit of the emergency life-saving facilities most vessels came equipped with, or the support of Her Majesty's Coastguard. By his calculation, they were still a good hour away from the Port of Tyne…if they made it that far.

"What'll I tell Gaz?"

"Shut yer gob and let me think," Mick growled.

Noddy hugged himself and stared out of the old, cracked windows. He didn't know which was worse:

seeing the terrifying vastness of the dark ocean, or merely imagining it from below deck, surrounded by the crashing of the waves from all sides and the putrid stench of their cargo.

"Can't we use the radio?" he asked.

"Don't be bloody daft," Mick snapped, and then swore volubly. "Just bugger off back to the hold and stay there."

Noddy knew better than to question an order, and hurried off, skidding and swaying as he made for the cargo hold, head-bent against the Arctic wind.

Left alone again, Mick swiped a hand over his face, amazed to find he was sweating despite the frigid temperature.

"Come on," he muttered to himself. "Think, man. *Think*."

Just then, he caught sight of a tiny flicker on the horizon—no more than a pinprick, winking against the midnight sky. He peered through the rain and sea spray that crashed against the flimsy marine glass, rattling its rusty frame.

Land.

There were only a few lighthouses that remained fully operational on the North East coastline. Given their position, he guessed the light he could see was coming from Roker, fifteen-odd miles south of the city of Newcastle upon Tyne. It wasn't ideal, and he'd need to make a call to arrange a new collection point, but it was better than the alternative.

Grinning fiercely, Mick began turning the wheel hard to port.

In the bowels of the fishing boat, Lawana tried once again to break free from the handcuffs which held her captive, forcing her skin through the metal as far as she could, uncaring of the blood and broken flesh. Meanwhile, icy water continued to seep through the cracks in the wall, forming a puddle around her feet.

"*Mae!*"

Panting, she looked across the room to where her daughter, Achara, was similarly chained, her body lying limply against the wall as she wept and cried for her mother. The fight had gone out of her, along with every ounce of the meagre energy she'd had to spare.

"*Poom jai, Achara!*"

She called back to her daughter and other female voices joined in, their sound a terrible, desperate cacophony. Around them, the air was heavy with a foul mixture of faeces and vomit, their bodies having rejected the nauseating rhythm of the boat and the toxic cocktail of drugs and bad food they'd been fed over the past week or more.

Where was the boy?

The young one, with the shaven head?

He was cruel, and there was a look in his small, piggish eyes that spoke of more cruelty lying dormant within his wasted heart, but it worried her that he'd left them.

To go where?

Had he left them to drown?

Lawana might have wept, but her tears had been spent long ago. Her mind was numb with pain and fatigue, her body frozen by fear, but she began to sing a Thai lullaby in as loud a voice as she could muster:

Hear the song of the

Wind in the trees,

Singing softly through the leaves.

Blowing from far, so far away.

Bringing to a wee one

Luck, they say.

Listen to the breeze…

She broke off as the door above them opened again and rain and seawater poured into the hold. Blinking the water from her eyes, Lawana saw a man's silhouette against the dim light of the cabin at his back, and heard him shout something to the other one they called, 'Gaz'.

Relief blossomed into hate, then unmitigated joy as she watched him take his first step down the ladder, then lose his footing and fall into the shallow, festering water. Through the darkness she waited, hoping he would not raise himself up, knowing she would have held him down until his lungs filled.

But, when she heard his gangly arms and legs thrash, and then the pitiful sound of him emptying his belly, she knew that he lived.

At least, for now.

Lawana didn't know how much time passed before the crash came.

Since she and Achara had taken their first, fateful steps onto the van in Chiang Mai, they'd lost all real sense of time, but it might have been twenty or thirty minutes after Noddy re-entered the hold when there came the splintering sound of wood against rock. The boat lurched, tipping upward, where it was suspended for a second or two before crashing down again, at the mercy of the sea which rushed through a gaping hole in its starboard bow.

The women screamed as their bodies were thrown forward, then back against the hard wooden walls of the hold, wrists in agony as the handcuffs held them tightly against the opposite force of the impact.

"*Mae! Mae!*"

Lawana thought she heard her daughter's voice, and struggled again to free herself, prepared to break her own bones to reach the girl she'd borne and for whom she'd wanted a better life.

"*Achara!*"

The water level was rising fast now, and she saw the young man *Nodi* scurry towards the ladder to save himself, like a rat. He didn't make it far, for the hold door was thrust open again and the devil they called *Pos'man* appeared, pushing the other back down before jumping into the water himself. He pointed towards the women and drew out a set of keys, throwing them at the younger man, who moved quickly to unlock their restraints while the other waited, counting them like cattle.

Soon, the third man came, and Lawana watched them as the sea rose higher, until she could no longer feel her body and her chest felt so tight, she could barely breathe.

Her eyes darted between them, knowing this would be her only chance.

Finally, *Nodi* reached her, his thick hands fumbling with the lock at her wrist while he spoke cowardly obscenities she did not understand. She smelled his fear and felt stronger, even on the precipice of death, and watched the whites of his eyes while the sea surrounded them. Eventually her hand fell from the wall to slap against the water, and he might have moved on to the next woman, but she rose with a strength she didn't know she had, teeth bared, fingers curled into claws.

Taken by surprise, Noddy fell back, and his face was submerged. For a beautiful, blissful moment, she threw herself on top of him, fighting his flailing arms to hold him beneath the water, before a strong hand grasped a fistful of hair and yanked her away.

"Bitch," Gaz growled, and raised his other hand to exact revenge.

"Get her off the bloody boat!" Mick shouted. "There's no time!"

Lawana was propelled towards the ladder to join the others, who scrambled upward as best they could, hurrying to abandon the boat before it sank into the murky depths of the sea to join the other skeleton ships that lay like sentinels on the ocean's bed.

Frantically, her eyes searched, but there was no sign of Achara.

"Achara!"

A fresh hell awaited her on deck, where the boat tipped and swayed perilously on its rocky pivot, scattering the women towards the gunwale and over it, into the sea. Lawana threw out her good arm and grasped a rough length of rope while she continued to search for Achara in the surrounding darkness, muscles screaming, begging her to let go and surrender. Beyond the wreckage, she saw nothing except the looming outline of an enormous rock rising up from the sea, its walls obliterating the lights lining the nearby shore like a dark reaper, come to claim their souls. She heard nothing but the waves and her own screams, felt nothing but her own grief.

But there was more to come.

The same thick, workmanlike hand covered her own and began to prise her fingers from the rope, and she let out a helpless sob as her body slid towards the edge of the rocking boat, like a ragdoll. Noddy followed, and she thought she heard him laugh; high-pitched and maniacal. Then, he was dragging her upward, turning her to face the water.

"Swim," he spat, and planted his boot in her back to send her sprawling over the edge of the boat, down and down, into deep, dark oblivion.

Only those with the will to survive were able to cover the short distance from the wreckage to the shoreline, which was little more than a thin sliver of pebble beach against the cliffs. Though the tide was beginning to recede, even in the shallows the current remained strong, and the rain drove down upon their exhausted bodies from all sides.

Achara collapsed against the sand, her body shaking uncontrollably in a mixture of shock, cold and withdrawal, her fingers gripping the earth to anchor herself there while her body heaved and spluttered. Dimly, she heard voices carrying on the wind, and she curled into a foetal position, closing her eyes while the rain fell against her broken body.

"There's one o'er here!"

Her fingers left drag marks against the sand as she was hoisted up again, her legs barely able to support her weight as the man pushed her towards the small corral of women who had been rounded up, under the watchful eye of *Pos'man*.

"That's eighteen," he growled, as Achara stumbled to the sand at his feet. "We're still missing two."

"Startin' to lighten up a bit, now," Gaz warned him. "We need to move."

Though she couldn't understand the words, Achara followed his line of sight across the water to the far horizon, which was beginning to shift from midnight blue to dark purple, as the sun began its slow ascent once more. She cast her eyes around the other women, scrubbing the salty water from her eyes to search their faces for the one she loved.

But her mother was not there.

"*Mae*," she whispered, finding her voice croaky and hoarse. "Mae!"

"Shut it," Noddy said, and gave her a hard, back-handed slap which sent her weakened body sprawling against the sand.

"Oi! Watch it, y' stupid git," Mick told him, without much rancour. "Remember, he doesn't want any of them marked."

Noddy laughed.

"Fat chance of that, after what we've just been through," he said. "They'll be fit for nowt—"

"Not everybody's as fussy as you," Gaz said, and the three men laughed.

"That'll be Callum," Mick said, pointing towards a flashing light further along the beach. "The Cavalry's arrived, lads."

"What about the other two?" Noddy asked.

Mick scanned the shadows of the beach once more, then looked back at the rock rising up from the water, where he'd once played as a child. Back then, there'd been an arch connecting the rock and a smaller stack of limestone, but it had crumbled away in the intervening years, leaving only the tall, rugged outcrop against which their boat had met its end.

Maybe the boat wasn't the only thing to have perished.

"Collateral damage," he said simply, and reached down to grasp one of the women's thin arms. "Howay, let's go."

CHAPTER 2

Elsdon, Northumberland

Forty miles northwest of where The Postman herded his living cargo along the beach and into a waiting van, Detective Chief Inspector Maxwell Finley-Ryan watched the rain patter against the skylight in his bedroom, unable to sleep.

That wasn't unusual; over the course of his life, Ryan had suffered with bouts of insomnia—which was hardly surprising, given the unique nature of his chosen profession. Investigating the most serious of crimes that one human being could inflict upon another, and witnessing the waste and destruction of its aftermath, was not often conducive to eight hours' uninterrupted sleep. Throw in a new baby with nocturnal tendencies, and he might as well give up altogether.

As if on cue, he heard the rustle of the baby stirring on the monitor, and he was already preparing to slink out of bed to intercept any bellowing cries when his wife's sleepy voice stopped him.

"I don't mind going," Anna said, and gave a jaw-cracking yawn. "You haven't been getting much rest, lately."

Ryan heard the note of concern, and brushed his lips over hers.

"I'm fine," he said, with admirable cheer, given the ungodly hour. "Try to get a bit more sleep."

Anna's brow furrowed, but her eyelids had already begun to droop.

"Okay," she murmured. "Love you."

Ryan smiled for a moment in the inky twilight, watching the way the moonlight fell across her face, and then grinned as he heard his daughter's indignant cry, louder than before.

"I'm a slave to these two," he muttered.

Unfolding his long body from its warm cocoon, Ryan shoved a tired hand through his dark hair, tugged on a pair of pyjama bottoms and padded across the hall to greet Her Ladyship.

"What time d'you call this?"

As always, he experienced a fierce surge of love. Emma was wide awake, standing up inside her cot with arms extended, ready to be set loose upon the world.

"I suppose it's not *that* early," he relented, and lifted her up into his arms, nestling her small body against his chest, breathing in her baby smell. "Let's go and have some breakfast."

Emma made a gurgling sound of agreement, and then sank her new teeth into his bare shoulder.

"*Fu*—fiddlesticks!" Ryan amended swiftly, and thought he heard his wife's laughter wafting through from the next room. "No biting daddy. Or mummy. Or anyone, for that matter. In fact, don't bite any*thing*, unless it's food…"

He began to head downstairs, while his daughter giggled.

"This is no laughing matter," Ryan said, conversationally. "For all I know, I might need to get a tetanus shot. You're practically feral."

Emma gave him another drooling smile, and watched from her highchair while Ryan made up a bottle of warm milk and some gloopy porridge.

As their eyes met across the kitchen, Ryan was struck forcibly by a new and certain knowledge; something that had skirted around the edges of his mind for the past two months and, perhaps, even before then. Looking into her beautiful face, so full of love and trust, he knew that he couldn't continue to do a job that would put his family in danger. Too often, his work had been responsible for bringing evil to their door. Too many times, he might have lost everything that was important to him in the world.

And, for what?

Justice for the dead, his mind whispered. *To make the world a safer place for others.*

Ryan shook his head and sat down to feed her while the world slowly awakened.

"Luck doesn't last forever," he whispered, brushing a gentle hand over his daughter's head. "What would I do, if something happened to you, hmm?"

A battle waged in his heart, between fulfilling his vocation in life, the work some would say he'd been born to do, and the family he loved.

"There are other vocations," he told Emma, as she looked up into his turbulent silver-blue eyes. "Higher callings."

Ryan glanced out of the window and across the Northumbrian hills, watching the skies melt from deepest navy to purple and mauve. Somewhere out there, he knew another parent might be suffering the pain of loss; the impotent rage of having that which was most precious to them snatched away.

You can help them, his mind whispered again. *You can avenge their loss.*

He closed his eyes for a moment and saw their faces swimming before him, the dead whose lives had been stolen before their time. He saw their killers' faces, too;

could picture the bright, ice-blue stare of Keir Edwards—*The Hacker*—as he'd wrapped his fingers around the man's throat, and the contemptuous sneer as he'd stepped back again, unwilling to sacrifice his own soul for the sake of vengeance. Pulling the weeds of humanity had given him a sense of purpose, something he'd always lacked in his youth, and the thought that there would be one less degenerate roaming the streets had made every risk worth taking.

But was it time to hand over that responsibility to others, equally as capable? Any one of his friends and colleagues at Northumbria CID could continue their work without him, and perhaps he'd sleep better at night without the addition of any more nightmarish faces to haunt him in the wee, small hours.

Maybe it was time for a *normal* life, whatever that meant.

A nice, ordinary nine-to-five job, with a bit of work-life balance. No pressure, no stress, just an easy, clock-in, clock-out type of existence leaving plenty of time and energy to spare.

Except, he couldn't quite imagine it—wouldn't even know where to start.

While Emma finished the milk in her sippy-cup, Ryan sat there for a while longer with these troubling thoughts circling his mind, and wondered whether the world would send him a sign.

If only he believed in signs.

CHAPTER 3

Marsden Bay
Sunrise, Saturday 13th February

Marsden was beautiful in the early morning light.

Over the centuries, the North Sea's relentless tide had fashioned the limestone cliffs into a bay and grotto, with stacks and caves that had provided shelter to smugglers and entertainment to local children, not to mention a picturesque tableau for the many photographers who strived to capture it.

Jill Price was one of them.

Though she made her living as a wedding photographer, snapping pretty, blushing brides in lace and tulle, her heart was in the landscape of her birth. It called to her on crisp, bright mornings, the sea and sky beckoning her to find that perfect image of sunrise over the water, never the same from one day to the next.

That morning was no different, and, since there were no wedding bookings in the diary, she was free to make the short journey from her home in South Shields to the bay at Marsden, armed with her camera bag and a flask of coffee to stave off the worst of the February chill.

The streets were quiet at that time, since most people were still at home in their beds, and Jill pootled along the familiar cliff road until she reached a public car park, where she brought her natty little Suzuki to a standstill. Resting her arms briefly on the steering wheel, she looked out of the windscreen and smiled as the sky began to change. Soon enough, the misty shades of pale pink would dissolve into warm yellows and bold blues, and she didn't want to miss it.

Zipping herself into an all-weather jacket, Jill tugged a well-worn beanie over her curly grey hair and began to make her way towards a steep set of stairs leading down to the beach. Technically, the stairwell was closed to the public for renovations—the concrete at the base of the stairs having fallen foul of generations of saltwater erosion, as had the old coastguard storage hut which used to sit beside it. Consequently, a large set of metal gates had been erected with appropriate signage warning of danger ahead, which she studiously ignored.

She slipped through a gap at the side of the freestanding fence and made her way down the concrete steps leading from the clifftop to the beach, dropping down onto her rear end to jump the distance between the ragged edge where the bottom steps used to be, onto the damp sand below. Her feet gave a satisfying crunch as she made her way south along the beach, feeling the brisk wind against her face while she watched sea birds circling high overhead, hearing their long cries that were as much a part of the fabric of her childhood as sandcastles and rock-pooling.

The beach was empty and, judging by the lack of cars, Jill realised she might be one of the first to head down to the bay. It gave her a thrill to know it, and she was eager to reach her favourite perch where she knew she would be able to capture Marsden Rock and the cave grotto opposite as the new day came alive.

"*Oh, bring me a boatman, I'll pay any money…*" she hummed, trailing off as she caught sight of something she'd missed earlier.

Footprints in the sand.

Automatically, she snapped pictures, and wondered how so many people could have beaten her down to the beach, even before the sun had risen. Although the people of the North East were a hardy tribe, not averse to a brisk morning walk in adverse weather conditions, the temperature remained cold and she'd have thought most people would have waited for the sun to warm things up a bit, especially at the weekend. Yet, she counted several sets of prints converging beneath the shadows of the cliff, all coming from the direction of the rock and heading one way, back towards the slipway running up towards the car park. There were no footsteps to show how the early risers had accessed the beach, in the first place—the only prints leading from that direction were her own.

Puzzled, she followed their trail towards the rock, passing around its weathered western edge with the cliffs to her right. As she rounded the edge, she was met with the full force of the wind, which rolled in from the sea and whipped the hat from her head.

She managed to catch it before the wind carried it further off, and yanked the wool back over her ears—only then, did she focus properly on the scene that awaited her.

Shipwreck!

Her eyes widened like saucers. The shock and awe at having stumbled upon a real-life shipwreck momentarily overtook any finer feelings, and Jill fumbled for her camera again, marvelling at the aesthetic of the boat's carcass wedged against the rock, sunken into the sand now that the tide had abandoned it there. Sea birds circled from their nests high on the rockface, clustering around the boat's stern, and she found herself moving closer.

What had they found?

Fish, perhaps?

Her feet sank into the dense silt and, as she moved further out, it became harder to walk. She thought of turning back, but the same pull that had driven her from her bed that morning drove her to seek the answer to a question which, she would later realise, she had already known. Her trigger finger snapped again and again as she drew near to the boat—which had certainly seen better days, even before its ignominious end—and she congratulated herself on capturing the morning sun rising over the boat's remains, casting it in silhouette.

With every passing footstep, the sound of the birds grew louder.

Suddenly, Jill no longer felt the urge to capture the broken boat or the sunrise—the rock she'd tried to climb as a teenager and the beach where she'd walked countless times before felt alien, and she was no longer merely alone, but *lonely*. By now, the path she'd taken along the beach was obliterated from sight, the rock and the cliffs beyond it blotting out any comforting view of civilisation. Jill shivered, hugging herself for warmth.

She could go back.

She *should* go back.

And yet…

And yet, the birds continued to circle.

With a growing sense of foreboding, Jill forced herself to continue towards the stern of the boat, stepping over planks of wood and other detritus littering the sand as she followed an instinct as old as mankind itself.

Curiosity.

And then, she saw it.

The camera strap fell from her limp fingers and onto the sand at her feet, acid bile rushing to her mouth as she sought to reject the horror of what lay washed up and tangled in the folds of sand. The body of what had once been a woman lay in a twisted pile of wasted flesh and bone, laid bare to the ravages of the sea and sky.

With a shaking hand, Jill reached down to retrieve her camera and held the weight of it in her palm, while she warred with herself. It was her life's passion to record the full spectrum of humanity and the natural world, and death was surely a part of that—wasn't it?

There would never be another opportunity like it.

Jill knew she could sell the images to the local papers—maybe, even the broadsheet nationals. There were bills to pay, and she couldn't afford to be sentimental.

Except, it would make her the worst kind of voyeur.

There were many things that could be cropped, filtered, corrected, or adjusted…

But death?

Death had no filter.

CHAPTER 4

As Jill Price put a hasty call through to the emergency services, Detective Sergeant Frank Phillips opened one sleepy, button-brown eye and then the other, while his superior nose sniffed the air like a bloodhound.

"Here, Denise—d'you smell that?"

His wife and, as it happened, his immediate senior in the police hierarchy, mumbled something unintelligible, cocked one eye at the clock sitting on her bedside table, then rolled over to glare at him.

"*Jesus, Mary and Joseph*…Frank! It's barely eight o'clock in the morning," Detective Inspector Denise MacKenzie said, irritably. "What's the emergency?"

"Bacon," he said, reverently.

"*What*?"

"Fried bacon—smoked, if I'm not mistaken."

"Frank…" MacKenzie was lost for words. "Are you feeling all right—in the head?"

"Never better," he said, and gave her a smacking kiss. "Stay right where you are, bonny lass, and I'll bring you some breakfast in bed."

MacKenzie considered pointing out that she might have preferred another hour's kip, but one look at his cheerful expression silenced her. Frank was, for the most part, the kindest and most thoughtful of men, who only ever acted with the best of intentions. It was just unfortunate that he had a blind spot when it came to the subject of fried meat.

And pasties.

And custard cream biscuits, Kit Kats, Jaffa Cakes...

Mind you, she had to credit him with having been very restrained, lately. Lord knew, she loved him no matter how he looked, but Frank wasn't getting any younger and she was glad he'd taken himself in hand. There was already a noticeable difference to his waistline, and the muscles she'd always suspected lay beneath his Winter Hibernation Layer were beginning to re-appear. Twice-weekly sessions at Buddle's Gym had helped, as had the lunchtime jogs he'd been enjoying with Ryan, when work allowed.

Phillips was about to trot downstairs, when her voice stopped him.

"You know, Frank, with all this working out and eating salads, you must be feeling *awfully* tired. Perhaps you should come back to bed for a while."

She patted the spot he'd recently vacated.

Frank hesitated for less than a second, the lure of bacon sandwiches almost too great to bear, but—fortunately for his health—it was quickly overtaken by the more pressing invitation from a green-eyed, red-headed goddess.

"Well, y' nah, come to think of it…"

Playfully, he let one side of his terry towelling robe fall off, and wriggled his preposterous eyebrows, to make her laugh.

He was about to pounce back on the bed, when the door burst open.

Phillips let out a squeal—there was no other word for it—and clutched the lapels of his dressing gown.

"Morning!"

Their daughter Samantha lounged in the doorway, oblivious to the fact she'd been perilously close to seeing a whole lot more than she'd bargained for.

"You know, it's customary to knock," MacKenzie said, gently.

At the age of twelve, Samantha was still learning about social niceties and, as her new adoptive parents, they were getting used to the fact that their life could no longer be as spontaneous as it once was.

"Oops, sorry," Sam said, and raised her knuckles to knock belatedly against the doorframe. "I just thought I'd let you know I've cooked up some bacon sandwiches, if you fancy one."

Phillips reflected that, whilst there were many things he loved about their adoptive daughter—her spirit, quick intelligence and fun-loving nature being chiefly amongst them—he decided that her sense of timing could use some work.

Then, he caught another whiff of the bacon, and decided he was being too hard on the lass. What father could complain about a daughter who, without any prompting at all, was independent enough to make breakfast for her parents at the weekend?

She was one in a million, and he told her as much.

MacKenzie might not have had Phillips' nose for bacon, but she could sniff out plenty of other things.

"Not that I'm complaining," she said, giving her daughter the beady eye, "but what's all the fuss in aid of? I usually have to sound a foghorn to get you out of bed in the mornings."

"Well, the thing is—"

MacKenzie pursed her lips. "Mm hmm?"

Sam fiddled with the hem of her pyjama top, which featured an embroidered slogan in bright pink that read, 'YOLO'.

"Well, the thing is," Sam began again. "This boy at school has asked me to go to Dibley's for ice cream tomorrow, for Valentine's Day…"

MacKenzie eyed her husband, who looked as if he might blow a gasket. "Frank, now, stay calm—"

"*Boys!*" he burst out. "They're nowt but trouble—take it from me! I was one, once!"

He chose to ignore the look of disbelief on his daughter's face.

"You're too young to be thinkin' about boys, and… and…and *ice cream*. I don't know who this lad thinks he is, but he can just forget it—"

"What's his name?" MacKenzie asked, cutting across Phillips' diatribe. "How old is he, love?"

Sam blushed.

"He's called Sam, just like me," she said. "We're the same age, except he's in another class at school. He's my friend."

MacKenzie experienced a moment of maternal grief as she thought of how quickly they grew up, and yet, how sweet it was that Sam had come to tell them all about it—better still, to ask their permission. She'd have worried if the opposite had been the case.

"Do you mind if I check the messages you've been sending?"

They had an 'open' policy in their household, and it wasn't merely because Frank and Denise were police officers. They were parents, first and foremost.

"Sure!" Samantha handed over her mobile phone, for which MacKenzie already knew the passcode.

A moment later, she was smiling again, having read the most innocent of childish exchanges about flavours of ice cream and favourite movies.

"I don't see any problem with you going to have ice cream together," she said, handing the phone back to her daughter and giving Frank a reassuring nod. "I'm proud of you for coming to ask us, first. If you don't mind, once we've dropped you off, we'll sit on another table, a little way away so we don't spoil things. That's just so that we get to meet him and his mum or dad, and everybody stays safe. Okay?"

Samantha decided it was a fair deal. Unlike some children, she already knew there were good and bad people in the world—and had developed wisdom enough to know when to argue, and when to feel grateful that she now had two people in her life who cared about her so much.

"Okay, cool! I'll tell him. Thanks!"

She skipped off, already wondering which flavour of sundae she'd choose.

"I'm not sure about this," Phillips grumbled, folding his arms across his chest. "What do we know about him? His family might be notorious. What—"

"Are his intentions?" MacKenzie finished for him, with a loving smile. "Probably just the same as yours, at that age—to pinch a kiss, but settle for holding her hand. They're not all reprobates, Frank; it's just that we see more than our fair share of the wrong sort and it skews our perspective, sometimes."

Phillips supposed there was a grain of truth to that.

"Aye, well, I'll be keepin' my eye on him," he said. "It might be ice cream tomorrow, but then it'll be fish 'n' chips and MacDonald's happy meals down at the multiplex…I mean, where will it end?"

At that precise moment, his stomach gave a loud rumble.

"With a bacon sandwich?" MacKenzie laughed, and then shooed him out. "Go on—I'll have a cuppa, while you're at it!"

CHAPTER 5

When Anna joined Ryan and Emma downstairs a little after eight, she found them both in the living room, stacking wooden alphabet blocks. She stood for a moment in the doorway and watched her husband, whose long body was stretched out on the rug beside Emma, dressed in the tartan pyjama bottoms gifted by his mother the previous Christmas, bare-chested as the morning sunshine shone through the window at his back. He might have been a statue cast in bronze, were it not for the blossoming welt on his left shoulder.

Sensing her presence, he looked up with penetrating eyes that could, on occasion, be ice-cold, but were now as gentle as a calm sea.

"Morning, beautiful," he said.

Six years, Anna thought, *and his voice could still make her stomach flutter.*

"Thanks for letting me sleep," she said, and leaned down to kiss him, before lifting Emma up into her arms for a snuggle. "I take it this is the little nipper responsible for that injury on your shoulder?"

Ryan shrugged it off. "Looks worse than it is," he said, and rose to his feet to stretch out his back. "She's still teething."

"I think you could be right," Anna said, and grimaced as she felt a line of drool slither down her back. "Do you have work, today?"

"I'm not on shift, unless there's a major incident," Ryan said, and decided to broach the subject uppermost in his mind. "Actually, I was hoping we could have a chat."

Anna searched his face and found it troubled, which was not a good omen.

"Is it about one of your cases?" she asked, and held the baby a little tighter.

Ryan noted the protective gesture and was sorry for it. A mother's instinct was to ensure her child's safety against external threats—she should never have to worry about threats from within.

"It's not any specific case," he said, and led her through to the kitchen, where he began to make a fresh pot of coffee. "It's the job, itself. I've been thinking…it may be time to move on."

Anna was shocked.

"From Northumbria Constabulary?" she asked. "Why would you want to do that? You've got such a great team, there."

When he said nothing, she realised he hadn't been talking about transferring to another regional area command.

"You mean, you want to leave the Force altogether?"

Ryan's lips twisted.

"We're not supposed to call it a 'Force', now. It's a 'Service', don't you know."

She couldn't quite work up a smile.

"Are you serious?" she asked. "Why would you want to leave a job you love so much?"

Ryan looked her squarely in the eye.

"Because I love you, and Emma, much more."

Anna looked away, blinking rapidly.

"You don't need to choose—"

Ryan shook his head.

"The job I do has brought danger into our home, which should be sacrosanct. I look at the front door and remember when it was smashed open. I look at your study and remember when you were forced to hide Emma in the cupboard, before you were taken. It should never have happened."

Anna was quiet for long seconds before she replied.

"The selfish part of me would like to accept your decision at face value," she said quietly, turning back to him with shining brown eyes. "I'd like to think of long, easy days without stress or drama, without any fear of history repeating itself."

"It wouldn't—" he started to say, but she put a gentle finger to his mouth.

"That's only the smallest part of me," she continued. "It's the fearful, risk-adverse little girl who longed for stability and security, when I was growing up. Did I ever tell you about my childhood dream? It was to glide through life working as a historian, burying myself in the past so I didn't have to worry about the future, too much. I wanted to marry and have a couple of kids, and bake cookies or whatever 'perfect' mothers do. Maybe write a blog about how best to organise my kids' wardrobe and puree organic vegetables, or something equally banal."

"Are you sure this wasn't a childhood nightmare?" Ryan joked.

"Really, I wanted an ordinary life," she explained. "Everything I didn't have, I suppose. And, if I didn't happen to find the right partner, well, I told myself I'd be happy on my own."

"Then, you met me," Ryan said. "I didn't give you your dream."

Anna stared at him—at the tall, raven-haired, blue-eyed, half-naked dreamboat who was her husband—and laughed richly.

"Yes," she said, composing herself. "It's a real hardship."

When he looked at her blankly, she gave him a playful shove.

"You know, for an intelligent man, you can be a numpty, sometimes."

Ryan had been in the north east of England long enough to understand the vernacular, and he knew that 'numpty' was only a shade away from full-blown 'moron'.

"But you don't have that life with me," he said, still not understanding her. "Our life can be unpredictable, at times."

"It can also be *exciting*," she admitted. "Ryan, my old dream was built on fear. It was a child's idea of what the perfect life would be, because I had no idea of knowing what it would really look like when I found it; I only knew what it *didn't* look like. From the moment I met you, my assumptions have been challenged. Just by being who you are, you've chipped away the old fear I used to have about life…about *living*, really."

"You haven't really had a choice," he said.

"I've *always* had a choice," she reminded him, firmly. "I've always known about the job you do, and you've never sugar-coated it. I've also seen the impact you've had on the families of victims, their communities… you have a positive effect on almost everyone you meet, including me."

Emma began to chatter, and slapped her hands against her chubby knees.

"And Madam," Anna added, with a smile.

But Ryan wasn't so easily convinced.

"Did you think that when you were trapped in the boot of that car?" he asked, quietly. "And, before then, when your cottage was burned to a cinder?"

"You didn't lock me in there, or strike the match," Anna said. "You aren't responsible for the actions of others—only your own, and yours have always been exemplary. It's the reason your team loves you, and why I love you, too. Your moral compass never wavers, even in the face of intense provocation."

"I'm no angel," he said.

"Don't I know it," she quipped, with a private smile that drew a reluctant smile from him, too. "Look, I know it's been especially bad, lately. A lot of people have asked how I'm doing, after my experience, but I wonder how many people ask how you're doing?"

Ryan shook his head, ready to brush it off.

"My feelings are nothing in comparison—"

"I disagree," she said. "I can't imagine the pressure you were under when I was missing. Then, when you found me, you were the one who kept me alive, performing CPR until the paramedics arrived. That's traumatic, too."

To Ryan's embarrassment, a lump rose to his throat and he swallowed hard.

"I thought I'd really lost you," he said, huskily.

Anna reached across to take his hand.

"You didn't," she said, and gave his fingers a squeeze. "I'm right here, and so is Emma. It does no good to live in the past—I know that, better than most. Life is for living, Ryan."

He looked down at her fingers and lifted them to his lips.

"I feel torn," he admitted. "If I stay and do the job, I worry I won't be a good husband or father—at least, not the kind you both deserve. If I leave, and find something else to do, I worry I'll leave a part of myself behind with it."

Anna gave him a reassuring smile.

"I've always known your work was a part of who you are. Oh, I don't mean that you're institutionalised, or anything like that. I mean, it's a vocation for you, not just a job."

She lifted her hand to curve around his cheek.

"You have special skills, and it would be a shame not to use them where they're most needed. As for thinking you're not a good husband or father—do you see either of us complaining?"

Ryan looked down into his daughter's happy face, then back at his wife, whose eyes were warm and loving.

"Remember, how you see yourself isn't always how the rest of the world sees you," Anna told him. "Do you want to know what it is that we see? A wonderful, kind person—an idealist, who makes us want to be better people. There's a spark inside you, Ryan; a fire that ignites others into action. The world needs people like that."

She shook her head.

"Trying to keep you at home, wrapped in cotton wool, would be like trying to cage a bird. It's not right, and I'll never be the one to do it."

"It wouldn't be a cage for me," Ryan said, but a part of him wondered if that was true. "I'll only ask you one more time, then I won't ask again. What do you think is for the best?"

"I think you already know the answer to that," she said. "But, if you want it from me, then I'll tell you my view. I think that, whatever makes you happy is for the best. There's no such thing as the 'perfect' life, but I'd say ours is pretty close. We love each other, we have wonderful friends and family, and work that we enjoy. What more could we ask for? There are others who can't say the same, and it makes them vulnerable to the wrong sort of person. They need you, Frank and Denise, Jack and Mel, all of you, to help them. Otherwise, who will?"

Ryan was still digesting her words when his phone began to jingle. At that hour of the morning, he knew it could only be a call from the office.

He looked at it, then at Anna.

"Answer it, chief inspector," she said, with an encouraging smile.

After a second's hesitation, he answered, then paced a few steps away, his back straightening as he heard the news. When he ended the call, his eyes were hard.

"A body's been found at Marsden Bay," he said. "I need to get down there, as soon as possible."

"It's a sign," Anna said. "You'd better hustle."

Ryan nodded, and began striding from the room, before turning back to enfold her in his arms.

"Thank you," he murmured, and kissed her deeply.

A moment later, he was gone.

CHAPTER 6

Marsden was only a short drive from where Detective Constables Jack Lowerson and Melanie Yates had recently purchased their first home together, in the village of East Boldon, which meant they were the first of Ryan's team to arrive at the scene shortly after eight-thirty. They parked in the same car park as Jill Price, whose Suzuki remained stationary in one of the bays, surrounded by a number of squad cars belonging to the local police unit and a dark, unmarked van they recognised as belonging to Tom Faulkner, the Senior Crime Scene Investigator attached to the Northumbria Criminal Investigation Department. Despite the best efforts of the first responders to cordon off all access points to the beach, the usual complement of 'lookie-loos' had gathered along the promenade, some still in pyjamas and overcoats, uncaring about social propriety in their haste to catch a glimpse of the drama.

"Bloody rubberneckers," Jack said, as they slammed out of the car. "How does the word spread so quickly?"

"Twitter, Snapchat, Facebook…" Mel replied, tugging the hood of her 'big coat' around her ears as the wind blasted them from all sides. "Social media's like a wildfire and it only takes one person to set it off."

"Here we go…shipwreck down at Marsden Bay," Lowerson said, scrolling through his phone. "There's a picture of the boat, but you can't see it in detail because it must have been taken from the clifftop. That's something, at least. The *Evening Chronicle* has picked up the story, so it won't be long before the others do. We'd better make sure everything's secured before the press rock up."

"And Ryan," Mel said.

Their boss might also have been their friend, but he didn't suffer fools gladly, no matter who they were. Too many prosecutions had failed at the final hurdle—or been quashed on appeal thanks to sloppy procedural oversights—for them to ever take the basics of their job for granted.

"It's too early for a bollocking," Jack agreed. "This wind is Baltic, mind. Wish I'd brought gloves—"

Yates fished out a spare pair from the pocket of her coat. "Thought you might forget them, so I grabbed them as we were heading out."

Jack smiled broadly, and then pulled a face. "Am I that predictable?"

"Yep," she replied, with a laugh. "You forget where you leave your phone, and it's always in one of three places: on top of the toilet cistern—which is gross, by the way—on the hallway table, or down the side of the sofa. Don't get me started on your morning routine."

Jack chuckled.

"One of these days, I'll surprise you," he said, and thought of his plans for Valentine's Day with a mixture of trepidation and excitement.

Was it too soon? he wondered.

"Jack?"

He snapped out of his daydream to find Mel looking at him with a quizzical expression.

"Sorry, I was miles away. What did you say?"

"I said, I'm going to ask Ryan if I can take the morning off, on Tuesday," she repeated. "I meant to put in the request before now, but the date sort of crept up on me. I hope it'll be all right."

He was confused for a moment, then he remembered and could have kicked himself.

February 16th was the anniversary of her twin sister's death, and Mel liked to mark the occasion by spending a few hours at the site where they had chosen to scatter Gemma's ashes, at Bolam Lake. The loss was still a gaping, open wound for Mel and her family; one she tried and often succeeded in patching up, so she could carry on living. But he knew that she brought out the old case file, sometimes, and picked over the facts to check she hadn't missing anything crucial—though, of course, she hadn't. It remained one of those unfortunate instances where a perpetrator had never been found, though not for want of trying.

"I'm sure it'll be no problem—Ryan is a decent bloke, and he knows how important that date is to you."

Mel nodded.

"Would you like me to come with you, this time?" he asked.

She hesitated and then, to his surprise, nodded. "All right—if you can get the time off, it would be nice to have the company."

Despite the circumstances, his heart swelled. Mel had never chosen to share that special time with anyone, not even him, before now.

At that moment, they spotted Phillips' Volvo pulling into the car park, and talk turned back to the business at hand.

"Mornin', lads 'n' lasses! Bit nippy today, isn't it?"

Phillips rubbed his mitten-clad hands together, sucked in a lungful of air and made a loud *brrrrgh* sound between his cheeks.

"Any sign of the Big Man?" he asked.

Lowerson and Yates shook their heads.

"I had a message to say he's on the way," Jack said. "He'll be another fifteen minutes, I reckon."

"If Ryan's at the wheel, make that seven and a half," Phillips joked.

"Where's Sam, today?" Mel asked.

"At a friend's house—a few of the girls are having a sleepover tonight," MacKenzie replied. "It's our turn next weekend."

"God almighty," Phillips muttered, and wondered if there was any legitimate way he could manage to be out of the house while his daughter and five of her friends stayed up till all hours giggling and watching telly.

"Don't even think about it," MacKenzie told him, with a warning note to her voice. "We're in this together."

Was the woman telepathic? he wondered.

They made their way from the car park towards the police line, which cordoned off a slipway leading from the main cliff road down towards the beach. At the end of the slipway, the road turned into a series of wide, concrete steps which were closed to the public by a set of tall freestanding gates.

"They're renovating this area," Yates explained.

"What about other access points?" MacKenzie asked, not being especially familiar with that stretch of coastline.

"You can usually get down using the elevator beside the grotto," Lowerson said, and pointed towards a tall, boxy grey building similar to a chimney, which spanned the full height of the cliffs, and was connected to the promenade by a walkway. "It gives access to the pub and hotel which is built into the grotto, and the beach on the lower level—but it's only open at certain times of day. It saves people having to walk down the narrow cliff stairs, which run down the side."

He pointed towards the steps, and they were pleased to see another cordon had been set up, in front of which a constable had been posted, warding off the crowd that continued to grow larger by the minute.

"You can also get down to the beach at low-tide, if you walk from the direction of Souter," Yates chimed in, referring to a disused lighthouse which stood at the southern end of Marsden Bay. "You can go even further and walk all the way from Seaburn and Roker lighthouse, if you time it right, but that'd be a good stretch of the legs."

As they approached the top of the stairwell leading down to the beach, they caught sight of Marsden Rock, standing tall and proud against the bold blue sky. From their vantage point to the north, its girth blocked any sign of a shipwreck, but they could see tiny, ant-like figures dressed in polypropylene suits scattered on the sand nearby and were reminded that it was no ordinary day at the seaside.

"Could have been a nasty accident," Phillips said, with his usual optimism. "Storm Edith was blowin' a gale, last night, so it's small wonder a fishing boat ended up adrift."

"Yes, but the question is, why did the coastguard have no record of a mayday signal, nor any record of its position?" Ryan put in.

All four jumped at the sound of his voice, and spun around to find him grinning at them.

"Howay, man! You can't go around scarin' folk half to death, like that!" Phillips patted his heart through the layered folds of his bright green puffer jacket, for effect. "How the heck did you get here so fast, anyhow?"

"Because I don't dawdle on the motorway singing along to Barbra Streisand's Greatest Hits, unlike some I could mention," Ryan drawled.

Phillips lifted his chin, while the others chuckled.

"The woman's a musical legend," he said, with dignity. "And, if you ask me, she was robbed of the Oscar for *Yentl*."

Ryan exchanged a look with MacKenzie, who held up both hands as if to disclaim any involvement.

"Just don't get him started on Tina Turner," she warned.

"The mind boggles," Ryan muttered, and then made a bee-line for the nearest constable, who came to attention at the arrival of their Senior Investigating Officer.

There was a momentary pause in the wake of his departure, before Phillips piped up again.

"Look, all I'll say is, *What's Love Got to Do With It?* was a crackin' film."

There was a collective groan, and they began trudging down the stairs, deciding that working on a crime scene would be preferable to any further debate about songstresses of a bygone era.

CHAPTER 7

It was a pitiful sight.

Their first, jarring look at the decomposing carcass of what had once been a person was never easy, and it certainly didn't get any easier with time or experience. Though Ryan and Phillips had seen more than their share of human waste, this time was particularly difficult, the sea having swollen the woman's body to twice its normal size before leaving it beached on the sand for carrion to have their pick—which they had, with ruthless efficiency.

"Poor lass," Phillips said, gruffly, and scrubbed a hand over his mouth.

Ryan cut a striking figure beside him; a tall man who stood perfectly still while the wind brushed the hair from his brow, revealing calm eyes which surveyed the scene and missed very little.

"Look at her left wrist," he said.

Phillips shuffled around to get a better look, and promptly wished he hadn't.

"Looks like some sort of restraint has been used," he said. "Wire, maybe?"

But Ryan shook his head.

"It's hard to see, considering the skin is so swollen, but the injury line seems heavier than if wire or cord had been used," he murmured. "Faulkner, what's your take?"

The Senior CSI looked up from where he'd been in the process of photographing the woman's feet, which were clad in cheap white trainers.

"Size four," he muttered. "Quite small, on average, these days."

"I meant the wound on her wrist."

"Oh, that," he said, rolling back onto his heels. "Yes, definitely some kind of restraint. You can see there's a deep, even lesion all the way around the wrist and several other semi-circular marks from where she may have tried to detach herself. Obviously, decomposition has been vigorous in that area since the skin was already broken when she died, and you can still see some faded bruising which would suggest injuries that were sustained ante-mortem. Pinter will be able to tell you more, of course."

"He's expecting to receive the body sometime this morning," Ryan said, referring to their Chief Pathologist.

"Sooner the better," Faulkner said. "We've tried to protect it from the elements, but we're fighting a losing battle, here, and we need to get the wreck transported elsewhere before the tide comes in again, after lunch."

It was true; the small forensics tent they occupied had been driven into the sand surrounding the woman's body, but it remained at the mercy of the North Sea wind which buffeted against its eastern wall and leaked through the cracks, leaving it liable to blow away at any moment.

"Weather report said to expect another storm in the next day or so," Phillips said. "Dennis, or Wayne, or Kevin. Don't know, for the life of me, why they always have to name it after some bloke who plays darts down at the Working Men's Club."

The other two laughed.

"Doesn't look like she was from around these parts," he continued, now they'd had a moment to recover themselves.

What remained of the woman's skin was of a medium tone and her hair was long and black, suggestive of Asian or Indonesian heritage.

"That doesn't necessarily tell us where she was born," Ryan said. "But I know what you're thinking, Frank, because I'm thinking the same thing."

People trafficking.

"Any paperwork found on her at all, Tom?"

Faulkner shook his head.

"Absolutely no personal effects," he said. "I've got my team combing the sand, in case anything interesting has washed up, but there's been nothing so far, except a few clothes and the usual rubbish you might expect. You might have more luck finding something inside the boat."

Ryan nodded.

"How old would you say?"

Although Faulkner was no clinical expert, he'd seen enough cadavers to make an educated guess.

"Hard to estimate," he replied. "Twenties—early thirties, maybe?"

They fell silent, each man thinking of a life that had barely been lived. Ryan forced himself to look again at the woman's ravaged face and thought of Anna's words to him, that very morning.

There are others who are vulnerable to the wrong sort of person…

Perhaps he was still needed, after all.

Outside the stifling confines of the forensics tent, they drew in some deep, nourishing breaths to cleanse themselves of the cloying scent of death, then cast their eyes around the vicinity. Immediately to their right was the broken fishing vessel, hanging limply on its side at the base of the rock, which rose up over a hundred feet and was teeming with cormorants, kittiwakes and seagulls whose colonies nestled in its limestone crevices. A short way off, MacKenzie was in discussion with the coastguard, whilst they could see Lowerson and Yates further up the beach, tracing the cliff wall to the south, towards Souter.

"I remember when there used to be another limestone stack, and an arch connecting the two," Phillips said, suddenly. "I think the arch finally collapsed in '96, and the smaller stack was unsafe, so they demolished it the year after. I came down to watch it crumble."

"I've seen pictures of how it used to look," Ryan said, shielding his eyes against the sun as he craned his neck. "I think Anna mentioned that people used to sit on top and have picnics."

"Aye, they built a stairway up the side, back in Victorian times, and folk used to sit up there, for a jolly. Wouldn't fancy it, myself; all those birds, doin' their messy business? Probably honks to high heaven."

Ryan grinned, and raised a hand to MacKenzie as she crossed the sand to join them.

"I just had a quick word with Marine Services at the Port of Tyne in North Shields, and there's no record of this boat having been logged on the VTS," she told them. "It's the same story at the Port of Sunderland, which is the only other obvious place the boat might have been heading."

Phillips cleared his throat.

"VTS...aye, that would be the...ah, Vessel... Tugging..."

"Vessel Traffic Service," Ryan told him. "It's a monitoring system, similar to air traffic control, which uses a boat's Automatic Identification System, radar and VHF radio to keep track of all the vessels coming in and out of port. It's a public system, which means that, when another boat comes within range, it's flagged up, to help avoid collisions. If a boat wants to dip under the radar, all it has to do is disable the AIS system—we've seen it before."

"Exactly," she said. "The coastguard were busy last night, thanks to the storm, but there was no call-out to Marsden and no report made whatsoever."

Ryan had already ascertained the same thing, since he'd been the one to call in the coastguard shortly after receiving word from the Control Room.

"Do they know anything about the boat, itself?"

"Nothing, so far," she said. "But they say they're ready to transport it out of the tidal zone so we can assess it safely, whenever you're ready. We might find some more answers once Faulkner's had a chance to go over the boat's interior."

"Agreed." Ryan nodded, and cast a weather eye towards the waterline, which was creeping ever closer towards the shore. "I want to have a quick look around, first, then they can take her away. Tide's coming in, again."

"Why are boats always female?" MacKenzie found herself wondering.

"It's tradition," Phillips said. "Mariners believed a mother or goddess protected a ship on its voyage, so they got into the habit of referring to their boats as 'she'."

Ryan glanced over in surprise.

"How d'you know that?"

"Common knowledge," Phillips said, and then nodded towards the pub that was built into the cliffside. "Has anybody checked with the people at the grotto, to see if anyone at the pub saw anything, last night?"

The unusual architecture of the building meant that its windows all looked out towards the sea, which should have provided a panoramic view of the action.

"The local team have taken preliminary statements but, given the time of year, there was nobody staying at the hotel last night, and the pub closed for last orders at eleven. The landlord—who's also the owner—locked the doors around midnight and went straight to bed, with his wife. They battened down the hatches and tried to sleep through the storm, so they didn't see a thing," Ryan said. "The first they heard of any shipwreck was when they got up and looked out of the window, but, by that time, the first responders had already been alerted."

"Unlucky." Phillips tutted.

"Or convenient?" Ryan wondered aloud, before stalking off to take a look around what was left of the boat.

The 'boat' was, in fact, a fishing trawler.

At twenty metres long, by Ryan's estimation, it was middling in size: not anywhere near as large as some commercial fishing vessels he'd seen, but not especially small, either. He'd learned to sail as a child and had taken the helm on one or two memorable occasions since then, but he couldn't claim to be an experienced sailor. All the same, he could see by the cut of her rusted jib that the blue and grey trawler had seen plenty of action in its time. Added to which, the absence of any painted name or number to identify her seemed to confirm that they were dealing with a suspicious vessel.

A thorough inspection of the boat's perimeter confirmed there were no safe entry points to allow Ryan access to the interior of the vessel, but he'd seen enough to draw some reasonable conclusions.

"Jack!"

He jogged across the sand to speak to Lowerson, who met him halfway.

"How was the sand, when the first responders made their way down?" Ryan asked. "Specifically, were there any footprints, and where did they begin?"

Lowerson turned and led him towards a series of small yellow forensics markers.

"Here's where the concentration of footsteps began," he said, pointing to a spot due west of the rock, near the cliffside. "They lead back towards the stairway that's under renovation."

Ryan followed their direction, then stuck his hands in his pockets.

"What time did the tide go out, this morning?"

"I can find out," Jack said.

"Do that. While you're at it, find out whether the witness took any photographs of the beach this morning—if she did, we're commandeering them. I want to know what the sand looked like, before half of Northumbria CID trampled all over it."

"Why?"

Ryan smiled.

"If we know what time the tide started to go out, when it was fully out, and where the footprints began, we can estimate the earliest possible time they could have been made by calculating the average distance the tide recedes per hour."

"Elementary," Lowerson said, with a grin.

"I want you to get hold of any CCTV footage you can, and look for mini-vans, transit vans or people carriers, in particular."

"You think there were others, besides the victim?"

Ryan cast his eyes back towards the tent, where a black body bag was now being stretchered out.

"The kind of low-life who traffics people for a living tends to go by the old maxim that things are cheaper by the dozen," he muttered. "I'll set up a meeting with somebody from Vice, Drugs, Fraud and the Serious and Organised Crime Squad. There may be something useful they can tell us."

"Fraud?" Lowerson didn't see the connection.

"Traffickers like to exploit their victims in lots of different ways, Jack. If they're not being forced into servitude, of some form or another, they're being used as the vehicles to perpetrate identity or benefits fraud. People forget that side of things, but it's often the way to unravel the bigger picture."

"I'm surprised we don't see more of it," he said.

Ryan merely shook his head. "On the contrary, Jack. It's all around us, hiding in plain sight. People trafficked to this country don't always know they're being trafficked, until it's too late. They might know they're being smuggled, or find themselves tricked into debt bondage, where they believe they're paying for an immigration service which ties them in to working for free at the other end until they've paid back the astronomical 'fees' their captors charge. They live in squalid housing, and work the hardest, menial jobs, for a pittance that they won't ever see. Car washes, nail bars, fisheries...you name it. They don't speak out, and they're often supervised under extreme coercion, in any case. That's the rosy end of the spectrum," he added.

Lowerson's eyes filled, and he looked away in embarrassment.

"Bloody wind," he mumbled.

"There's no shame in feeling it," Ryan said, and put a hand on his friend's shoulder. "In fact, we *should* feel it. We should feel ashamed that we can't root these bastards out, once and for all, and protect the people they exploit."

On that note, he took out his phone and gave the order for an All-Ports Warning to be issued, with immediate effect, knowing he might already be too late to prevent the onward transit of whichever poor souls had escaped the water, but not the fate that awaited them on land.

CHAPTER 8

Mick Donnelly awakened shortly after noon in a puddle of his own piss.

He swore half-heartedly, since it was hardly the first time, and tried to remember how many beers he'd drunk before passing out on the bed, sometime around dawn.

Eight? Nine?

There'd been a couple of tequila shots, too…

He rolled into a sitting position, his paunch bursting over the rim of his sodden underpants, and hoisted himself up. The action made him dizzy, and the dull ache in the back of his neck swiftly became a full-blown headache.

He reached for the stale remnants of whichever amber liquid floated inside the glass on his bedside table, and knocked it back, just to take the edge off.

Then, he reached for his phone to check the messages, and swore again.

The Dragon wanted an update.

Well, he wanted a shower, first.

"Mick? You awake?"

Gaz didn't bother to knock, uncaring of whatever he might have found on the other side of the bedroom door.

"You'd better come and see this," he said, and wandered out again.

Mick pulled on some fresh boxers, considered himself decent, and made his way down the landing of his nondescript semi-detached house, then downstairs to the living room, where an enormous television took up the entirety of one wall and was currently streaming the local news channel. Noddy was stretched out along one sofa, his skinny, sunburned legs covered in nicks and bruises, while Gaz sat on the other sofa beside a caramel-coloured cross-bred Staffie and a chubby boy of sixteen called Ollie, who happened to be his son.

"I've heard enough news about the Royal Family," he said, yawning widely. "Who gives a flyin'—"

"Wait for it, Mick," Gaz said. "They've found a body."

"Is that all? They were bound to wash up, sometime or other, weren't they?"

Then, the relevance of what Gaz had said penetrated his fuzzy mind, and the newsreader's voice confirmed it.

Police have closed off Marsden Bay, today, after a body was discovered early this morning alongside a shipwrecked fishing vessel which had, apparently, collided with Marsden Rock, sometime during the night. No further details are known, but we'll be reporting on this developing story throughout the day...

"One body," he muttered, and yet, they were missing *two* bodies from their own head count.

Where was the second?

"I swear, Mick, I looked around the beach before we left, last night," Noddy said, with a touch of desperation. "It was dark—"

"Shut up," he growled, while his mind came into sharp refocus. "Look, the other one's either dead and hasn't washed up yet, or she's alive and hiding somewhere."

"Somebody could have found her," Gaz said.

Mick shook his head.

"If they had, we'd have heard about it," he said. "But none of them would talk to the authorities, anyhow. They're too scared, after what we've told them happens to illegal immigrants, and what they know would happen to their families back home, if any one of them blabbed. It wouldn't be worth the risk."

"So, what do we do?"

Mick thought it over, and looked across at the boy, who'd been making noises about playing more of an active role in his dad's business.

"They can't keep the beach shut, forever," he said. "The tide'll be in again now, for one thing. Gaz? You take Ollie and the dog and head back down there, around four. The tide should be out again, by then, and they'll have reopened the beach. If anyone sees you, they'll think you're dog-walkers."

Gaz nodded.

"What're you going to tell *him*?"

Mick scratched his belly.

"I'll tell him we want more money, for the bloody inconvenience."

The others grinned.

"He'll be round sometime today or tomorrow, to have his usual pick," Mick told them. "Better make sure the merchandise is presentable. Who's watchin' 'em?"

"Callum's takin' a shift," Noddy said, and flicked the channel. "But he says we're runnin' low on hash to keep them quiet."

Mick walked over to the window, which overlooked a tarmacked yard stacked with bricks. There was a large warehouse with a small chimney covering two sides of the quadrangle, accessible only via the courtyard and locked to prying eyes. The house formed part of the property, around which a tall, brick-and-wire fence had been built, with several, top-of-the-range CCTV cameras dotted along the perimeter.

He turned suddenly, and looked over at the boy.

"What d'you tell your ma, when you come here?"

"She doesn't know owt, Mick—" Gaz began. "She's off her tits, most days, anyhow."

"Let him speak for himself."

Ollie felt their eyes turn to him, one by one, and he licked his lips.

"I just tell her I'm doin' an apprenticeship, Mr Donnelly," he said, and Mick approved of the formality. They weren't at the back-slappin', hand-shakin' part, just yet. "She thinks I'm learnin' a trade."

"So you are, son," Gaz said, and the others grinned. "She'd 'ave you all dolled up like a bloody dog's dinner in a suit and tie, scratchin' a livin' every day. That's a mug's game, that is."

"Listen to your Da," Mick said, with a sharklike stare. "There's doors that'll open to you, if you play the game, and play it right. D' you understand?"

Ollie glanced at his father, then nodded.

"Y-yes, Mr Donnelly."

Mick gave another loud, hacking cough, before continuing.

"I'm glad about that, son. I really am. Because, you see, you're entering one of the world's oldest professions—did you know that?"

Ollie looked at him blankly.

"Didn't you like pirates, when you were a kid?" Mick asked, weaving his charm around the boy. "Swashbuckling adventures, smuggling, and all that? Bet you never knew your da' was one of the best, eh?"

Gaz grinned. "Bloody Bluebeard, that's what I am," he said, and the others guffawed.

"It goes back a long way," Mick continued, his eyes never once leaving the boy's face. "But there's rules to the game. The most important one is *loyalty*."

He moved to stand in front of where Ollie was seated, and the lingering scent of urine wafted off his skin, at close quarters.

"D' you understand what I mean by loyalty?"

"He knows, Mick," Gaz said, with a nervous laugh. "I've told him straight."

Mick held up an imperious hand.

"What d' you know, then, Ollie? Tell me."

The boy was sweating now; he could feel it, running down the crack of his arse.

"I don't talk business outside these four walls, and never to anybody without your permission," he said, looking to his father for reassurance.

"Don't look at him, look at me," Mick warned him.

"S-sorry, Mr Donnelly."

"It's all right. What else?"

"Never speak to the pigs, not even if you're going down for murder, and no matter what they offer in exchange for information."

Mick nodded. "What if you haven't killed anybody, but we asked you to take the hit. What would you say?"

Ollie swallowed. "I—I'd say it was for the good of the family."

"What if one of them says they'll do your mam over for possession, or threaten to take one of your little sisters into care? What then?"

"I'd still say nothin'," Ollie told him, but the thought of it made his stomach quiver.

"Good lad," Mick breathed, and dropped onto his haunches in front of him, so they were eye to eye. "Cos, you know what we pirates do, if one of our own betrays us?"

Ollie's eyes widened, and he shook his head.

"We make him walk the plank, o' course," Mick said, and the room erupted into laughter.

He rose to his feet and gave the boy's head a ruffle with a none-too-gentle hand, but the look he sent Gaz held a warning.

Any slip-ups, and there would be consequences.

"You can count on us, Mick. You know that."

The Postman smiled.

"Just as well, Gaz. We've got some deliveries to make."

CHAPTER 9

Was this death?

Lawana couldn't tell.

The darkness was penetrating, and the stone where she'd fallen was cold, and hard. Her body was a mass of pain; every nerve ending screamed, and she wondered if this was divine punishment.

Had she been so very bad?

She was one of six children, born in a tiny village on the outskirts of Chiang Mai, but she hadn't seen the city properly until she was nine, when she'd been sent to work at the factories making clothes for rich, pale-skinned women.

She'd made money in other ways, too; ways she didn't care to think about.

Was this her punishment?

The work had given her Achara, her beautiful angel, so she could not regret it.

Life had been a terrible struggle for the past sixteen years since her daughter had been born. Then, one day, she'd seen a man coming around the clubs and bars, speaking to the girls and women, telling them about his immigration service. He'd worn nice, clean linen trousers, and had a friendly smile. He hadn't asked for any freebies, and he'd told them all about the United Kingdom, joking with them all about Yorkshire puddings and gravy.

You want to bring your daughter?

His smile had widened, even further. Of course, she could bring her daughter.

Not enough money to travel?

No problem, he'd said. You can pay us back, later. You'll earn five, or ten times what you earn in Chiang Mai, doing a few hours' strawberry picking.

Don't want to work outdoors?

That's okay, you can learn how to do nails and work in a fancy nail salon. He said he knew lots of women who'd saved up and bought their own shop. After a while, they sold up, kept the profits and moved back home, to live the good life.

Worried about immigration?

We'll handle all of that, for you. The authorities could be very strict, but they'd manage everything.

The weather isn't as good, he'd joked. *But there'd always be enough to eat, and plenty of honest work.*

A single tear rolled down her cheek, as she thought of that particular lie.

Back home, she might have used her body, but she'd done it honestly and for good reason. Day after day, she'd sacrificed herself to benefit Achara, and had scratched together the money to send her to school—something she'd longed to do, herself. She hadn't done all of that, only to watch her child suffer a worse fate than she herself had known.

The reality had become clear—oh, so clear—soon after their suitcases had been confiscated.

That's when his smile had vanished, along with all her hopes.

Lawana lay there, passing in and out of consciousness, her mind replaying the events of the past few days. Mostly, she remembered the fear—the overwhelming terror of the icy sea engulfing her, its current dragging her beneath the waves. She'd battled through exhaustion to break to the surface, disoriented, her wrist limp and broken, and had kicked her legs as hard as she could, gritting her teeth against the cold, powering through the driving rain and wind with only one goal.

To find Achara.

Finally, her feet had found purchase against sand, and she'd fallen down in relief and shock, splashing through the shallows, hearing their voices carrying on the wind somewhere further up the beach.

She'd called to her daughter, but her voice had been drowned out by the wind, and there was no answering cry.

Achara!

After a while, she realised they'd left her, alone and trembling, and her daughter was gone from her forever. She had no idea of the direction they'd travelled, and could see no footprints in the darkness—only the murky outline of the cliffs and a tall tower of some kind, with no obvious way out.

Desperately, she'd stumbled along the beach, keeping close to the cliffside to shelter from the worst of the wind. She didn't know how far she walked, but eventually she came to a kind of pier, where the stones were not as high as before, and light shone above them. She didn't hesitate, but began climbing up the slippery rocks, clinging to the jagged stones as she dragged herself up and over the incline.

A road.

The distant rumble of a car's engine, driving away from her.

Her feet had tripped and stumbled over the turf at the top of the cliffs, but she'd kept going, mumbling words of comfort to herself as she'd hurried towards the lights of the village. When her legs met with a barrier and a sign she couldn't read, she'd propelled herself over it, past caring about her own safety in her haste to discover Achara's whereabouts.

Suddenly, the ground underfoot had given way and she'd fallen, swallowed alive by the grass and soil until she'd landed with a sickening crunch of bone, and the darkness was complete.

CHAPTER 10

While Lowerson and Yates oversaw the recovery of the fishing trawler and completion of the forensics work at the beach, Ryan, Phillips and MacKenzie made their way back to Northumbria Police Headquarters, which was located in the eastern end of Newcastle, not far from the old shipping heart of the city and a stone's throw from the Port of Tyne.

"I wouldn't mind paying the harbourmaster a visit," MacKenzie said, as they crossed the car park towards the main entrance. "Marine Services were helpful on the phone, but nothing beats a face-to-face."

"It's the most obvious place for a drop-off, presuming the boat came from the Netherlands," Ryan agreed.

"They've got some balls," Phillips remarked.

"You can say that again," Ryan muttered. "I've been out on a boat in a storm like that one, and I was lucky to come out the other end of it with mine still intact."

Phillips was puzzled.

"I meant, The Pie Van has those little chocolate coconut balls," he said, pointing to the takeaway van parked nearby. "Vegan, or somethin', but they taste nice enough. Anybody want one?"

Ryan stared at him, then let out a short laugh.

"Why not," he said, with a glint in his eye. "I didn't know you liked eating balls so much, Frank."

"Words I never thought I'd hear you say," MacKenzie put in, while Phillips stalked off, muttering to himself about the younger generation.

"I surprise myself, sometimes," Ryan said, and then remembered something important. "Morrison was hoping to catch us both for a word, on Monday."

"What does she want to talk about?" MacKenzie asked.

Ryan decided to leave it to the Chief Constable to put forward their idea.

"Nothing urgent, just a discussion about your career progression, and where you'd like to take it."

It occurred to MacKenzie that, no matter how busy or distracted Ryan was with the daily grind, he never forgot to consider those around him, and what their needs and goals might be. It was a particularly laudable trait in their chosen profession, which was not especially known for its equal opportunities record.

"Thank you," she said. "I have to say that, lately, I've been feeling at a bit of a crossroads, now we have Samantha to think about."

Ryan gave her a keen look.

"Have you come to any conclusions?"

"I concluded that I wanted any daughter of mine to respect me, not only as a parent but as a productive member of society. On that basis, I still want to work, and find the right balance at home."

"How will you know when you've found it?" he asked softly.

MacKenzie thought of the days she spent sifting through case files, interviewing witnesses, managing staff and investigations—and the evenings and weekends she spent with Samantha and her horse at the stables, at the shopping mall, bankrupting herself buying all manner of pink, glittery tat, or having dinner with Frank while they talked over their day.

She couldn't think of a better balance than that.

"You just feel it," she said, simply. "Don't you?"

Ryan thought back over his conversation with Anna that morning, looked across at Phillips who, even now, was jiggling his little cellophane-wrapped balls suggestively, and smiled.

"Yeah, you do."

At lunchtime, the three detectives reconvened in one of the smaller meeting rooms of the Criminal Investigation Department, where they were joined by four other senior officers: DCI Dan Wentworth from the Vice Squad; DI Alec Gross from the Drugs Squad; DI Kieron Chambers from Serious & Organised Crime; and, DCI Mo Farooqi from the Fraud Squad, all of whom were male and in their mid-forties.

"Thank you all for coming, especially during your lunch hour," Ryan said. "Please, help yourself to sandwiches, let's try and keep this informal, for now."

"I think we've all seen the news this morning," Farooqi began, and poured himself a cup of strong coffee. "What's the line?"

"Trafficking, we suspect, or some other illegal smuggling," Ryan said. "The body was found with suspicious markings on her wrist, the boat was unmarked and had no VTS record…"

"Standard ploy," Chambers put in. "Have you managed to identify her?"

Ryan assumed he meant the body rather than the boat, and shook his head.

"The body's been transferred to the pathologist for post-mortem, but we're assuming it may take some time to identify her—unless we receive word from overseas that they're missing a foreign national. Of course, it's possible the woman was a British national, but it seems unlikely given the surrounding circumstances."

"Any missing persons reports?" Wentworth asked.

"None matching the woman's description," MacKenzie answered, having already checked her daily alerts, and the Missing Persons Database.

"At this stage, what we need to know is whether there's a link to any active investigations. We want to know whether this was a one-off, or part of a wider, organised operation."

"And what we *really* want to know is whether there's a new honcho in town," Phillips said, with his usual forthrightness. "There's always some tussling back and forth, while the gangs fight over turf, but who fancies themselves as the new boss in town, nowadays?"

The man in the 'know' was DCI Chambers, who polished off the last of an egg sandwich, brushed the crumbs from his tie and then linked his fingers together on the desk.

"As we all know, following the success of Operation Watchman, last year, the 'Smoggies' were largely disbanded, and their leader, Bobby Singh, is now behind bars enjoying the hospitality of HMP Frankland," he said, with the ghost of a smile. "The Smoggies were the biggest and most powerful threat to community safety I've seen since 'Jimmy the Manc' was alive, so I'm happy to see the back of them."

"Hear, hear," Phillips intoned.

"Of course, the minute we get shot of one gang, another one's lined up to fill its boots," Chambers continued. "From a Serious and Organised Crime perspective, 'County Lines' is still a major problem in these parts, like it is across the whole of the UK. We don't have dealers working through syndicates in the pubs and clubs, anymore—or, at least, they don't limit themselves to the usual places where people gather. Supply is outweighing demand, so they're having to work harder to shift the merchandise, and that means pushing out into the countryside."

"We're pickin' up a lot more kids and teens in the villages," DI Gross agreed. "We had a meeting with reps from a few of the NHS trusts across Northumberland, Tyne and Wear, and Durham, and they've all reported a rise in drugs-related healthcare complaints, overdoses and all that."

Ryan listened with a heavy heart, thinking of how often his team had been called out to bear witness to children and young adults having lost their lives through drug abuse. It was a vicious cycle, and one that never seemed to end but, as Anna had observed, he was not one to give up on the fight, nor the people.

He would never give up.

"Gettin' harder to trace the money, too," Farooqi observed. "The kingpins use kids as go-betweens, and get them to do the dirty work so the dealers don't even have to handle any cash. Then, they find somebody vulnerable, move themselves in, and do their business from there, so they don't have to use their own address."

Cuckooing was a growing trend, and one that was very hard to root out, since the victims were often disabled or otherwise incapacitated, living in fear at the mercy of ruthless men and women who cared about nothing and nobody except their bottom line.

"As far as we can tell, there are four major gangs operating across Northumberland, Tyne and Wear, and Durham," Chambers continued. "Three of them are home-grown, family-based operations, and the fourth has Russian links which we're trying to unravel at the moment."

He went on to list the names of the families, all of whom were well-known to the police.

"What about trafficking?" Ryan pressed. "Which one of them would have the logistics and set-up to run that side of things?"

"Any one of them," Chambers said. "I'd put my money on the Russians, though. They'd have more established international connections. The problem we have is that, even when manage to bust 'em, none of them will talk and there's zero paper trail. It's a slick, complex operation, which makes it bloody hard for us to trace the source or be able to predict when they're planning to bring in their next boatload."

"From our side of the fence, we don't see a lot of new faces," DCI Wentworth said. "When they traffic women into the country for sex work, they don't parade them on the streets; they hide them away at undisclosed addresses, with a minder keeping an eye on them, at all times. We've had undercover officers working on-and-off for months now, posing as punters trying to get a lead on where some of the addresses might be. We've managed a couple of busts, but they've been low-level and nobody would give up the names of who was behind it all."

"What kind of scale are we talking about, here?" Ryan asked.

"Hard to say," Wentworth told him. "These guys run national operations, so it's not just a case of manning the ports in our neck of the woods. We'd have to stop every single van, people carrier and car entering the district from other parts of the UK or Ireland, which is completely impossible. They blend in, and it happens right under our bloody noses."

Ryan ran a frustrated hand through his hair.

"What about your informants?" he asked. "Haven't they heard rumbles?"

"I'm sure they have," Wentworth said. "But they don't tell us about it. Listen, mate, it's hard enough to develop trust with people who've built up a lifetime's worth of hate for the authorities. They know, as well as we do, that these people would kill them, if word got around that they'd turned grass."

He paused, as if considering whether to tell them something else.

"Look," he said, leaning forward. "There's a particular shelter I know of, run by former sex-workers, for sex workers and their children. The woman who runs it was trafficked to the UK when she was a teenager, but became an informant for three years before she was discovered. Luckily for her, and for us, she managed to kill her assailant before he killed her, but she's got a long scar here, as a memento."

He traced a finger along his right cheek.

"I can't give you the location," he said. "I don't even know where it is, myself. But I'll speak to her, and see if she'll agree to talk to you. Or, maybe, DI MacKenzie."

Denise nodded, understanding that these things could be easier coming from another woman.

"She has new women coming into her care all the time, so it's possible one of them might know something."

Ryan thanked him, and the other men, for their time.

"Take a bit of friendly advice, Ryan, and don't beat yourself up over this one," Gross said, as they were leaving. "It's sad and all that, but, if there were others on that boat, they're probably down in London or Birmingham, by now. You could spend months tryin' to chase down some small-time operation, using up all your resource budget in the process. Put it down to experience and focus on the bigger picture—that's my advice, son."

"That's the fundamental difference between us," Ryan said, once the door clicked shut behind them. "Every life matters to me, regardless of how long it takes."

He turned away to look out of the window, across the car park and beyond, to the rooftops of the city. Last night's storm had washed away the clouds, leaving bright blue skies in its wake. Pigeons cooed on the window ledge, and he could see women with buggies walking along the road towards the supermarket, chatting to one another. It was all so *normal* and *wholesome,* he thought, but under that same sky, there were people suffering all manner of degradations, behind closed doors.

Sad, and all that, Gross had said.

Unacceptable, Ryan would say, and made a mental note to refresh his team's training on the identification and reporting of potential victims of human trafficking and modern slavery. If there were victims walking amongst them cleaning cars, filing nails, caring for children and homes without pay, dignity or other basic human rights, he wanted to know about it.

"We can only do our best, lad," Phillips said, reading his friend's mind with ease.

"Maybe it's time we raised the bar a bit higher," Ryan said, and his eyes strayed to one of the coffee mugs sitting on the table, which featured the bold, red, white and blue of the Union Jack. "We're responsible for building the kind of country and the kind of society we want for ourselves and our children. The day I stop striving for better will be the day they bury me six feet under."

It was a matter of pride.

"You know your problem?" Phillips said, gently. "You expect too much from people. Not everybody's a high-flyer, like you."

Ryan's lips twisted, and he downed the rest of his coffee in one gulp.

"I don't expect anything from anybody else that I don't also expect of myself," he said, fairly. "Besides, don't tell me you don't always give the job one hundred per cent, Frank—same goes for you, Mac. Every last one of us brings our best effort, even if we're having a bad day or haven't slept well, or whatever the hell it might be."

"Aye, but we're like the A-Team, us lot. You can't judge everybody by our exceptional standards," Phillips said, a bit smugly.

"You're not getting a pay rise," Ryan told him.

"Well, it was worth a try."

Ryan and MacKenzie laughed.

"Come on, Mr T," Ryan said. "We've got work to do."

CHAPTER 11

Gaz and Ollie timed it perfectly to arrive at Marsden shortly after four o'clock. Mick had been right about the police having re-opened the beach to the public; the tides waited for no man, and the forensics team had been hard pressed to complete their work before the sea rolled in to sweep away whatever trace evidence there might once have been. Meanwhile, the crowds who had gathered at the top of the cliffs that morning had now returned to swarm the beach like vultures, presumably hoping to find another body washed up against the rock, or something equally macabre. As it happened, Gaz wouldn't have minded if one of them found another body—it would save him and the kid wasting their afternoon scouring the shoreline.

She'd been trouble from the start, that one.

It was funny how you got to know them, over the years. Gaz could categorize a woman in less than a minute, and not just the ones he brought in off the boat, either. Lasses he met in bars and clubs, ones who served his food at the local café, even the kid's schoolteacher, that one time he'd been forced to go along and listen to her harp on about how his kid wasn't *applying himself* and how his attendance was too low. Women all had their common traits, and nationality didn't matter so much as the nature of the beast.

In many ways, he mused, they were a lot like dogs—only less obedient.

Break their arm, then give them a shot of heroin or a few pills to ease the pain, and they'd love you for it. Leave them to sweat for a while, to get a taste for the good stuff and learn to miss it, then give them a little more so they'd become desperate, reliant, and, most importantly, *compliant*. It wasn't nuclear science so much as basic training.

He hadn't wanted his wife to be like that, of course. A man wanted a different kind of woman to share his name, or else, why bother? It wasn't drugs that had ruined Keeley, but drink.

She couldn't go half an hour without a drink.

Of course, she blamed him for that but, the truth was, he never forced a bottle down her gob. She did that, all on her own, after that first fight. The wisp of a memory played at the back of his mind, of his fist connecting with her jaw, but then it frittered away to be replaced with the more palatable narrative he'd created since then, which absolved him of any blame.

Marrying her had been a mistake, but at least she'd given him Ollie. A man needed a son he could mould in his own image. As for company, he was never short of a woman, and he could always help himself to the merchandise, if he was really desperate.

"Here, have you lost it, yet?" he asked, suddenly.

Ollie was confused.

"Lost what, Da?"

"You know bloody well, what. You're sixteen. You must have had your leg over, by now."

Ollie's pale skin turned a slow shade of puce, and he scrambled for something to say.

"Yeah, loads of times," he muttered.

Gaz wasn't fooled.

"You better not be bloody gay," he told him.

"I like girls," Ollie muttered, defensively. *They just didn't like him*.

"That's all right then," Gaz said, with some relief. "We'll sort you out."

Ollie couldn't find the words to tell him that he didn't want any so-called 'help' in that department, so he fell back on bravado.

"The girls at school are all stuck up," he said, and thought of Molly, a girl he'd liked for two years and for whom he'd written out a Valentine's card.

"They'll be the ones after you, when you've got a bit of money in your back pocket," Gaz said, with a sneer. "They're all the same."

Not Molly, Ollie wanted to say, but held his tongue.

"That's another rule to remember, son," Gaz continued. "No matter how much you think they're the dog's bollocks, you don't *ever* tell a woman about our business. I don't care if she's got the biggest pair on her you've ever seen—you keep your trap shut. Got it?"

Yeah, Ollie thought. *He got it.*

When they reached the bottom of the stairs, they found the beach swarming with people. It was as though nothing had ever happened; there was no sign of the wreck, nor any way of knowing a woman had once lain dead in the sand. The sun was shining brightly and, though the air remained chilly, it was nothing in comparison with the freezing conditions they'd experienced during the early hours of that same morning.

"What are we lookin' for, Da?"

"Hidin' places," Gaz muttered, and let the dog roam off its lead, causing other dog-walkers to give them a wide berth.

Ollie tugged on the door of a beach shed at the base of the grotto, but found it locked.

"Da? Why did Mick land the boat here?"

"Best he could do," Gaz muttered. "He was aimin' for Roker."

"Were you scared?"

Gaz was taken aback. "Bugger off."

"I just mean when the boat hit the rock. Wasn't it scary?"

Gaz thought of the women's screams in the darkness and the crashing of the sea.

"No," he barked. "Now, shut up and get to work."

Ollie didn't ask any more idle questions and they carried on walking in a southerly direction towards Souter, tracing the line of the cliffs as they made their way along the beach, past the rock and the grotto. It took more than half an hour to cover the ground while they made a careful check of every inlet for any sign of their lost cargo, dipping into the natural caves using their phones as torches to check the darkest corners, but finding nothing. Eventually, as they neared the pier, they spotted another cave entrance, this time only half the height of a man.

"You'll have to go in," Gaz said. "I can't fit in there."

Ollie broke into an immediate sweat at the thought of being confined in a small, dark space.

"D' you really think she would have walked this far?"

Gaz thought back to the woman he remembered who, even at short acquaintance, had been one he'd categorised as a fighter.

"If it's the one I'm thinkin' of, then, yeah, she would. Get in and check, because we're not goin' back until you have."

"What—what if I get trapped in there?"

"Stop bein' a bloody pussy and get inside!" Gaz thundered.

Ollie obeyed, squeezing himself through the small opening into a short, dank tunnel. The darkness was suffocating, and he began to breathe in short gulps as his heart raced in his chest. Spots danced in front of his eyes and he felt himself losing control, pins and needles pricking his fingers as he gripped the cold rock. He began to shake, fighting the overwhelming urge to belly back out into the sunlight, where he knew his father would give him an earful.

"Well?" Gaz shouted. "Can you see owt in there?"

Ollie blinked the sweat from his eyes and squinted through the gloom. The tunnel was narrow, but seemed to widen further ahead into a small cave, its walls illuminated by thin shafts of light.

Light?

Though it could never be said that Ollie was the sharpest tool in the box, he had sufficient wherewithal to know that it was unusual for there to be light in an underground cave.

"I—I dunno, I'm goin' in a bit further to have a better look!" he called back.

He inched his way through the tunnel, feeling the rock digging into the soft flesh of his arms and legs, until he his fingers met with something that was neither sand, sea, nor rock.

It was soil.

Ollie lifted his hand to stare at it dumbly, wondering how soil had found its way down there, then fumbled for his phone torch to shine it around the cave. Emerging from the tunnel, he was able to stand, and in his haste to scramble upward, immediately bumped his head. Rubbing it with one hand, Ollie shuffled forward, kicking tufts of soil and grass out of his path until he found he could go no further, his passage blocked by a small mound of earth. It was illuminated by weak shafts of light, and he tipped his head upward to find a hole in the cavernous ceiling, thirty feet above. It appeared small from his vantage point, but could have been two or three metres in diameter, half-obscured by the ragged edges of turf which still clung to its edges.

Sink hole.

There were several scattered along the clifftop, cordoned off by fencing and signs that warned of the danger to pedestrians. The ground was liable to crumble at any time, as this one obviously had—sometime recently, it seemed.

The significance of his own observation didn't register fully, and Ollie was about to make his way back through the tunnel when the light of his torch skipped over something shiny and gold, winking at him through the semi-darkness. Like a magpie, he was drawn to it, and his fingers made a greedy grab for the thin gold bracelet that was half-buried in the soil.

His disappointment in finding it made of inexpensive plated gold was nothing to compare with his horror at finding the bracelet still attached to its wearer, whose skin was so caked in dirt as to be camouflaged against the soil.

He let out a strangled cry and skidded backward, banging his head again.

"How, man! What's takin' yer so long?"

Ollie opened his mouth to call back to his father, but the words died in his throat. It might have been the pitiful sight of the woman's thin body lying twisted amid the mound of collapsed earth which stopped him from raising the alarm, or the thought of what his father and the others might do to her, once they knew she'd been found.

But it wasn't.

It was the possibility that the woman was already dead, and unable to cry out or alert any passers-by, which gave him pause. He'd seen many things in his young life but, so far, Ollie had never witnessed a dead body, particularly not at close quarters. One of the effects of having experienced the myriad of childhood traumas his parents had inflicted upon him was that he found it extremely difficult to feel any empathy for his fellow human beings; he simply couldn't drum up the emotion, his brain not having developed in the same way as other children. Consequently, once he'd recovered from the initial shock of finding her there, the sight of the woman's body became more of a curiosity to him, little more than a jumble of flesh and bone.

He moved forward to get a better look at it, rubbing dust from his eyes with dirty fingers, until he stood directly above the woman's inert form. She was clad in the simple jeans and motif sweatshirt she'd travelled in, bearing the logo of a famous sports brand. Every inch of her was covered in a layer of cracked mud, the soil having solidified against her wet skin the previous night.

Cocking his head to one side, Ollie stared at her for a minute or two, and found himself pleasantly surprised.

She didn't even look dead.

She might have been sleeping.

"Ollie!"

"Comin', Da!" he turned away to bellow.

When he turned back, he found himself staring into a pair of unblinking brown eyes.

Lawana stared at the boy while her mind floated slowly back to consciousness.

Her first thought was that he bore a passing resemblance to a young Buddha, with his rounded cheeks, shaven head and rolls of fleshy skin which strained against the t-shirt he wore.

Her second thought was that he was frightened.

Of her?

She tried to speak, but the words came out as a rasping, painful whisper.

"Hel'," she said, softly. "You hel' me?"

The boy hugged his arms around himself and shuffled his feet, feeling uneasy.

"Pleez," she added, with difficulty. *The pain is so bad. Please, help me. Help me find my daughter.*

He swallowed, and ran agitated fingers over his head, casting quick glances back towards the tunnel. She barely had time to wonder what lay beyond it, when a disembodied voice filtered through the layers of stone.

A voice she recognised immediately.

Gaz.

Horror, fear, loathing…it all must have shown on her face, and she was suddenly galvanised, fighting the pain in her body in an effort to scramble off the altar of soil and seek out some other means of escape.

The boy watched her for a moment, immobilised by indecision, before rushing forward with his arms outstretched.

She shrank away, bracing herself for a blow of some kind, but it never came.

"Don't—don't move," he whispered. "You'll hurt yourself."

She didn't understand the words, but the tone was remarkably gentle.

"I'll—I don't know what to do…" Ollie trailed off, panicking again. "Just—just stay there."

She searched his face, and did not trust it.

He turned to go, then surprised himself again with an act of kindness.

"Here," he whispered, holding out a half-melted bar of chocolate he had in his pocket. "Go on, take it."

When she didn't, he left it within reach and then hurried away, already knowing that he had crossed the invisible line Mick had warned him about.

Loyalty, he'd said. *Loyalty above all else.*

And yet, he couldn't forget the look on the woman's face; couldn't erase the new and uncomfortable feeling niggling his gut, worming its way into his heart.

Pity.

"Oi, bloody deaf lugs? Didn't you hear me callin' yer?"

"Sorry, Da, it goes back quite far in there," Ollie muttered, as he squeezed himself back through the entrance of the tunnel to land on the sand with an ignominious thud.

Gaz watched him heave himself upward and start brushing himself down.

"Well? Anythin'?"

Ollie kept his eyes averted, and made a show of re-tying the shoelaces on his trainers.

"Nah, nothin'," he said.

"You're sure you looked all the way in?"

He nodded, and stuffed his hands in his pockets. "D'you think we should carry on?"

Gaz eyed him closely, then shrugged. "I divn't nah what Mick thinks we're goin' to find round here," he said, and whistled for the dog to come to heel. "There's no sign of her, which means she's probably dead in a ditch somewhere, or she's hitched herself to somebody's wagon. Either way, it's never gonna come back to us. She doesn't know any names, any addresses—nothin'."

Ollie remained silent.

"Howay," Gaz said, with a jerk of his head. "I'm gaggin' for a pint, and the light's almost gone now, anyway."

Ollie realised that the sun had dipped low in the sky while he was inside the cave, and thought of the woman lying there in the darkness, without even the scrap of light trickling through the sink hole above her head.

Terrifying.

"What'll Mick say?" he asked, working hard to keep the wobble from his voice.

Gaz shrugged again. "He'll chalk it up to wastage, and put the loss down to unforeseen circumstances," he said, with breath-taking logic. "Fancy some chips?"

Ollie felt his stomach roll, but gave a weak nod.

As they re-traced their steps along the beach, he told himself not to look back. He'd lied to his father—he didn't fully understand why—and there was no choice now but to carry on. Any small, tell-tale sign would be enough to expose him, and the consequences would be dire—not only for himself, but possibly his whole family.

His mind raced as he thought of how to backtrack.

The most obvious thing to do would be to tell his father the truth, but there would be untold retribution, and he'd be out on his ear.

Or…

He could leave her there. Pretend he'd never seen her, never spoken to her.

Never helped her.

Nobody would be any the wiser, because there was little chance that she'd be able to drag herself out of the cave without help from someone—and who would possibly find her?

The odds were stacked against her, and against him, now.

It was every man, or woman, for themselves.

CHAPTER 12

Achara stared at the wall with eyes that burned.

Tears had been shed until her body was wrung out, and could produce no more. It had been a few hours since her last forcible injection, and she was shivering beneath the thin blanket in her cot, identical to those occupied by seventeen other women who lay curled up in rows. A large, industrial heater had been set up beside the door on the far side of the room, and some of the women had gathered around it, blocking any heat from circulating to the rest of them.

She didn't care.

All she cared about was that her mother, the only person she'd ever loved in the world, was now gone. Drowned or left to die of exposure, she didn't know, but either was a harrowing, miserable way to die, in a foreign land far from everything and everyone she'd ever known.

And now, she, Achara, was utterly and completely alone.

Another shiver racked her body, and she clasped her arms around her legs, focusing hard on the grimy wall. It was clear that she wasn't the first person to have lain in that very spot—not only because she could smell the last incumbent's sweat and other bodily fluids on the blanket and stained mattress, but because they'd left a message for her on the wall, written with a shard of pebble or glass picked up from the remnants littering the warehouse floor.

Unfortunately, the message was written in a language she didn't understand.

She liked to think it was a message of hope, or a poem from the person's homeland, and began to construct a tale of how they'd escaped the confines of that terrible place to be rescued by a kind stranger. Not all English people were like *Pos'man* and his gang; she had to believe there were some…some who would help.

Just then, she heard the rattle of a key turning in the heavy lock on the outer door and knew that they'd come to administer the next dose. Her skin was crawling with need and she sobbed her frustration, *hating* the new and powerful addiction flooding her mind, hating them all for the disease they'd spread through her veins where none had existed before.

"On your beds!" Noddy barked at the small group gathered by the heater.

They were beginning to learn the ritual, by now, and the women stumbled back to their cots without argument, too weary and too afraid to fight.

"That's better," he said, while the other one they called *Caloom* entered with several large brown paper bags. "Look, Callum's brought you a bit of dinner. You lot feelin' hungry, eh?"

Noddy grabbed one woman's face in a hard grip, squeezing her cheeks until it hurt.

"How about a bit o' sausage, darlin'?"

The woman might not have understood the words, but she understood his meaning well enough, and tried to scuttle as far away from him as possible.

"Like that, is it?" he sneered, and made a grab for her again, this time armed with a syringe.

Achara watched him from across the room, dreading her turn and yet craving it, at the same time. When the two men finally reached her, she kept her head bowed, trying to appear subservient.

But, they didn't reach for her ankle, straight away.

"Here, Noddy, I think we've found our winner," Callum said, eyeing up the girl's face and figure. "I'll bet you fifty quid he'll pick this one."

"Piss off, man," Noddy said, and gave her a thorough assessment himself. "Anyone can see she's the best of the bunch. Course he's gonna pick her."

Achara listened to their fast stream of words and wished she knew what they meant.

"She's hangin' already—look at her," Callum said. "Must've given her too much, yesterday."

Noddy shrugged, and began loading up the next syringe.

"She won't put up a fight then, will she?"

When Achara sank back against the bed a few minutes later, her body euphoric, they dropped a lukewarm burger by her feet.

"D'you think he'd know the difference?"

"What d'you mean?" Callum asked, keeping a beady eye on the rest of them. "Know what?"

"Nothin'," Noddy said, watching the rise and fall of her chest. "Listen, I don't mind takin' the night shift, later."

"Cheers, mate," Callum said, and moved off to the next bed.

Through the foggy high, Achara felt Noddy's fingertip trail over her leg and wanted to kick out, to break every bone in his hand, but she was so sleepy...

As the world slipped away, she thought again of the kind stranger in her daydream and wondered if such a person might exist, or whether they were nothing more than a fairy tale.

Ryan faced the assembly who had gathered for a late afternoon briefing, shortly after five o'clock. Outside, the sun had set, and the conference room was illuminated by a series of garish white strip lights which seemed to bounce off their sun-starved, winter skin. An unpalatable odour of pine-scented cleaning detergent lingered on the air, but they hardly noticed, their minds being otherwise occupied with the even less salubrious matter of murder.

"All right, settle down," he said, in clipped tones.

Ryan waited for the stragglers to take their seats and nodded towards Chief Constable Morrison, who dipped inside at the last moment to observe from the corner of the room. He'd grown used to it, by now, and respected her for taking the time to familiarise herself with the active cases on her beat, albeit she no longer played any active role in investigating them. Morrison's world was one of politics and policies, diplomacy and game-playing. Though she did it with integrity, hers was not a job he envied and, he dared say, the same was true in the reverse.

"Thank you all for coming," he said, when the rustles had died down. "Hopefully, you'll already be aware of the incident reported to us this morning at Marsden Bay, and it's seen extensive coverage in the local press—but, for those of you who haven't, let me bring you up to speed."

He turned to a long whiteboard on the wall behind him, upon which had been written, 'OPERATION SHORELINE' in bold capitals, alongside a number of blown-up photographs and scribbled notes. He indicated the first image, which was of the wrecked boat, taken by Faulkner's team that morning.

"Control received a report from a local photographer by the name of Jill Price at around seven-thirty," Ryan said, and began to roll up his shirtsleeves as he replayed the timeline of events in his mind. "She'd been down there to catch the sunrise and take some pictures, when she stumbled across the wreckage of what we now know to be a fishing trawler, of around twenty metres in length."

He moved onto the sleeve of his other arm and, from her position on the front row, Yates found her eyes drawn reluctantly to the action and to his forearms. Never more conscious of Jack seated beside her, she dragged her eyes away and fixed her attention on the murder wall, feeling all kinds of guilt.

Ryan continued with his summary, blissfully ignorant about having been the unwitting source of any turmoil.

"At the same time, our witness also discovered the body of a young woman," he said, and his voice softened a fraction in deference to her loss. "I haven't posted an image of how she was found, but you can find a series of photographs taken by Forensics in Appendix B of your packs."

There were one or two shuffles of paper, followed by soft murmurs of regret.

"Yes," Ryan nodded. "She died badly, and her body was exposed for hours prior to discovery."

He let the significance of that hit home.

"We've been unable to identify the woman from any existing police or DNA records but, given her ethnicity and the circumstances surrounding her death, we're taking a punt and liaising with international colleagues to see if anyone has been reported missing overseas," he continued.

"No update on that yet, boss," Phillips chimed in.

Ryan nodded.

"Let me know when you hear from them. In the meantime, the body has been transferred to our pathologist at the RVI," he said, referring to the Royal Victoria Infirmary, which was the largest hospital in the area and served as the base for their Senior Police Pathologist, Doctor Jeffrey Pinter. "I've requested an express turnaround, so I'm hoping to receive an initial report tomorrow morning. At a glance, we can already see there were lacerations on the woman's wrists and other contusion marks on her body, so we'll wait to see what Pinter can tell us about their origin and post-mortem interval but, taking into account all known data, we're treating this woman's death as suspicious."

He paused to hitch a hip on the side of a desk at the front of the room, and reached for a mug of cold coffee, deciding it was better than nothing.

"As for the trawler, we haven't been able to identify its origin and it bears no markings of any kind," Ryan said. "The Coastguard and Marine Services have both confirmed they received no signals to indicate the vessel was in distress, and they have no record of its movements, owing to the fact its Automatic Identification System was, most likely, disabled."

There were a few murmurs around the room.

"I've taken statements from the Harbour Masters at North Shields and South Shields," MacKenzie said. "They've both confirmed they have no record of any boat matching its description having requested to dock, and they don't recognise the vessel."

Ryan nodded.

"Faulkner's team are combing the trawler as we speak," he said. "It'll take them several days to work through the damage to try to salvage anything of use to us, but they've already been able to confirm one thing."

He reached for a cardboard folder, and pulled out a clear evidence bag, inside of which rested the broken remains of a pair of rusted metal handcuffs.

"There were several of these found attached to the walls of the boat's hold," Ryan said, in a flat voice. "A similar pair has been forwarded to the pathologist for comparison purposes, to see if these are likely to be the source of the marks we found on the woman's wrists, but I think we can draw a safe conclusion that they were. We can also deduce that there may have been several people in that trawler, last night."

He let them fall back onto the desk with a meaningful thud, to illustrate that these were no fluffy toys but hard tools of restraint.

"Joining all the dots, our working theory is that our unidentified woman was a victim of trafficking—"

"Not an illegal immigrant?" one of the team piped up.

Ryan shook his head.

"When you have people travelling in the full knowledge of the risks they'll be taking, there's no need to restrain them," he said, simply. "Whereas, when you're moving people against their will, or in a manner they weren't expecting, they're much more of a flight risk."

He stuck his hands in his pockets, and thought of the storm which had raged the previous evening. It had rattled the windows of the nice, secure home he shared with Anna and Emma, howling through the sleepy valley to waken its sleeping inhabitants, but none of them had truly known fear; not as that poor woman must have known, in her final hours before the sea claimed her.

It was a sobering thought.

"We've already spoken with colleagues in Vice, Drugs, SOC and Fraud," he said, thinking of his meeting earlier that day. "They'll ask around, but there were no leads that might connect our investigation with any active cases they're working on, at the moment. As far as they're concerned, any of the leading gangs could have been responsible; they've all got the resources and the connections to run that kind of operation."

Ryan paused, thinking of how to frame his next point.

"The fact is, the main thrust of resources in SOC and Drugs are being spent trying to combat County Lines," he said. "It's a worthy pursuit, when you consider how far-reaching its effects can be, and how many lives can be ruined. But it doesn't leave much in the way of time or money to spend on surveillance or effective investigation into people trafficking in our neck of the woods."

He cast his eye around the room, compelling them to listen.

"I propose we give our colleagues a helping hand," he said, with a small smile. "Our investigation into this woman's death may, or may not, lead us to uncover much broader connections with vice, fraud or serious and organised crime—everything is connected in some way or another, and we will, of course, be co-operative in sharing any relevant intelligence with other divisions, when appropriate."

There were nods around the room.

"It goes without saying that co-operation cuts both ways," he was careful to add. "Colleagues in Vice have already facilitated a meeting with one of their contacts who might prove helpful to us."

He turned to MacKenzie.

"Mac? Tomorrow morning, we have a meeting set up with the woman we discussed earlier, who was trafficked into this country for the purposes of sex work, but managed to get out. She may have some very useful insights."

She nodded, and Ryan turned back to the others.

"What I need you to understand is that we've stumbled across something we were never intended to see, never intended to know about," he said. "It's a tiny crack in the doorway to another world, a seething underbelly of organised crime we're trying constantly to bust open. As you all know, that's easier said than done, and it'll be a lifetime's endeavour."

He paused, and surprised them all by smiling broadly.

"Luckily, that's precisely what we've all signed up to do," he said. "So, here's the plan: Lowerson, Yates? I want the pair of you to investigate the shipping angle. Look into routes and any other historic information on that score, past busts and whatever else you can find."

They nodded, and made a swift note.

"Frank? I want you to focus on the local angle. See what the word is, on the street."

"Happy to," he said, and knew the first place he would try.

Ryan appointed a reader-receiver, and dished out a few other administrative roles.

"The rest of you, I want to piece together a comprehensive picture. Assume this is part of a broader scheme, which we're only just beginning to unravel. I want no stone left unturned. Go over closed cases and, furthermore, I want you to unearth reports that were made but not followed up. It's a lot of work, granted, but there might be a key in there, somewhere, that we've overlooked. It's because of that lack of focus that trafficking operations continue to flourish and—as the saying goes—not on my bloody watch."

They broke into smiles, and he was relieved to know that morale was high. He only hoped it would last, because there was no telling how long a case like this could drag out.

"Well? What are you waiting for? Let's get cracking."

CHAPTER 13

After the briefing, Ryan's team spent another hour working their way through the various statements and other pertinent information they had amassed throughout the day, before deciding to call it a night.

"Howay," Frank said, stretching his arms above his head. "It's Saturday night, and there's nowt more we can usefully do, this evenin'. Why don't we head down to the pub for a swift one? What d' you say, love?"

MacKenzie tried to remember the last time they'd been free to have an adult beverage that had been poured by someone else.

"Why not," she said. "It's been a long day, we've put in a good stretch, and Sam's staying at her friend's house, tonight. I fancy a glass of something fruity."

"Jack? Mel? What about you two love birds?"

"What do you reckon, Mel? Shall we have a quick one?"

Yates glanced across at Ryan, who was on the phone to his wife, and swallowed a constriction in her throat.

"Sounds great," she said, brightly. "Count us in."

"That's the ticket!" Phillips said, and rubbed his hands together. He happened to know it was karaoke night down at their local, and it had been too long since he'd treated the company to a rendition of *Sweet Caroline*.

At that moment, Ryan ended his call and leaned back in his chair, yawning widely.

"What about you, lad? Fancy joining us down the road for a hot toddy?"

Yates hated herself for caring so much about his answer, and for the immediate disappointment when he shook his head.

"Not tonight, Frank. Anna's been home all day with Emma, and she's due a break." *Besides, he missed them both.* "Have one for me."

He bade them all a fond farewell and, soon after, the foursome set off to walk the short distance to their nearest pub. Phillips and Lowerson fell into conversation about football, and Yates was glad to find herself in the company of MacKenzie, whose wisdom and advice she trusted implicitly.

Keeping an eye on the two men, who walked a short distance ahead, she cleared her throat and wondered how to broach the subject that was uppermost in her mind.

She needn't have bothered.

"Why don't you just spit it out?" MacKenzie said, keeping her voice down. "What's on your mind, Mel? Have you and Jack had an argument?"

Yates might have laughed.

"No, we haven't—at least, nothing worth mentioning," she amended. All couples argued from time to time, but she wasn't worried about that. "Um, it's just—Denise, is it normal to find yourself...sort of, attracted to other men, even when you're with somebody else?"

"Well, Lord knows, I love none but Frank," MacKenzie said, putting a hand on her heart. "But, as the Lord *also* knows, if that Henry Cavill came knockin' on my door, you'd best believe I'd ask him to stay for dinner and dessert."

She let out a bawdy laugh which, ordinarily, would have elicited a laugh from her friend, but the best Yates could manage was a weak smile.

"Just *how* attracted are we talkin' here?"

Dreams, hot, sweaty dreams, Yates thought, with a fresh stab of guilt.

"Um, quite a bit, I suppose."

"I see," MacKenzie said, and she did see, quite clearly. "I'm guessing the object of this, ah, attraction, is one person in particular?"

Yates nodded, miserably.

"Oh, Mel—"

"I know," she muttered, and was glad to see the men had already entered the pub ahead of them. "Believe me, I don't want to be having these thoughts. I love Jack, for goodness' sake!"

She turned to her friend with wide, panicked eyes.

"We just bought a house together," she hissed. "So, why am I thinking about somebody else?"

"Look, it's normal to get cold feet, sometimes," MacKenzie said, although, she had to admit, she'd never experienced that with Frank. "You've both had a rocky start and it probably feels like a big step, moving in together with your names on the title deed."

Yates seemed unconvinced, so MacKenzie decided to take the bull by the horns.

"Look, Mel, I'm sure you don't need me to tell you that Ryan is already very happily married," she said, with just a touch of steel. "And I know you like and respect Anna as much as we all do."

Yates was mortified.

"Oh, God, Denise, I know all of that—Anna couldn't be nicer! I'd never want to do anything to jeopardise their relationship, or mine."

MacKenzie nearly remarked that Ryan would hardly have given her the chance, but held her tongue.

"It's just so embarrassing…" Melanie whispered. "I don't know what to do about it. I thought I was well and truly over that daft crush I had, when I first joined the team."

MacKenzie searched her friend's face, and was worried.

"Look, sweetheart, you're going to have to do some soul-searching, here," she said, and put a motherly arm around her shoulders. "If you let this silly infatuation get the better of you, there's an awful lot you stand to lose. Not only Jack, but your place on the team—"

Mel looked up in surprise.

"Do you think Ryan would keep you around, if he found out what you've just told me? He expects professionalism, at all times, even amongst friends—and, frankly, I wouldn't blame him, if he were to arrange a transfer for you. It's what I would do, in his position."

"Do you think he suspects?" Yates asked, tremulously.

MacKenzie shook her head.

"I'm quite sure he has no idea."

Despite his physical attributes, she knew that Ryan was not a man who walked through life assuming he had anywhere near the kind of effect on the opposite sex that he so obviously did. If he knew the reality, the poor man would probably never leave his house.

"That's something," Yates muttered, and was silent for a long moment, thinking of all that MacKenzie had said, which was only the truth.

"It isn't fair to Jack," MacKenzie added, for completeness. "But, you know that already."

"I do," Melanie agreed. "And, it isn't as though we don't lead a happy life together. In fact, in many ways, I've never been happier. But—"

"Yes," MacKenzie said, sadly. "But."

By now, they had reached the doorway to the pub, and Yates found she'd lost all appetite for a social tipple.

"Thanks for the advice, Denise, I really appreciate it. Would you—can you just tell them I have a bit of a headache, and I've gone home? Tell Jack not to rush back, he should enjoy himself."

Without giving MacKenzie any time to argue, she turned and walked swiftly back in the direction of the police car park, swiping away sudden tears which rained down her cheeks.

MacKenzie watched her young friend hurry back along the lane and realised there was a much bigger question that remained unanswered.

Did she really love Jack Lowerson?

Only time would tell.

When she stepped inside the warm pub, MacKenzie found her husband guarding a small round table set for four, while tapping the toe of his boot to The Bee Gees, which were playing on the sound system.

"Where's Jack?" she asked, unable to see him amid the crowd of Saturday night revellers.

"He insisted on gettin' the first round," Phillips said, with a smile. "I said you'd have a glass of red—how's that?"

"Perfect," she said, and hoped it was a large one.

"Here, where's Mel?"

"She went home," MacKenzie said. "She wasn't feeling up to it, after all."

"Ah, that's a pity," Frank said, with genuine feeling. "It's been a long day, I s'pose."

"Mmm," she said.

"Here we are!" Lowerson sang out, as he set four glasses on the table. "Has Mel gone to the Ladies'?"

"No, she said she had a bit of a headache and that she'd see you back at home," MacKenzie told him.

Instantly concerned, he began to reach for his coat.

"I'd better get back and see if she's feeling all right—"

MacKenzie put a staying hand on his arm.

"Honestly, Jack, I think she just needs a bit of time alone," she said, truthfully. "She said you should have a good time."

"Well…" he said, uncertainly. "I'll drop her a text, just to make sure."

Once that was done, he looked between the pair of them.

"I feel like the third wheel, now," he complained.

"Not at all, son," Phillips assured him. "It's not often we get to share a pint with a friend, these days. Parenthood is busy work."

"You two do it so well," Lowerson said, with a smile. "I hope I'll get to be a dad, some day."

MacKenzie took a sip of her drink and eyed him over the rim.

"How does Mel feel about having children?"

"I—come to think of it, we haven't really talked about it," Lowerson realised, and made a mental note to rectify that, as soon as possible. "I hope she feels the same way I do because…well, I think she's the one for me."

MacKenzie swallowed her wine with difficulty.

"In fact," Jack continued, with a private smile. "I was thinking of asking her to marry me."

She almost choked, at that.

"To marry you?" MacKenzie squeaked.

"That's what the man said!" Phillips exclaimed. "That's fantastic, lad. We're so happy for you—for the pair of you."

"Well, I haven't asked her, yet," Lowerson said, nervously. "I don't want to count my chickens."

MacKenzie couldn't have said it better, herself.

"When—when are you planning to ask her?" she wondered, and hoped he hadn't bought a ring. "You haven't been together that long…"

"I was planning to ask her tomorrow, on Valentine's Day," he said, and MacKenzie was lost for words. "Then I remembered, it's the anniversary of her sister's death on Tuesday. I don't know whether it would be the best timing."

"Yes," MacKenzie said, clutching at the straw. "It might not be the best time, if she's going to be reminded of her sister's murder—don't you agree, Frank?"

But Phillips was blithely unaware of any undertone to her question, and failed to read the meaningful look in her eye.

"I dunno, pet. I think it might be nice for her to have a happy memory around that time, to offset the bad ones."

MacKenzie could cheerfully have throttled him.

"That's a good point," Jack said.

"Yes," she said, and glared at her husband. "But, all the same, why don't you play things by ear? Maybe see how she's feeling tomorrow? You'd want the timing to be perfect, wouldn't you?"

Jack nodded thoughtfully.

'You're right," he said eventually. "No sense in rushing things. We've got all the time in the world, after all."

At precisely the same moment Frank Phillips took charge of the karaoke mic, Ryan stepped inside his front door at Elsdon. Rather than finding Neil Diamond crooning on the radio, he heard the soft strains of Louis

Armstrong coming from the direction of their living room.

He hung up his coat, and followed the music.

"Anna?"

He found his wife swaying softly with their baby in her arms, the lights turned down low.

"Ssh," she whispered. "I've nearly got her over to sleep."

Ryan glanced over her shoulder at the baby, who lay comfortably against her shoulder with her eyes wide open.

"Mm hmm," he said, and grinned. "Want me to take over?"

"Why don't you join us?"

Ryan did just that, transferring the child from her weary arms to rest against one shoulder, before holding out his other arm so that Anna could snuggle against the other. They swayed like that for a while, the three of them, as the music shifted from Louis to Ella Fitzgerald, and on to Bing Crosby, until Ryan felt his daughter's tiny body slump against him, having fallen asleep at last.

"I'll take her up," he whispered.

Anna nodded, and sank onto the sofa with a grateful sigh. Though their child was by no means difficult, she was a bright little thing who seemed to have boundless energy. While she was pregnant, she was sure other mothers had advised her to sleep while her baby slept… but, what if the kid barely slept at all, day or night?

It seemed that Emma hardly needed any rest before she was up and raring to go again—whether her parents were ready, or not.

Still, these were special times, and Anna wouldn't have changed a thing.

"She's tucked up," Ryan said, re-entering the room. "Let's see how long it lasts."

Anna smiled, and tipped her face up for a kiss.

"How was your day?" she asked him.

But Ryan was more interested in hearing about hers.

"We'll come on to that," he said. "Why don't you tell me how your day was, first?"

Happy enough to oblige, Anna told him about their exploits, from 'paint splodging' to petting the horses at the nearby stables.

"Emma loved the horses," she said. "I've never seen her so excited."

"We'll have to give her a ride on a miniature Shetland, when she's a bit older," he said. "Perhaps Sam would be able to teach her—she'll be older, by then, too."

"Emma loves Samantha," Anna said, with fondness. "She always has so much time for her, which is pretty good, for a twelve-year-old."

Ryan nodded, and then grinned.

"I'm not sure how long that will last," he said. "According to Frank, Sam has a date with a boy from school tomorrow."

Anna could imagine Phillips' reaction to that, and chuckled.

"So, I assume he's been cobbling together an iron chastity belt," she joked.

"Drowning his sorrows in Newcastle Brown Ale and Barbra Streisand's Greatest Hits, more like," Ryan said, with another grin. "But, one day, that'll be me, so I won't laugh too loudly. Emma's bound to grow up, one of these days."

"Not just yet," Anna said, and gave him another kiss. "You can keep your shotgun locked away, for now."

Ryan thought of his little girl as a grown woman, and had only to look at his wife to imagine it.

She'd be a beauty.

Almost immediately, he thought of another woman whose beauty had been swept away by the tides, and a shadow crossed his face.

Sensing it, Anna took his hand.

"Tough day?"

Ryan nodded.

"No more so than any other, I suppose, but…" He rolled his shoulders to ease the ache. "I think it's different for me, since having Emma. I see things from a different perspective, or maybe I feel it more keenly. We found somebody else's daughter, today, and they don't even know it yet."

"Can't you contact them?"

"It's more a case of being unable to identify the victim," he said. "Without an ID, we have no way of knowing where she comes from, or who her family might be."

Anna squeezed his hand.

"You'll find out," she said. "You always do."

"I'll do my best," he qualified. "It isn't always enough, when you're battling against an unknown foe."

She gave him a quizzical look.

"What do you mean?"

"The whole thing—the wreck, the body—it reeks of organised crime," he said. "They're parasites, every last one of them. They prey upon the weak, and sleep soundly in their beds at night. Not only that, they've evolved so that it's becoming harder and harder to detect the real honchos, the ones with the clout. We might pull in a couple of soldiers from time to time, but never the top dog."

"Try telling that to Bobby Singh," she reminded him.

"He was a rare exception," Ryan said. "He'd been operating for years before we could bring him down. It's the wasted time that makes it hard to bear."

"That's because you always want everything done yesterday," she said, and rested her head on his shoulder. "There are some people in life who will always look for a way to get one over, to skip a queue, to flout a law or further their own interests at the expense of others.

I should know, I've spent my whole career reading about some of the most infamous operators around."

"Oh? Even worse than Jimmy the Manc?" Ryan said, with a playful smile. "Which historical figure could top him for nefarious deeds?"

"Well, there was the Roman emperor Nero," she said, off the top of her head. "He had homicidal tendencies, as did Genghis Khan, of course…then, there's King John, who ruled England between 1199 and 1216. He tried to seize the throne while his brother, Richard the Lionheart, was away crusading, and had his own nephew murdered. Arthur had a better claim to the throne, you see."

"Naturally," Ryan said.

"Ivan the Terrible, of Russia," she continued. "He was known to be especially cruel and ruthless. He had one nobleman eaten alive by dogs, when he was only a teenager. He took over vast areas of Russia for his personal domain, and gave a mounted police force carte blanche to execute anybody who didn't like it. Oh, and he killed his own son in a fit of rage, so the story goes."

"He sounds like a peach," Ryan commented, and was surprised to find he was enjoying himself. "Anybody else?"

"Well, Henry the Eighth was no boy scout," Anna mused. "He engineered the deaths of two of his six wives, and quite enjoyed burning heretics at the stake.

There's a pattern of good and bad people throughout history because that's just human nature. You're always going to get some rotten eggs, and unfortunately some of them are born into, or manage to claw their way into, powerful positions."

Ryan smiled slowly. "Did anybody ever tell you, you're sexy when you're talking about history?"

Anna laughed. "I think I can safely say, you're the only one who's ever told me that."

"Just as well," he said, and kissed her deeply.

CHAPTER 14

There was only a single toilet and shower in the dormitory the women shared but, since the former was perpetually occupied and the latter came with no towels or other means of drying themselves, they were forced to remain for long stretches in their beds until the heroin highs wore off. For some, the return to relative lucidity was unwelcome—the faraway world they occupied under the influence of the strong opiate being far preferable to the horrifying reality of their captivity—whilst, for others, it was a relief.

For her part, Achara was glad to find herself in possession of her own body and mind once again, even if it came with the crushing knowledge that her situation remained unchanged, and had not been some dreadful nightmare from which she would awaken. Reality was brutal, and cold, and she knew she must take measures to survive.

Her eye fell upon the small, wrapped package at the base of the bed, and she dragged herself up to reach for it. Though she'd have liked to throw the burger away, hunger was a more pressing concern, and she fell upon the cold bread and cheap meat with a ravenous appetite, only to feel nauseous soon after it was gone.

Had they drugged the food, or was it simply that food didn't taste the same after heroin?

She didn't know the answer to that question, but found herself running to the toilet, desperate to expel the meagre amount lining her stomach. Finding the cubicle occupied as usual, she banged hard on the door and muttered a stream of fast Thai, beseeching the other woman to come out, but there came no answer. Desperate, and since there was no lock on the cubicle door—*Pos'man* being firmly of the opinion that he should be able to access his merchandise at all times—Achara took the chance to yank it open.

Only to find a woman collapsed on the floor, surrounded by a puddle of her own vomit.

Overdose.

With a shaking hand, she leaned across to feel for a pulse at the woman's throat, calling to the others for help. But there came no running feet, no rush of action, the other women being ill-equipped to deal with any other trauma besides their own.

"*Chuay duay!*" she shouted again.

In desperation, she did the only thing she could think of, which was the one thing she'd been warned never to do.

She screamed, and kept screaming until somebody came.

"What's all that racket?"

Mick muted the sound on his television screen and looked over at Callum and Noddy, both of whom lay sprawled across the other sofas in the room.

"Cal, get over there and tell them to keep the bloody noise down," he said. "I'm tryin' to watch *Line of Duty*."

"I'll go," Noddy said, immediately. "I said I'd take the night shift, anyway."

Mick gave him a searching look.

"I said Cal would go," he repeated, very clearly.

The other men said nothing, and soon after Callum hurried from the room to do his bidding. In the residual silence, Mick pointed a finger at Noddy and looked him hard in the eye.

"Now, look here, you little prick," he snarled. "Don't think I haven't got the measure of you, cos I have. D' you think I'm a mug? Is that what you think?"

Noddy began to sweat.

"N-no, course not, Mick—"

"D' you think I'm blind, then? Or deaf? D' you think I'm a bloody idiot who's never been round the block?"

Mick rose to his feet, scattering crumbs onto the floor, and moved across the room until he stood nose-to-nose with the younger man.

"Well? Is that what you think o' me?"

Noddy shook his head vigorously.

"No, Mick, I don't think that—"

Mick stared at him for endless seconds, watching the man's eyes dilate in fear, and was satisfied.

"Good," he said, and stepped away again. "Because if you think I haven't seen you sniffin' round that skinny one through there, the one with the green eyes, you've got another thing comin'. This isn't a bloody free-for-all. I'm the one who says who gets to have a turn, and that's *none* of us, till The Dragon has had his pick. You know the rules."

Noddy ran a hand over his heated brow. "Aye—sorry, Mick."

"First rule of business, lad," the other man said, reaching for the television remote. "Always think of your bottom line. She's fresh meat, but she'll be worth nowt to him, and nowt to us, if you go helping yourself. That eats away at our margin, and I'd have to dock your pay. Understand?"

Noddy hadn't thought of it like that.

"Now, one of the older birds," Mick said, magnanimously. "If you'd had an eye for one o' them, that might be different. Nobody cares about them, so much. They'd be servin' a completely different clientele."

On which note, he unmuted the television and continued to watch his favourite police drama without any irony whatsoever.

"Mugs," he said, every so often, and took a swig of his beer.

In the confines of her stone prison, Lawana built a cocoon for herself inside the soil, for warmth, and wondered whether, in doing so, she had been responsible for her own burial. There must be few people who could boast of such a thing, and there was a strange comfort in the knowledge that she would die in her own company, swallowed whole by the earth, beneath a starry sky.

She could see one or two of them twinkling far above her head, in the scrap of sky that was just visible through the sink hole. She said silent prayers for her daughter, offering herself to whichever deity was listening.

Let her break free, where I failed.
Let her live a long and happy life.
Let her know the joy of children, and none of the pain of hardship.

Hunger ate away at the lining of her stomach, churning back and forth, while the pain in her back continued to rage.

She couldn't move her legs.

It hadn't come as so much of a surprise, after the fall she'd taken, but it severely curtailed any chance she might have had to escape, or find help. She could have tried dragging herself from the mound of earth and along the rocky floor using her arms, following the pathway the boy had taken earlier that day, but she could hear the crashing of the sea against the outer wall and into the mouth of the tunnel, trapping her inside.

And so, she waited, and hoped.

If she survived the night, she would leave at the first opportunity rather than wait any longer for *Gaz* or one of the other men to claim her.

She'd die, first.

Lawana thought of the boy, and wondered whether he had told them where she was.

Of course, he had.

He was one of them, and the only reason they hadn't come for her was probably because they were waiting until the cover of darkness to steal her away—only to find themselves thwarted by the tides. But, come daybreak, they'd be back, she knew it.

Lawana lay there in the darkness and tried to conserve her strength, willing herself to survive for another night, so that she might see the sunlight one last time.

It was not too much to ask, was it?

Just one last sunrise.

CHAPTER 15

"Ollie! Get your arse downstairs an' give me a hand!"

The boy heard his mother calling to him from the kitchen, and even through the layers of wall and plaster he detected the slur to her speech. Automatically, he checked the Spiderman clock he still kept on his wall, and saw that it was almost nine o'clock, which meant she would be almost a full bottle of gin into her nightly routine.

"Ollie!"

He left the quiet of his room to trail downstairs, unsure of what he would find. As he passed the living room, he dipped his head inside to find his younger sister watching cartoons, long after her bedtime. Her hair was unkempt, and she wore a stained pinafore dress he was sure she'd worn the day before.

"Stay there," he told her. "I'll come back in a minute."

"I'm hungry," she wailed. "Mammy said she was goin' to get me beans on toast—"

"All right," he said. "I'll make you something."

He closed the living room door, then made his way along the corridor towards the kitchen, which was brand new and filled with high-end appliances, just like the rest of the house. Business had been good for Gaz and his family, if nothing else.

"Mam?"

He found her slumped on the floor, leaning back against the dishwasher. For a second, he just looked at her, in much the same way he'd looked at the woman he'd found in the cave: with a mixture of curiosity and fear. His eyes swept over her dishevelled, platinum blonde hair, and over the smudged make-up on her lined face. Once, he could remember it being beautiful, just like her voice. He remembered how it had sounded while she sang softly to him, at night, when he was very young…but, not now. Now, it was hard and gravelled, its tone no longer that of a naïve girl, but of a grown woman whose dreams had been shattered. The low-cut t-shirt she wore was stained and smelled of booze, most likely from the bottle which lay empty beside the back door, where it had obviously rolled after she'd missed the bin.

"I fell," she said, and let out a giggle he found annoying. "Give us—give us a hand, son."

"Where's Dad?"

"Who gives a—" she began, and tried to reach for the countertop. "He'll be out with some woman or another, won't he?"

There was no anger, anymore. Just acceptance.

"Just make su—sure, you're nowt like him," Keeley managed, before sliding onto the floor again.

"Here," he said, tiredly.

She'd put on a bit of weight over the last few months, and it was a task to raise her up, but he managed it. Keeping her upright was another matter.

"Becki's still awake," he said, with reproach. "Mam, she's only four—"

"It's only fi—five o'clock," his mother argued, and squinted at the clock on the wall. "Isn't it?"

"No, Mam. It's past nine."

She looked at him, then back at the clock, before her face crumpled.

"I'm sorry," she cried, and tears began to roll down her face. "I'm sorry—I promise, I promise this is the last time—"

Shut up, he thought. *Just shut up.*

"Come on," he said, and half-dragged her towards the door. "Walk, Mam, I can't carry you all the way."

Her body refused to co-operate, and he was panting by the time he managed to take her upstairs to the master bedroom, where he laid her on the bed in the recovery position, which he'd learned at a First Aid class in school. If she threw up, at least she wouldn't choke.

He dragged a blanket over her body and, when she made no further sound, he realised she must have blacked out.

With a sigh, he left the room and made his way back downstairs to see to his sister, who was probably starving. A brief recce in the fridge confirmed that pickings were slim, nobody having remembered to go to the supermarket, but he dredged up a can of tuna and some dry pasta, which he set to boil. There was no milk or juice, so water would have to do, but it was better than nothing. While the pasta bubbled, he found his mother's purse, took out her debit card, and placed an online order for groceries to be delivered the next day. If he did that, maybe his father wouldn't blame her for not looking after the house properly, and might even think she'd had the foresight to remember.

"Ollie?"

Becki came into the kitchen and yawned.

"Is there anything to eat?"

He nodded, sat her on one of the shiny bar stools before serving up a plate of pasta and tuna.

"I don't like it," she said, wrinkling her nose.

"It's all we've got," he said, and nudged the plate towards her again. "Please, Becki. Just eat it, okay?"

He watched his sister munch her way through the swirls, then picked her up and carried her upstairs. It was too late to give her a bath, although she probably needed one, so he found a nightie and helped her into it, before tucking her into bed.

Ollie waited outside her door for a while and then stuck his head around to check she was asleep. When he was satisfied that Becki was out for the count, he checked his mother's room, and heard her deep snores.

Then, he stood on the landing and considered his next move.

His father might come home at any moment, and wonder where he had gone. Gaz liked to know his whereabouts, even if he was largely absent himself, and had made it clear that, as a new recruit to the business, he was expected to be on call at all times, day or night. Any unexplained absences must be accounted for.

The thought was enough to hold him there, until another thought entered his mind.

The woman's face, as she'd appealed to him for help.

Ollie clutched his hands to the sides of his head, trying to rid himself of the unwanted image, wishing he'd never found her, never seen her…

But he had, and her image could not be erased.

He'd spent much of the day thinking of the best course of action, considering numerous possibilities and rejecting each one, until he'd fallen back on a simple, old-fashioned solution to his problem.

Call the police.

It was extremely risky, and would require bravery, which was a commodity in short supply. There was no way he could make the call from home, or from his mobile phone; not even from any of the burner mobiles his father left lying around the house. There must be no way for the police to trace the call back to him, or he'd be punished as a rat, and his whole family ruined.

He thought of his sister lying asleep upstairs, and even of his mother.

If he left the house, he would be committing an act of treason against his family, and an act of mercy for a complete stranger.

It went against everything he had ever known, but he knew what he must do.

Jingling the loose change in his pocket, Ollie hurried downstairs and put on a dark jacket and cap. Then, he checked the peep hole and, finding the pathway clear outside, slipped out into the night.

"Emergency. Which service?"

Ollie watched the seconds drain away on the pay phone, and felt his mouth run dry.

"Caller, you've reached the Emergency Services. Which service do you require?"

"I—the police. Police."

"I'll just connect you now."

He waited, eyes scanning the deserted street for any movement.

"Hello, you've reached the Police. What is your emergency?"

"It's—I've found someone. A woman, and she's injured—"

"I can transfer you to the Ambulance Service—"

"No! No, you need to go and find her," he whispered, clutching the phone with both hands until his knuckles turned white. "She's trapped."

"Where are you calling from?"

"It doesn't matter," he almost shouted, and then caught a movement in his peripheral vision, which sent his heart racing, before he realised it was only a stray dog. "Just head for Spottee's. She's not far from there."

He hung up the receiver before the operator could ask him any more prying questions, then used the back of his sleeve to scrub any fingerprints from the cracked plastic. The faces of half-naked women touting their wares stared back at him from the many adverts plastered to the inside of the phone box and he felt dirty, all of a sudden. Standing there in an old phone box which smelled of dog excrement, he found himself in possession of a new, hitherto unknown knowledge about the nature of his own existence.

Don't be like him, his mother had said.

But, he realised he and his father had something in common, after all.

They were both brave, in their own ways.

CHAPTER 16

Later that evening, Jack Lowerson found Melanie sitting cross-legged on the floor of their living room, surrounded by papers and old photographs from her sister's file.

"Hi," he said, gently.

She looked up at him with bloodshot eyes.

"Hi," she said in return. "Did you have a nice time?"

"Yeah," he said, thinking of Frank's roof-raising baritone and MacKenzie's infectious laughter. "Wish you were there, though."

"Sorry about that," she said, looking away. "I just didn't feel like socialising, after all."

"It's okay," he said. "It's a difficult time of year for you."

She frowned, then looked down at the paperwork in front of her.

"Yes," she said, feeling guilty again. "Um, d' you want a cup of tea?"

"Stay where you are and I'll make it," he offered, and she watched him bustle off to the kitchen, pausing to scratch the cat's ears as it trotted over to curl lovingly around his legs.

A good man, she thought, and tears sprang to her eyes.

A few minutes later he returned with two steaming mugs, and seated himself on the rug beside her.

"Want to talk about it?" he asked, indicating the old summaries and statements.

"I do this every year," she said, and shook her head. "I don't know why I keep torturing myself."

"Because you loved her, and you haven't given up on the possibility of avenging her death," he said quietly.

She nodded, and took a sip of the tea he offered.

"Thanks," she murmured. "I needed this."

"That's what I'm here for—"

"No," she said, with a bit more force than she'd intended. "No, it isn't, Jack. You're not here to wait on me, or make me feel better when I'm low. It should be a two-way street."

"Isn't it?" he asked, in genuine confusion. "You'd do the same for me."

She supposed that was true.

"I'm a bit wound up," she admitted. "Sorry."

She looked down at the papers strewn in front of her, and was angry, all of a sudden.

"I don't know why I'm wasting my time with this," she muttered, and began shuffling them into a stack. "There isn't anything new to discover, and it's not as though I'm about to have some great epiphany. Gemma's gone, and it's one of those things, that's all."

"Except, it wasn't 'one of those things,'" he said. "You don't need to pretend that it was."

Mel let out a harsh sob, and rose to her feet, kicking the papers as she went.

"All right, then, she was brutally murdered. Is that what you want me to say? Do you want me to tell you about how they found her, weeks after her death, so she couldn't even be identified without dental records? Whoever did that to her left her in plastic bags, Jack, as though they were taking out the rubbish." He said nothing, letting her get it all out.

"It's been over a decade, and still no DNA match," she said, dejectedly. "There was only one usable sample they found on her whole body, just a single hair that didn't belong to her, but was caught on her nail—probably as she tried to fight. For years, I kept thinking I'd get an alert to say a match had been found, and we'd have the bastard after all, but it's never come."

"There's still time," he said, although he could make her no promises.

"She was my twin," Mel said, so softly he strained to hear. "She was always just a little brighter, a little more beautiful and a little bit kinder than me. Everyone loved her."

He wanted to argue that she was all of those things, too, but it was not the time.

"All my life, I've compared myself to her, wondering how she'd be, if she was still here," Mel continued. "I've felt guilty that I'm here while she's gone, and I've wondered—wondered if it should have been the other way around—"

Her voice broke, and Jack rose to his feet, moving swiftly to envelop her in his arms.

"Don't say that," he said urgently. "Don't even think it."

"I think of her every day," Mel admitted. "Not for long, but often in the morning, or just before bed. I say, 'good night' to her, and 'good morning'. Does that make me crazy, Jack?"

"No, love, it just makes you human."

And, just like that, Melanie Yates had the epiphany she'd hoped for. There, in the quiet comfort of the home they'd built, she looked at the man beside her—*properly* looked—and felt her worries melt away.

"I love you, Jack," she said, with feeling. "I'm sorry if I don't tell you enough."

He looked down to find tears in her eyes.

"Hey—no need for that," he said, and brushed them away. "I don't need to hear it all the time, to know it."

She swallowed. "Thank you," she said huskily.

"For what?"

"For…being patient with me, that's all."

Lowerson shook his head, and decided he would never fully understand the strange and mystical mind of a woman, even one he happened to love.

While the world slept, Lawana lay awake, listening for a change in the tides.

While the hours ticked by, she watched the subtle shift in the colours of the sky, from deepest black to royal navy, as the night slipped into the early hours of a new day. When the sound of the sea became less of a roar at the mouth of the cave, she knew it had receded and it was time for her to move.

She pushed the soil from her body, breaking free of the shell she'd made for herself, and shivered as her skin was exposed to the air once more. Then, using hands that were still tender from their onslaught on the boat, she lowered herself from her perch and onto the rocky floor, which was damp to the touch and covered in hardened shells and lichen.

Her legs came last, thudding onto the floor like dead weights.

Breathing fast and shallow, she dragged herself towards the entrance to the tunnel, commando style.

Every movement was an enormous effort, every inch of ground a hard-won victory, until she detected a sound that made her freeze.

She lay on the floor of the cave, shivering, while she waited to hear it come again.

There, she thought. *A rustling sound, as though something were sliding along the tunnel towards her.*

Terrified that Gaz and the others had returned, she tried to slide backwards, searching frantically for a hiding place but finding none.

The noise came closer and closer, and she watched the entrance to the tunnel, holding her breath.

"Hello?"

A voice echoed down the tunnel, a man's voice she'd never heard before, and the light of a torch beam broke through the darkness. Soon after, she spotted a bright yellow stretcher appear at the head of the tunnel, sliding along the floor with a *whoosh* of hardened plastic against rock.

She waited, and then he followed.

Her rescuer.

She watched his head emerge from the tunnel, saw him shine the torch around the cave until it found her. She could not see his face, but she heard the kindness in his voice, even without understanding all the words.

"Help has arrived," he said softly. "Let's get you out of here."

"*Hel'*?" she whispered, and began to cry.

"There now," he murmured, and bent over to make his way across to where she lay sprawled on the floor.

With a pair of strong, gloved hands, he dragged her across the ground to the waiting stretcher and spent precious minutes strapping her onto the back of it, making sure she was securely tied.

"Time to go," he said, cheerfully.

The man led the way back out of the tunnel, dragging her behind him by way of a rope he'd attached to the base of the stretcher, and the journey out of the cave was long and uncomfortable, for which he apologised profusely.

"Not far now," he said, in the same cheerful, unthreatening voice.

Lawana could barely describe the feeling of relief and exhilaration at having been found. This man was all her prayers answered, and she would have complied with anything, if he'd only take her away from that dreadful place.

There was a short pause while he dropped onto the sand and checked the beach in both directions, before reaching back inside to drag her the remaining distance with swift, strong movements.

When her feet appeared at the tunnel's entrance, he abandoned the rope and grabbed her legs, tugging her out onto the wet sand and into his waiting arms.

"This is what we call the Fireman's Lift," he said, and hauled her over his shoulder like a sack of potatoes.

Keeping a secure hand banded over her legs and another on the rope attached to the yellow stretcher, he walked purposefully along the beach towards the grotto, keeping to the edge of the cliff. He stopped briefly beside one of the coastguard huts, where he nudged open the door he'd forced earlier and returned the stretcher, having been careful to drag it through the shallows as they made their way along.

After disposing of it, he turned his attention to the steep set of stairs beside the grotto, and let out a long sigh.

"I hope you're not afraid of heights," he said, and began making his way up the hill, gripping the bannister rail for support as he made the arduous journey to the top of the cliff.

Lawana closed her eyes tightly against the sight of the beach directly below, which grew further and further away as they ascended. It was another relief when they finally reached the summit, and she opened her eyes again to seek out his emergency vehicle. In Thailand, rescues were usually made in pairs or teams, rather than sending a single coastguard or policeman, but she didn't know anything about how things worked in England. Perhaps this was how things were done.

But, there was no police car or ambulance in sight.

In fact, the street was deserted, except for a small van parked on the other side of the road. To her surprise, he began walking towards it, whistling beneath his breath.

A delayed sense of self-preservation began to creep in, snaking its way through her body until it rang like a siren in her mind. She tried to move her legs, but they would not respond to the signals from her brain. She moved her head from side to side, seeking out any sign of life, but saw only a series of streetlights shining along the cliff road.

Quick as a flash, he crossed the road, pleased to have left the back door to his van unlocked and ready. Before she could utter more than a small cry, he shifted her in his arms, reaching for the rag he kept in his back pocket, for emergencies such as these. Sometimes, he managed a very wholesome conversation for at least part of the journey to their new home, but it seemed that was not to be, with this one.

"Open wide," he said, and stuffed the rag into her mouth before depositing her in the back of the van.

Taking one last look around, he joined her in there, battling his own rising excitement to make sure her hands and legs were securely tied for the remainder of the journey.

Soon after, the van moved off into the night, disappearing into the foggy morning as though it had never existed.

CHAPTER 17

Sunday 14th February

Anna awakened to the scent of roses.

Vases and jugs of all shapes and sizes had been stuffed to the brim and arranged around the bedroom. Surprised, and a little overwhelmed, she sat up and turned to find a card propped on her bedside table.

She opened it to find the 'artwork' courtesy of Emma Taylor-Ryan, but the message had been written by her father:

Anna,

You know I don't believe in Hallmark calendar dates—I love you every day of our lives, not only today. But I want to say how much you are appreciated. Thank you for every time you have supported and encouraged me to be a better man. Thank you for believing in me, when I forget to believe in myself. Thank you for being my best friend, my lover, the mother of my child and the best person I have ever known. I am the luckiest man in the world to have you walking by my side as we navigate this thing called Life.

Happy Valentine's Day.

With all my love, now and always,

Ryan x

Beneath which, there was a small painted handprint, and a translation which read:

Dear Mummy,

Thank you for all the cuddles, kisses and tickles.

Lots of love,

Emma x

Anna sat there for a minute or two clutching the card to her chest, and thought that, no, she didn't need to hear the words very often, but, when she did, they meant so very much.

"Knock, knock," Ryan said, and appeared in the doorway with Emma in one arm and a small tray balanced in the other.

Find yourself a man who can multi-task, she thought, with a smile.

"Good morning," she said, with a blinding smile. "Did you rob a florist's shop, for all these?"

She lifted her arms to encompass the roses.

"I might have made a few calls," he said, with a wink. "Happy Valentine's Day."

He deposited the tray on the bed beside his wife, and then perched on the end with Emma, who immediately made a grab for the toast and eyed the small pot of jam beside it with intent.

"Oh, no you don't," he said, but relented by breaking off a finger of buttered toast. "Gnaw on this."

Emma did just that, happily gumming the bread while her parents enjoyed a quiet moment.

"Thank you for the card," Anna said, softly. "It's beautiful."

"I have something else for you," Ryan said, and walked across to a chest of drawers to retrieve a small gift-wrapped package.

"You shouldn't have gone to all this trouble!" she protested. "I don't need gifts—"

"Who said anything about *need*?" Ryan smiled, and handed her a small square box.

Inside, she found a pair of amethyst earrings, which was her favourite stone.

"Oh, they're beautiful," she murmured. "Thank you!"

Ryan retrieved the remains of a slice of gummed toast from the floor where Emma had dropped it, and then smiled.

"Just a token," he said.

"Actually, I got something for you, too," she said, and felt shy, all of a sudden. She knew it was ridiculous to feel shy around her own husband, but he was a man who could elicit that kind of emotion.

Anna slipped from the bed and opened her wardrobe door, where she fished around for a few seconds before presenting him with a rectangular package in the shape of a book.

"Let me guess," Ryan said. "Is it a book?"

"Booo" Emma repeated.

"It might be," Anna said, lifting her chin. "Just open it."

Ryan tore open the packaging to reveal an old and, if he wasn't mistaken, first edition copy of *A Study in Scarlet*, which was his favourite of the Sherlock Holmes detective stories.

"Anna, you shouldn't have," he said, but felt like a little boy at Christmas.

"You never spend anything on yourself," she said. "We don't go in for flashy things, most of the time, but I know how much you love this book."

"I do," he said, reverently, running his fingers over the delicate binding. "This is wonderful, thank you."

"Well, don't get used to it," she chuckled. "Next year, I'll buy you an ice cream."

He grinned, and placed the book carefully out of the reach of small, sticky hands.

"I have to go back into the office today," he said, with regret. "But I've booked a babysitter for this evening because, tonight, Doctor Taylor-Ryan, we're going out."

Anna flushed happily. Due to one thing or another, it had been a while since she'd been able to put on some pretty clothes and enjoy an adult night out.

"You've got yourself a date," she said. "What time should I be ready?"

"Sitter's coming at six-thirty, and the table's booked for seven, in Bamburgh."

The little village where they'd been married, she thought.

"You're stacking up the Brownie points, aren't you?" she teased him. "What are you after?"

Ryan turned, braced a hand on either side of the bed where she lay, and gave her a slow smile as he moved closer.

"That all depends on what you're offering," he whispered, before capturing her lips.

When Emma let out a protesting cry for attention, and banged her little hands on the mattress beside them, they both laughed.

"Get used to it, kid," Ryan told her. "There'll be plenty more PDAs to embarrass you, over the years."

With that, he ruffled her soft hair and padded through to the bathroom, soaking up every moment of happiness to sustain him through the long hours of the day, until they were reunited.

Jack Lowerson had big plans to surprise Mel with breakfast in bed, and a morning of indulgence before they needed to return to the office. However, when he awakened, it was to find that she'd had the same idea, herself.

"Spanish omelette, coffee and freshly squeezed orange juice," she said, as he padded through to the kitchen-diner. "I was going to bring this through to you, on a tray. Go back to bed!"

He smiled and shook his head, lowering it to nuzzle at her neck.

"I'd rather share it with you, here," he said, gesturing to the table. "You've beaten me to it."

Mel smiled, and thought it was definitely her turn to show some appreciation.

"Well, I know we haven't got long, but I wanted to say thank you for listening to me, last night."

"Any time," he said, and lifted his knife and fork. "Mel?"

"Mm hmm?" she said, while she added milk to their cups of coffee.

"Will you—"

Just then, his mobile phone began to jingle, and he swore, knowing it would be the office.

"Hold that thought," he said, and made a grab for it. "Lowerson."

Mel paused to listen to the conversation, watching the shifting contours of his face.

"What's the matter?" she asked, once he'd ended the call.

"That was a call handler I know from Control," Jack said. "We used to have a drink every now and then, when I lived over in Heaton. Anyway, he was on shift last night, and took a call he thought was a bit unusual."

"Why didn't he just write it up?" she asked. "Why call you about it?"

"Robbie says he's written it up, but his supervisor's labelled it a prank. He doesn't agree."

"Why not?" she asked.

"He says a young man, he can't be sure of the age, called around nine-forty-five last night asking for the police. When he came through to Robbie, he reported that he'd found a woman who was injured and trapped, but he didn't say where. Didn't give any personal details, either. All he did say, was that we should head towards 'Spottee's.'"

"Spottee's?" she queried.

"Spottee's is a cave on Roker seafront," he told her. "It takes its name from a foreign sailor who was stranded in the area and could speak no English, so he couldn't talk to the locals—they thought he was some kind of lunatic. Apparently, he wore a spotted shirt, which is what earned him the nickname."

"Hang on, I remember now," Mel said, thinking back to an outing during her childhood. "There are all kinds of caves around that stretch—some of them go all the way back to Hylton Castle, apparently."

"What d' you make of it?" he asked.

"I think it's too much of a coincidence that an anonymous call comes through about an injured woman along that stretch of coastline, so soon after what we found, yesterday. I think we need to call Ryan."

She rose to clear their plates.

"Weren't you going to ask me something?"

Jack gave her a rueful smile.

"It can wait," he said.

If there was one thing Frank Phillips had learned over the years, it was that the way to a woman's heart was through laughter. With that in mind, he tiptoed out of bed and borrowed Samantha's stereo—thanking his lucky stars that she had stayed overnight with her friend, and would be none the wiser. He set it up on the landing outside the bedroom he and Denise shared, then went in search of *The Full Monty Soundtrack: Music from the Motion Picture*.

Already chuckling to himself, he slipped it into the ancient CD player but didn't press 'play' just yet; first, he snuck off into the spare bedroom to retrieve the outfit he'd ordered online several weeks before. When he'd bought it, the sizing had been ambitious, but he was gratified to see that his fitness and weight loss efforts were obviously paying off, as the garment—though questionable—now fit him like a glove.

He grabbed the plastic truncheon to complete his ensemble, and prepared to give the performance of a lifetime.

He believed in miracles, and, after all, she was a sexy *thang*.

MacKenzie couldn't say what she'd expected of Frank on Valentine's Day. Every year, he thought up some new way to surprise her, but, she had to admit, this year he had outdone himself.

She'd never laughed, and loved, so much in her life.

Being treated to Frank's personal rendition of a comedy striptease, complete with a Velcro and polyester police uniform that definitely didn't conform to regulations, was something she would never forget. She got into the spirit of things, clapping and cheering as he shook his funky stuff, and was more than pleasantly surprised when the shirt came off to reveal a decidedly buff Detective Sergeant Phillips.

The Velcro might have got a bit stuck around the posterior, but it came off in the end.

Later, when he'd worn himself out with the dancing—and other exertions—she laughed again.

"Frank? You're one in a million, you know that?"

"Aye, it's often been said."

"I wasn't expecting that," she told him.

"They never do," he winked, and earned himself a jab in the ribs. "Besides, I wasn't about to waste the first child-free morning we've had in a good long while."

"Amen," she said, with satisfaction.

"There was one other thing," he said, and leaned across to retrieve a box from his bedside drawer, which he passed to her. "I heard that it's sometimes customary for new mothers to receive an eternity ring, and, well, it doesn't seem right, you not having one as well. You've been as much a mother to our Samantha as the poor lass who brought her into the world—maybe more so."

Denise stared at the delicate run of diamonds set in a slim gold band.

"If you don't like it—" he said, worriedly.

"I love it, Frank," she said, quietly, at a loss for words.

"Here, let's try it on for size," he said, and slipped it onto her ring finger.

She looked down at the double bands and thought that they represented the two people she loved most in the world.

"I don't need diamonds, Frank," she said, because it was true. "And you shouldn't go spending all your money on jewellery."

"Can't a man spoil his wife, sometimes?" he demanded.

She smiled, and leaned over to kiss him.

"Why don't you restart the CD?" she whispered. "We've still got an hour before we need to collect Samantha…"

He turned to her with a pained expression.

"I'm many things, lass, but I'm not bleedin' Superman. I'm gonna need a sausage and egg sarnie before we go for round two."

CHAPTER 18

Having dispatched Lowerson and Yates to investigate Spottee's Cave and its surrounds, Ryan and MacKenzie met shortly before ten o'clock in the café of a bookshop in the centre of Newcastle, while Phillips went off to collect Samantha from her friend's house. Despite the day dawning brightly, the skies had begun to turn overcast, heralding the onset of another storm expected later that evening, and they were glad to be inside its warm surroundings.

"The weather's been all over the place," Mac said, and took a sip of her hot chocolate, smiling privately at her deliberate choice of beverage.

"The forecast is for storms over the next three to five days," Ryan agreed, angling himself towards the door so that he could keep an eye out for their guest.

"How will we recognise her?" MacKenzie asked.

Ryan shook his head.

"Wentworth said she'd find us," he replied. "Although, the scar on her cheek might be a clue. This seems an odd choice of location."

"Perhaps the kind of people she hopes to avoid don't tend to frequent bookshops," MacKenzie said, casting her eye around the customers. "It's good of her to meet us, at all."

"Very," he agreed, and wondered why she had.

There was no time to speculate further because, at that point, the waitress came across to ask if they'd like anything else.

Ryan was on the cusp of politely declining, and then did a double take.

"It's you, isn't it?"

Her scar was concealed by expert make-up, and her hair had been dyed a funky shade of pink. If he wasn't mistaken, she wore coloured contact lenses, and her arms were covered in intricately designed tattoos which, he assumed, were as much an expression of creativity as a means to hide the other scars on her body, inflicted by some of the people she'd had the misfortune to know. She looked no more than twenty, but Ryan knew from his discussion with DCI Wentworth that she was closer to thirty.

They'd ordered their drinks from her at the counter, and never so much as guessed.

"I've got a ten-minute break, so we can talk, if you like."

She took a seat beside them, angling herself towards the door, just as Ryan had.

"I didn't want to meet you here," she said. "But I couldn't think of anywhere better. This is the last place any of them would come."

"Too public?" MacKenzie enquired.

"No, too intelligent," the woman replied. "The kind of people you're looking for don't waste their time reading."

Her English was flawless, and Ryan could only admire how she held herself, after all she'd been through.

"Can I see your badges, please?"

They obliged, and waited while she scrutinised their warrant cards.

"I've been watching you both for the past five minutes," she said. "I can see you haven't brought anyone else with you."

They nodded.

"That was the agreement," Ryan said, and looked down at the badge on her shirt. "Is that your real name?"

She shook her head.

"No. I change my name, every six to twelve months, for safety. You can call me Niki, for now."

"Thank you for agreeing to meet us," Ryan said, keeping his voice low. "We understand that you run a centre for women who've recently left sex work, or who've been trafficked and have escaped their abusers. Is that right?"

She nodded.

"I work there, part-time, and here, or other places, on weekends," she said. "I wanted to do something to help."

"Who runs it with you?" Mac asked.

But the woman shook her head.

"I can't tell you that."

MacKenzie nodded her understanding.

"We know you're going out on a limb for us, Niki, but what we don't understand is *why*."

"The woman you found yesterday," she said simply. "She was one of us."

"We believe so," Ryan said.

"Perhaps it was better for her," Niki muttered. "She escaped a different kind of hell."

It was one way of looking at things, Ryan thought.

"What we really want to know is who might have been responsible for bringing her over to this country," he said.

She laughed.

"I only know faces," she said. "And, after a while, they all look the same. In the brothels or the strip clubs, nobody gives a real name. Don't you know that, sweetie? When they sent me there, they told me my name would be 'Fuchsia.'"

She patted her hair.

"Just a little nod to the past."

"Who sent you there?" MacKenzie asked.

"They called him 'The Horse', but he was no horse," she said, with an ugly laugh. "Thomas Linekar was his real name."

Ryan recognised the name as being part of a well-known crime family who had operated ten or more years ago, before the Moffa brothers had moved in and stolen their turf.

"The strip clubs are supposed to be regulated," MacKenzie began to say, and the woman laughed again, without any mirth.

"Listen, white lady. There's one rule for British girls, and another for everyone else," she said, bitterly. "In the main bar, it's all a cheap laugh. Drunk boys and men on stag dos, sometimes women, gathered around the main stage to get an eyeful and feel big about themselves. It's *just a laugh*, right? Isn't that what they always say? Where's the harm?"

Ryan and MacKenzie didn't bother to argue, because it was exactly what some people said.

"The British girls do private dances, and that's it," she continued. "They take their money and go home. They tell people it's their choice, that they're enlightened, and give speeches about female empowerment."

She took a deep breath, letting the anger drain away.

"Maybe for them," she said quietly. "But, not for everyone. There was a room, more than one room, behind a red curtain. It was another part of the club—members only—where 'special' clients were invited to go for 'special' treatments. They could have whatever they liked, if they paid the right price. We were made to form a line-up, and they'd pick whoever they liked the look of. Some nights, I tried to look bad, to avoid being picked, but they can always tell."

"I'm sorry," Ryan said, huskily.

She looked into his eyes, and thought he was sincere. All the same, he didn't know the least of it, and probably never would. Like Gaz, she too could categorize people within a minute or two, especially men, and this one was a breed apart.

"You have a wife, Chief Inspector?"

And a daughter, he wanted to say.

"Yes."

"She's a lucky woman."

Ryan said nothing, but was sorry for the life she had led, and angry with members of his own sex who had put that scar on her face and the deeper scars on her heart.

"How did you get away?" MacKenzie asked her.

"They use drugs to control you," Niki explained. "From the very beginning, they try to make you dependent, so you learn to need them, even when you hate them. Then, they say you owe them money, so you have to pay it off. It's a cycle, and you're trapped."

She took a long, quivering breath, and lifted her chin.

"I learned a lot from them, about business," she said. "I became one of their best earners. It took years, but Linekar learned to trust me. That was his mistake. He fell asleep beside me, one night, and that was the chance I was waiting for."

She remembered the feel of the knife entering his gut, and clasped her fingers together.

"Who runs things now?" he asked her.

She looked into his face and was almost tempted. She saw his conviction and wanted to trust it, but her life was at stake.

So, she told him all she could.

"It's been a long time since I was in the game," she said. "But some of the newer girls who come to us talk about a place called 'Voyeur'—it's where The All-American Diner used to be, down near the railway station. Apparently, it's the place to go, if you want a certain kind of entertainment."

It was a place that was already on their radar.

"Tell them Fuchsia sent you, and some of the girls might talk to you," she added.

"Thank you," MacKenzie murmured. "What if we have some more questions—"

"I don't have anything else to tell you," she said. "Good luck, Inspector."

CHAPTER 19

Spottee's Cave was tucked into a wide limestone ravine off the Roker coastline, four miles further south of Marsden. It was a scenic spot, a large Victorian park with bandstand having been built on either side of the ravine, spanned by a bridge. However, there were no injured women to be found; only the occasional dog-walker and the usual crowd of beach combers who cast curious glances at the man and woman who, even dressed in plain clothes, were obviously police.

"There's nothing here," Lowerson said, as they made their way back onto the beach.

"Maybe the caller said 'Spottee's' because it was the nearest landmark," Yates replied. "We should have a look at the other caves in the area."

Lowerson looked north, towards Souter, and knew that Marsden lay beyond it.

"If this injured woman has anything to do with the wreck, it seems unlikely she'd have walked this far south, especially in the middle of a storm. You can't walk all the way from Marsden to here via the beach, anyway—the tides wouldn't allow it."

"It could have been a prank call, after all," Mel said.

"Maybe," he agreed. "Perhaps our anonymous caller panicked and said the nearest thing they could think of."

She nodded.

"It could be a genuine error," she said. "They just got the name of the cave wrong."

"Yeah, people often mix up the names and exact location of Spottee's, unless they're local," Lowerson said. "The only reason I knew it was here is because I used to visit my grandparents in Seaham all the time when I was a kid, and that's just around the corner."

"I've asked Digital Forensics to trace the source of the call," she said. "They know it came from a pay phone, but they're looking into its exact location. It might help."

"Good thinking."

"The call has to have come from someone connected to the operation," she thought aloud. "Anyone else would have reported having found her, in the usual way."

He looked out across the water, and thought that there were worse places to be, on Valentine's Day, than walking along the beach with the woman he loved—even when they were still on duty.

He reached for her hand, and tugged her close.

"Do you like kids?" he asked, and she gave him a startled look.

"Kids? Um, yes, I do. Why do you ask?"

"I've always wanted to have a family, some day. Nothing crazy, just the usual—you know, a nice house, couple of kids…"

"At least you're not expecting a football team," she joked.

"What about you?" he asked, seriously. "Is that something you'd want?"

She considered the question, which inevitably raised memories from her own childhood.

"I don't know how good of a mother I'd make," she said. "I'd like to think I'd do my best, but I'm not sure I'm ready for children, just yet. I need more time, just as a couple."

"I couldn't agree more," he said, pressing a kiss to the top of her head. "It was more of a general question."

"I'm not against having kids," she said, openly. "I just don't agree with the institution of marriage."

Lowerson tripped over a pebble, then righted himself.

"You—you don't agree with marriage?" *Why hadn't he known this before?*

"It works for a lot of people—take Anna and Ryan, or Frank and Denise. But I've seen how other marriages can be, and it isn't always pretty. Besides, if two people love each other, surely they don't need a piece of paper to prove it, do they?"

He looked out across the water, trying to unscramble the thoughts in his head. He'd had it all mapped out: the ring, the proposal, the happily ever after. He'd imagined her in a big white dress, and himself in a smart tuxedo. He'd visualised them dancing to their favourite song and saying 'I do' in front of all their loved ones.

She didn't want any of that, and it was a hard pill to swallow.

"Do you think it's something you'd ever change your mind about?"

He hoped he didn't sound too desperate.

"Well, I suppose, never say 'never', but I just can't imagine it right now. I didn't realise you were so traditional," she added, with a frown.

"Yeah, I guess I'm an old-fashioned guy, despite the shiny suits," he said, self-deprecatingly. "But, like you say, it doesn't really matter, so long as we're happy."

"Jack, if it's something you really want—"

"It has to come from both of us," he interrupted. "Or it's meaningless. Besides, as you say, who needs a piece of paper, eh?"

He nodded towards the next cave.

"I'll dip inside this one," he said, and was all business again.

The next stop on Ryan and MacKenzie's list was the mortuary.

It was not everybody's idea of an ideal Sunday morning excursion, particularly on what was supposed to be the most romantic day of the year, but any feelings of self-pity were easily overcome by remembering that there was at least one woman who no longer had the luxury of choosing where to spend her time—for, time had been snatched away from her.

"It never changes, does it?" MacKenzie remarked, as they made their way past the main entrance of the Royal Victoria Infirmary and towards the staff entrance that would lead them down into the bowels of the hospital.

Ryan looked around at the people coming and going: an eclectic mix of visiting relatives, recovering patients being wheeled out to waiting taxis and mini-buses for their journey home, and tired-looking clinical staff coming on or off shift.

"I've lost count of the number of times I've been here," he said. "It should be a depressing place, when you consider all the things we've seen, but somehow I find it uplifting."

She gave him a questioning look.

"For every person they can't save, there's another five they do," he told her. "That's something to be cheerful about."

His sister hadn't been one of them, Ryan thought, but there was nothing any of the world's finest nurses, doctors or surgeons could have done for Natalie. Her time had been snatched from her, too, and there was no bringing her back. Thinking of his sister, as he often did, brought with it bittersweet memories of the past, but it also re-affirmed his resolve. Her death had been the catalyst driving him to work harder and faster to bring the very worst kind of criminals to justice and, he supposed, being able to bring some small comfort to the families of their victims was the best way he could think of to honour her memory.

"Penny for them," Denise said.

Ryan shook his head.

"Ghosts," he murmured.

"Benign, or malicious?" she asked.

"Oh, definitely the Casper variety," he grinned, and, after keying in the access code, held open the door for her to precede him.

It was a small, chivalrous action, and, unlike with some other men, MacKenzie understood that it came with no sexist undertone; no implied belief that she was in any way incapable of opening her own doorways. It was an act of kindness he would have done for anyone, and that was all there was to it.

"Thanks," she said, and stepped inside.

Outside, wind from the Arctic had made its way across the North Sea and further inland, touching even the hardiest of people with its icy fingers. However, as they descended to the basement, the temperature became noticeably warmer thanks to the mortuary's industrial cooling system which pumped cold air in, and expelled hot air into the surrounding corridors through a series of ancient-looking vents.

They shed their overcoats as they made their way through the warren of corridors until they came to a set of wide metal security doors.

"I think the passcode changed, recently," Ryan said, and tried to remember what it was.

"It'll be something pretentious," MacKenzie said. "Pinter loves meaningful codes."

It was true: the last few codes he'd chosen had signified the year of death of a famous historical figure.

"I'm trying to remember which king or queen he's chosen, this time," Ryan said, and was struck by inspiration.

He typed in *1991*, and the doors buzzed.

"Freddie Mercury," he explained, and MacKenzie smiled.

"Much better than your average monarch."

Stepping through the double doors, they were treated to a blast of cold air, which immediately precipitated a wave of goosebumps that seemed only fitting for the occasion. They paused to sign themselves into the logbook beside the door, reached for a couple of guest lab coats to protect their clothes, and then sought out the master of the mortuary domain.

Doctor Jeffrey Pinter was alone that morning, his technicians being either at home for the weekend like normal people, or enjoying a well-earned cigarette break around the back of the hospital. They didn't spot him immediately, for he was partially obscured by the side of a large immersion tank on the far side of the wide, open-plan room.

"Morning!" he trilled out.

They didn't bother to enquire what was occupying his attention; ignorance was sometimes bliss, in an environment such as this.

"Well," he said, appearing after a minute or two. "Ryan, Denise, good to see you both."

Pinter was an outstanding clinician and, for all his foibles, a decent man, but he was not possessed of the kind of easy social graces that might have endeared him to strangers. Paired with a tall, lanky frame, sunken, shadowed eyes, and a wispy, salt-and-pepper head of hair, he bore an unfortunate resemblance to the Grim Reaper which, in his line of work, cut a little too close to the bone.

All the same, he wore the cheerful expression of a man whom life was treating kindly.

"What's her name?" Ryan asked, and wriggled his eyebrows. "You've got that look in your eye, Jeff."

Pinter made no attempt to be coy. His last relationship with a fellow pathologist hadn't lasted—it turned out that talking shop after hours was not the most conducive to a fulfilling love life—and he'd gone through a long dry spell before meeting the current object of his affections, who he was only too happy to shout about.

"Her name's Rae," he said. "She's a science teacher. We met over at the Centre for Life—I was giving a talk to some of her sixth formers about a career in pathology."

"Used to be nursing or secretarial work, in my day," MacKenzie joked. "The Careers Service is branching out."

He nodded.

"I don't know how keen the kids were, but Rae and I seemed to hit it off."

Ryan was happy for him.

"In that case, we're even more grateful to you for coming in on a Sunday."

"Don't mention it," Pinter said, with none of his usual belly-aching about overtime. "We've all got to pull together."

When he turned to lead them towards one of the private examination rooms, Ryan and MacKenzie exchanged an expressive glance. If this was the effect of romance on the mind of a gnarly old pathologist, maybe the government should consider dishing out free memberships to some online dating sites as a matter of public health policy.

"I've put her in here," Pinter said, as they came to one of the smaller rooms off a side corridor. "I hope you're feeling strong of constitution, this morning, because this one's especially difficult to look at."

It was good of him to warn them, but no amount of warnings could have prepared their systems for the sight which awaited them beneath that white paper shroud.

The woman's body was enormously bloated, its skin stained a jaundiced yellow thanks to a liberal application of a strong disinfectant, which left a strong stench of iodine hanging on the stale air circulating around their heads. Her body bore countless small and larger lesions and lacerations, the product of having been battered against the edge of the wreck, following which she'd been left to the mercy of the fish and the birds.

The three were silent for long seconds, allowing their bodies and minds time to adjust to the sight of violent death, as well as paying a small mark of respect to the dead. All the while, Ryan's eyes roamed over the gurney, noting every minor detail, every nick and cut.

"How old do you think she was, Jeff?"

Pinter might have expected him to ask about the cause of death, first, but he understood and sympathised with the line of thought.

"No more than twenty," he said, with quiet authority. "Looking at the bone mass, the teeth…I'd say that was an accurate gauge."

Ryan nodded.

"How did she die?"

Pinter sucked in a long breath and let it whistle back out again through his teeth, which was a habit he'd been wont to do for time immemorial, and had irritated them for just as long.

"Fatal asphyxia by drowning, owing to aspiration of fluid into the lungs," he said. "However, as you'll see from the top of the cranium here—"

He unclicked a small, retractable pointer and directed it to the top of her head, where they could see a gash of around three or four inches in length.

"—there's a large cerebral contusion, following a split in her skull. It's difficult to say whether this was sustained post-mortem, or ante-mortem, but there's every possibility the tide struck her against either the side of the boat or a nearby rock, causing her to lose consciousness and drown thereafter."

Ryan nodded.

"As you can see from the remaining injuries, many of these are superficial and were undoubtedly inflicted post-mortem as a consequence of the local wildlife."

MacKenzie looked upon the woman's body with sad green eyes.

"What about the marks on her wrists?"

Pinter nodded, and moved down to look at one of the woman's hands, which had been bagged in plastic casing that was beginning to balloon as natural gases seeped from her skin.

"Just as you'd expect," he said. "Faulkner sent across one of the cuffs his team recovered from the wreckage, and I've compared the shape and size with the line of her injuries. I'd say it was highly probable this woman was tightly restrained, and for a number of hours. Her skin still retained a number of embedded iron particles."

Ryan thought of all the other cuffs they'd recovered from the trawler, and was enraged.

"What about post-mortem interval?" he said, very softly. "How long had she been dead, when we found her?"

Pinter made a thrumming sound with his lips, pretending to think about it.

"Somewhere between three and five hours would be my best estimate," he said. "How does that compare with your timings?"

"It fits," MacKenzie replied, thinking of the tides and of the time Jill Price had first reported it to their Control Room. "The tide began to move out at around four a.m. yesterday morning, which would have enabled anyone coming off the boat to access a small amount of shoreline sometime thereafter. That also corresponds with the location of gathered footprints we found near the cliffs."

"Our witness called it in just before eight, which gives around a four-hour window between the time the boat was likely to have collided with Marsden Rock, and the time first responders arrived at the scene," Ryan added.

"Was there anything in her system?" MacKenzie asked. "Has the toxicology report come back?"

Pinter nodded, and moved across to a metal desk which held a computer, where he brought up the results of the report on the monitor.

"Aside from the abnormal quantity of fluid found in her mastoid cells, as you would expect, the report indicates nil in the way of alcohol, but high levels of diacetylmorphine—more commonly known as heroin."

Pinter rattled through the other items in the report, concluding that she probably hadn't eaten for at least twelve hours prior to her death.

"There are some very minor track marks on her left ankle," he said, rising to indicate the pinpricks, which were so tiny in comparison with her other, more obvious traumas, they would have been easy to miss.

"You must have eyes like a hawk," Ryan said, leaning down to look at the tiny abrasions.

"There are multiple puncture marks, when you look at it under the magnifier," Pinter explained. "Given that heroin has a very short half-life, to maintain the high, a user has to inject themselves every few hours. I've examined every inch of this woman, and this is the only concentration of markings consistent with intravenous drug use."

"You're saying, there aren't any other signs of drug use on her body?"

"None," Pinter agreed. "As for this area around the ankle, there are thirty-two puncture marks that I've counted which would tally with the diameter of a needle, and the beginnings of cellulitis surrounding those marks which would corroborate that."

Ryan digested that information, then nodded his thanks.

"If we assume this woman received, let's say, four or five doses of heroin per day to maintain the high and develop a dependency, that would mean the injections began anywhere between six and eight days prior to her death."

MacKenzie smiled, following his line of thought.

"Which will help us to build a timeline of events, once we hear from colleagues in Europe and beyond."

"Exactly," Ryan said. "Jeff, this was very helpful, and we're grateful to you. Is there anything you can tell us that might give us a steer on her identity?"

Pinter looked down at the woman with compassion.

"In terms of fingerprint analysis, there's no match to the databases we keep, and likewise as far as DNA is concerned, there's no match on any accessible database," he said. "Now, when it comes to this lady's genealogy, we can make assumptions as to her ethnic background by the colour of her skin, but, as we all know, that is by no means determinative of her country of origin or much else, for that matter. I've sent a sample of her DNA for more detailed testing, which I'm hoping to have back in the next couple of days, and that will compare the frequency of each of her autosomal DNA markers with various population groups, which should provide some indication of her geographic heritage."

MacKenzie cleared her throat.

"Do you still have the clothes she was found in?"

Pinter's eyebrows raised, but he nodded.

"Yes, they're being stored in the usual way—"

"I was only going to suggest that, perhaps, the tags on her clothing might prove informative."

Pinter opened his mouth to speak, then snapped it shut again.

"Yes," he said, grudgingly. "I suppose that might help."

Five minutes later, Ryan and MacKenzie held the woman's soggy clothing in their gloved hands, examining it for tags.

"Here," he said, holding out the small white label. "Made in Thailand—"

"She could have bought that in Primark," MacKenzie was bound to say. "Anything else?"

"All the washing instructions appear to be written in some language other than English—not Chinese, or Japanese, I know that much. Could very well be Thai."

He held it out for MacKenzie to see for herself.

"Yes," she agreed. "Looks like it."

"It's not determinative," Ryan said, conscious of Pinter's crestfallen face looming over his right shoulder. "We'll certainly wait for the results of Jeff's clinical enquiries, before we draw any firm conclusions."

Pinter perked up at that, just as Ryan had hoped.

"Oh, definitely," MacKenzie said, picking up his cue, whilst privately thinking that she would tell Lowerson and Yates to focus the thrust of their enquiries on known trafficking routes out of Thailand.

"I'll get those results across to you as soon as they come through," Pinter said, somewhat mollified. "There was one other thing…"

"Oh, yes?" MacKenzie said, as she slipped the clothing back into their evidence bags.

"This," he said, reaching for another evidence bag containing a water-damaged photograph. "When she came in, she was still wearing lace-up trainers. We found this plastered to the sole of her foot."

The paper was so badly damaged it was hard to make out the figures in the photograph, but it seemed to show three people: a man, a woman, and a child, standing beneath a flowering tree with the sun at their backs.

"Perhaps she was the child in this image," MacKenzie whispered, and was embarrassed to find tears prick the back of her eyes.

"Whoever she was, we know there were people who cared for her," Ryan said, casting his searing blue gaze back over to the silent witness in the room. "That means we're no longer just doing this for her. We're doing it for *them*, too."

CHAPTER 20

Ryan and MacKenzie weren't the only ones looking for answers.

Phillips kept a beady eye on the Person of Interest sitting on a table in the window, and an *especially* beady eye on their hands.

"Keep those on the table, where I can see 'em," he muttered, before scooping up a giant spoonful of rum and raisin ice cream.

Dibley's was a local treasure to the residents of Tynemouth and far beyond, who flocked to the little ice cream parlour not only to satisfy a craving for sugar, but to enjoy a slice of childhood nostalgia. A stone's throw from the sea, it was patronised by people of all ages, all of whom pressed their noses to the glass of the long counter with its colourful display of flavoured cream.

"It's cute, isn't it?"

Phillips had almost forgotten he was not alone.

The mother of the boy Samantha was currently giggling with—a bit too enthusiastically, for his liking—smiled at him from across the table with a look in her eye that suggested she understood exactly how he felt, and could sympathise. She'd introduced herself as, 'Annie' and, he was forced to admit, looked perfectly normal.

Cute? Phillips wondered, stealing another glance at the twelve-year-old couple swapping sundaes. She, with her long red hair intricately French braided by his own fair hands and tied with a pink butterfly bobble—not that Phillips was about to admit *that* particular skill to all and sundry—and he, with his experimentally-gelled hair and t-shirt which read, 'SURF LIFE'.

"Aye," he said, at length. "I s'pose."

Annie smiled to herself, and took a sip of coffee.

"Sam tells me you and Denise are both with the police?" she said, trying again to make conversation.

"Aye—I mean, yes, yes we are. Murder Squad," he added, without thinking.

She stared at him.

"That's…interesting."

He took another slurp of ice cream, and wondered if she looked nervous because she had something to hide.

"It has its advantages," he said, with another meaningful glance towards the window table. "What did you say your last name was?"

She swallowed her ice cream with difficulty, feeling like an interrogation suspect.

"Er, Priest."

Priest, he thought, and flipped through his mental files for any recollection of a troublesome family by that name.

"We, er, we run a bike shop down in Ouseburn," she added. "That's where Ben is now."

He made a note to check its filing status with Companies House.

"It's hard for me, too, you know," she said suddenly.

Phillips was caught off guard.

"Er, what's hard?"

She gave him a knowing smile.

"This," she said, waving the spoon towards their children. "Having to come to terms with the fact that they're not so little, anymore. I'd look forward to spending our free time together as a family, but he wants to go to the skate park with his friends…and now, he's having ice cream with girls. It's an adjustment."

Phillips sighed, and set his spoon down.

"It's daft, really, but…listen, my Sam had a rough start in life. When we adopted her, we promised ourselves we'd do all we could to make sure no harm ever came to her, not while we're around, anyhow."

And, oh, how he wished he could live forever, to see her grow into a woman, then a mother herself.

"It's not daft," Annie said. "I can only imagine how protective you must feel. Sam—my Sam, that is—hasn't been through half of what yours must have, and I feel like a giant clucking hen, at times."

He smiled at that.

"I've got a mate who's just had a little girl, and we were thinkin' of settin' up a support group for confused and sleep deprived parents."

"Let me know when you have your first meeting," she said. "I'll bring the sandwiches."

Phillips let out a rumbling laugh and, this time, when he looked over at his daughter in the window, he smiled.

By the time they covered the length of the beach at Roker, Lowerson and Yates were no closer to finding any sign of an injured woman. They went as far as they could along the sand before heading back up to the cliff road, to begin retracing their steps towards Souter and, beyond that, to Marsden. The stretch of land between Roker and Souter formed part of Whitburn Coastal Park, which had been reclaimed from the old colliery after its eventual closure. Now owned by National Heritage, the area was prone to landslips and erosion thanks to its geological make up and previous mining exploits, but it was still a popular draw for locals.

Soon, they approached an area around two hundred metres south of Souter Lighthouse, known to locals as 'The Leas'.

"It's beautiful here," Mel said, breathing in the sea air.

"Beware the sink holes," he replied, and pointed towards a sign and a permanent barrier, further along.

"Really? I didn't realise there were so many."

Jack nodded.

"People have fallen, but you still get the occasional nitwit who likes to skirt with danger."

The idea formed in his mind even before the words came out.

"Mel—"

"Jack—"

"You go first," she said.

"I was going to say, what if this injured woman fell, and that's why she ended up trapped in a cave?"

Mel nodded.

"Exactly my thoughts," she said. "These holes would be deadly, at night, and especially in the middle of a storm."

Lowerson took out his phone and put an urgent call through to the boss.

Marsden Beach and much of the neighbouring Whitburn Sands was inaccessible by the time Ryan arrived at the seafront, the tide already having closed in, but he made directly for The Leas, where Lowerson and Yates awaited him.

And, if Melanie noticed how the breeze swept Ryan's dark hair back from his face, or how he threw a stick for a passing dog with the kind of playfulness that made him seem less hardened than your average murder detective, she certainly thought nothing further about it.

"Jack, Mel," he said, nodding to them both. "Mac's gone over to have a word with Faulkner about the trawler, now he's had a chance to go over it, a bit. What've you got for me?"

They explained their theory, and where they had searched, so far.

"We checked all the little caves and inlets in Marsden Bay, yesterday," Lowerson said. "There was nobody in there, and no sign of there having been anybody in distress—no blood spatter, or anything of that kind."

Ryan nodded.

"Following the anonymous caller's instructions, we then headed directly to Spottee's, but, again, there was nothing to find and, frankly, nowhere for the woman to have become trapped. It's an open cave, with easy access."

"This is the only remaining stretch," Yates added. "Although we haven't had an opportunity to check the caves from the beach, we thought the sink holes could explain how this injured woman came to find herself trapped, sir."

Ryan thought that it had been a while since his immediate team had called him 'sir' in casual conversation, but let it go. Old habits sometimes died hard, he supposed.

"On the other hand, it could be a wild goose chase," Lowerson said, with admirable honesty.

Ryan looked at the barrier, then at the dark, gaping holes in the cliffside that were just visible from the safety of the footpath.

"It could be any one of them," he said. "So, let's look at this logically. For this anonymous caller to have found a woman at all, they'd almost certainly have accessed the cave from the beach. In that case, there are only a finite number of accessible caves from the beachside which correspond with the sink holes up here, on the cliffside. Agreed?"

The others nodded.

"In that case, let's try to tally them up."

"The photos," Yates muttered, and hurriedly brought up a reel of images on her phone, taken by the forensics team the previous day and showing the length of the cliffs along Marsden Bay.

Unfortunately, they didn't show the cliffs past Souter, where they now stood.

Yates was in the process of seeking out some reliable images of that stretch of coastline, when a movement caught Ryan's eye. He turned to see two men dressed in hard hats and high-vis jackets making their way underneath the cordon further up ahead, and he called out to them.

"Hey!"

Ryan jogged along the footpath with the others trailing after him, raising his hand to attract their attention.

One of the safety engineers turned to meet him at the barrier.

"Help you, mate?" he enquired.

"DCI Ryan, Northumbria CID," Ryan explained, flashing his warrant card. "Can I ask what's going on, here?"

The engineer, who turned out to be called Dave, was suitably impressed by the mention of CID, and called across to his partner.

"We got a call to come and check out a new sink hole," Dave explained. "Apparently some dog walker noticed it as they were passing."

"Where?" Ryan asked. "Can you show us?"

"I don't know about that," Dave said, dubiously. "Members of the public aren't supposed to come over the barrier, it's Health and Safety—"

Ryan gave him a long, level look.

"We'll try to restrain ourselves from diving into the hole," he said.

Dave saw the funny side.

"Aye, well, you all look sensible enough," he chuckled. "It's over here—mind where you walk."

He made them stand well back, in deference to the fact none of them was equipped with hard hats, and pointed out a new hole which hadn't been there a couple of days before.

"This was only reported to you today?" Ryan enquired. "By whom?"

"Couldn't tell you," Dave said. "It would've gone through to the main office, and they contacted us separately to get down here, pronto, and make sure it was safe for the public. They don't like havin' to deal with any complaints."

Ryan turned to the other two.

"Get onto the National Heritage main office and find out who that call came through to," he said. "I want to know who called this in, and when."

"On it, boss," Yates said, and moved away to make some calls.

First, 'sir', now, 'boss'? he thought, with a slight frown, before addressing the engineers again.

"Can you see anything down the hole?" he asked. "Any sign of an accident?"

They took a few minutes to rig up a safety rope, in case either of them should slip, following which Dave and his partner approached the edge of the sink hole with extreme caution to peer inside.

"There's a cave at the bottom," Dave called back. "It's too dark to see anythin' from up here, even with the torch!"

Ryan had been required to make borderline judgment calls throughout his career, and this was no exception. He was in the process of weighing up the pros and cons of calling in a specialist mountaineering team to abseil into the heart of the cave, when Yates hurried back across the grass to join them.

"I've just spoken to the regional office," she said. "The call they received was actually a voicemail message, received just before ten p.m. last night. They didn't pick it up until later today, because they admitted they'd forgotten to check their voicemails."

"Did the caller leave a name?"

"No name, no personal details," she said. "Only a brief message to let them know a new sinkhole might have appeared near Spottee's."

The two men exchanged a glance.

"Spottee's, again?" Lowerson said.

"Exactly. They said they'd sent someone out to check, but they've never had sink holes around that area, and it's run by the council, so doesn't fall under their remit. They passed on the message to Sunderland City Council, and sent the engineers out here to check over the existing sink holes, just in case that's where the caller meant to direct them."

"Looks like our caller isn't so hot on their geography," Ryan said. "But that makes two for two, which is good enough for me. Jack? Put a call through to the nearest mountain rescue team and tell them we need to borrow a couple of personnel. We need to get down there and have a proper look."

CHAPTER 21

Mick watched the early afternoon news with a growing sense of unease.

He leaned forward in his chair, barked at the others in the room to keep quiet, and listened intently to the newsreader.

At lunchtime today, engineers were dispatched to local beauty spot, The Leas, after a report was received about a new sink hole having appeared overnight. In a surprising turn of events, police have now cordoned off the area and are assisting National Heritage engineers in their assessment of the area...pedestrians are advised to keep clear of the area...

A short reel of footage began to play across the screen, showing the engineers alongside a small crowd of other men and women, some dressed in harnesses as they prepared to abseil into the sink hole, and a small group of other, plain-clothed police officers.

Why were they plain clothed? Mick wondered.

And then, he spotted one he recognised.

Ryan.

Even if he hadn't been so recognisable, and even if he hadn't garnered a bit of a cult following for all the collars he'd taken, Mick would have known him—he'd been given a list of names and faces to look out for.

He swore softly, and reached for the burner phone resting on the chair leg beside him.

"Whassamatter, Mick?" Noddy asked.

There came no reply, and Mick left the room to put through an urgent call.

"What's up wi' him?" Callum wondered.

Noddy yawned and then shrugged.

"Pro'ly just cheesed off that we're havin' to stay here longer than usual," he said. "We'd be long gone, by now."

"Aye, it's draggin' on, like," Callum said, keeping his voice down lest his boss should overhear. "The longer we hang around with the girls, the more chance there is of someone gettin' tipped off. We need to move."

Further conversation was forestalled when Mick returned, with a face like thunder.

"It's the woman," he told them. "She's gotta be down that sink hole."

The other two stared dumbly at the television screen, although the news had moved on.

"How d'you know that?" Callum wondered.

"It's that big bugger—Ryan," Mick spat. "He's CID, not some beat copper. There's no chance he'd be on site lookin' at a friggin' sink hole, unless there was owt to find down there."

"What if she's alive—and talks?" Noddy asked, with the kind of bald stupidity Mick found infuriating.

He turned on him like a shark.

"What d'you think happens, Nod? We all go on a bloody jaunt to Marbella?"

Noddy reddened.

"I just meant…won't he take care of it?"

Mick didn't reply directly.

"He's comin' round tonight," he said. "Apparently, he's got it fixed for us to move them tomorrow."

Callum and Noddy exchanged a relieved glance, but Mick didn't share the emotion. There was a long way to go, yet, and they'd already been delayed by over twenty-four hours. The risk to himself grew higher with every passing hour, and not just from the pigs—although, it didn't help that there was an All-Ports Warning in place. That only made the job harder.

But all of that paled in comparison with the single overriding concern which played over and over in his mind.

Why were CID investigating that sink hole?

Because they thought somebody was down there, dead or alive.

Why did they think that? They had no way of knowing for certain how many women were brought in on the boat.

Unless some bugger told them.

Mick looked at the faces of the other two in the room, considering what lay behind their eyes.

Callum was pushing forty, but had the mentality of a teenager, which made him pliable and easy to manage, most of the time. The fact he happened to have no sexual drive was an added bonus, and meant he could be trusted with the women—more so, than any of the others, or *himself*, for that matter. He'd been a part of the business for the past five years, and he'd known him a lot longer, since the bloke was his half-brother. The possibility of him having blabbed was so far outside the realms of possibility, he could barely imagine it.

As for Noddy…

He was more of a problem. He was young—and dumb, for that matter—but he had a strong back and a taste for power which could be useful in their line of work. It could also be difficult to keep in check. Ambition and delusions of grandeur had led many a promising young recruit to find themselves at the bottom of the Tyne, before all was said and done, because they'd forgotten themselves. There was a pecking order in all things, and he didn't need any hot-headed little upstarts swingin' their dicks about, tryin' to get the jump on him.

Mick stared hard at Noddy, who felt the heat of his gaze and looked up in surprise.

"Y'alreet, Mick? Can I get you somethin'?"

Mick shook his head slowly.

There was still enough deference in that one and enough healthy fear—if not quite respect. He couldn't be trusted around the women, at least not on his own, but he could be trusted to do whatever it took to bring in a healthy profit, which included not squealing to the police.

No, it wasn't Noddy.

That left Gaz or Ollie.

Mick paced across to the window and looked out at the courtyard beyond. A light drizzle had begun to fall, coating the rusted lawnmowers and other small-scale machinery he kept there, for show. He thought of the first time he and Gaz had opened the doors to 'Donnelly's Scrap Yard', full of big ideas and hungry for success. They'd been mates since school, when Mick had been the runt of the litter, always the one to take a beating in the playground, except when Gaz intervened. Gaz, the one all the girls wanted, the one all the lads wanted on their team. They'd palled up, the pair of them, when Mick had shown him a better, more profitable way to make money than delivering newspapers on a

Saturday morning. He supposed it had been his way of thanking his mate for the times he'd stepped in, when he hadn't needed to.

That was loyalty.

That was *friendship*, as far as it went, and was deserving of reward.

The possibility that Gaz could have betrayed his trust, betrayed the bond they'd shared for twenty-five years, was beyond the pale. Besides, Gaz had grown used to the life and all the perks that came with it—and knew the consequences of defection better than most, since he was usually the one to dole out any punishments when they were due.

But Ollie...

Ollie.

The boy was young, and still wet behind the ears. He might have been Gaz's son, but Mick had misgivings on that front as well. There was no physical resemblance, other than them both having dark hair, and the boy had more of his mother in him, than anything else. He was submissive, but he was too intelligent for Mick's liking. Too thoughtful, too quiet by far.

What went on, inside the boy's head?

He'd sent the pair of them to check that stretch of coastline, to turn it inside out and find their missing woman. They'd reported back with nothing, having sworn they'd checked everywhere.

And yet, the police were swarming around that sink hole.

It didn't make sense.

Mick turned back to the other two and reached for the packet of cigarettes in his back pocket.

"When's Gaz due back?"

"He's pickin' up some more brown sugar for the girls," Noddy told him. "Said he'd be back with some food around three."

Mick checked the time, which was half-past-two.

"Tell him to come and find me, when he gets in. I'm off to check the women."

A moment later they heard him leave and cross the courtyard beyond, boots clicking against the broken tarmac.

CHAPTER 22

Ryan spotted the television camera and sighed in a mixture of resignation and frustration.

How they managed to arrive so quickly, he didn't know, but there was seldom a time when they could simply get on with the job in hand without having to worry about having their every move recorded for posterity. Unfortunately, there was little he could do about it, unless they found a body, in which case they'd be intruding upon an active crime scene.

"How are you getting along?"

Two professional climbers from the Northumberland National Park Mountain Rescue Team, led by a woman by the name of Ginny, were rigged up and strapped into their harnesses, and were testing the strength of their supporting ropes which had been secured to firmer ground, away from the entrance to the sink hole.

"Just about ready to go down," Ginny said. "We'll record what we see using the body-cams."

They were also equipped with radios, so they checked their frequencies and Ryan stepped away again to allow them to make their way down.

"How will we get her out, if there is a body down there?" Lowerson wondered, keeping his voice low.

"Let's cross that bridge when we come to it," Ryan said, preferring to remain hopeful of a positive outcome. "There might be nothing there, at all."

As it happened, he was almost right.

The radio crackled into life, and soon enough they heard Ginny's voice reporting what she could see within the chasm of rock.

"No signs of life," she said. "There's nobody down here, Detective Chief Inspector."

Ryan frowned.

"Nothing at all?"

"Well, nothing except a wrapper," Ginny said.

"What kind of wrapper?"

"Looks to be a chocolate bar—Twix," she added. "It's discarded on the floor. Can't see anything else."

"Bag it up, please," Ryan said, before ending the exchange.

After a couple of minutes, they saw the ropes move again, signalling that the team were making their return journey.

"Could be kids," Yates remarked. "If the cave is usually accessible from the beachside, kids might play in there."

Ryan nodded.

"It's the most likely solution," he said.

And yet...

"All the same, we'll test the wrapper for prints and DNA," he said. "It's a hell of a coincidence that two calls were made within a fifteen-minute period."

"It might be the wrong place," Lowerson said. "It was a good bet, but we might have the wrong cave."

Ryan looked out across the sea, which glimmered like molten silver as occasional shards of light broke through the heavy clouds.

"Take a team and check every entrance again from the beach—the tide's starting to go out," he said. "It's time and money, but, if there's a life at stake, I want to be sure we haven't missed anything."

The others nodded, and made no complaint.

"I'll see you back at HQ at..." He paused to check his watch, and made a couple of swift calculations. "Four-thirty."

He paused to thank the mountaineering team for their time, before striding off along the cliffside, a tall, lone figure against the rugged landscape.

"The lads said you wanted to have a word?"

Gaz found Mick in the dormitory, checking on the woman who'd overdosed.

"How's she doin'?" asked.

Not because he cared about her welfare, but because he wanted to know if he needed to start making plans for disposal.

"She'll be all right by tonight," Mick said, throwing a blanket back over her shivering body. "I want them all cleaned up and looking presentable, by nine."

Gaz drew out a rollie and began licking the paper.

"Comin' over, is he?"

"Aye," Mick said. "Where's the lad, today?"

"Still asleep," Gaz told him. "Said he'd been on one, last night."

Mick gave his friend a lazy smile, and wondered just how much young Ollie had done, the night before.

"Howay, let's take a walk."

Gaz read something behind his friend's eyes, but didn't worry, too much. He hadn't done anything wrong, so there was no need to.

Or so he thought.

The two men made their way back out into the courtyard and, after a quick check of the road beyond, let themselves out of the main gates, pausing only to whistle to the dog who was hunkered beneath the remains of an old car. It lolloped across the tarmac and

Mick clipped a leash onto its collar, and they began making their way down towards the river.

It was by no means an Arcadian scene; the skyline was peppered with poor housing and dingy, high-rise flats, and there was little in the way of greenery. When they reached the river, it brought forth no idealised notions of *The Wind in the Willows*, its murky depths having concealed too many sins ever to inspire such purity.

The river path was empty when they arrived, so Mick unleashed the dog and let it snuffle around the reeds, nosing its way into the mess from other animals left to rot in the matted grass on either side.

"What's on your mind, Mick?"

Gaz lit up another rollie and waited.

"The police were sniffin' around The Leas," Mick said, and turned to face him with flat, emotionless eyes. "They sent a climber down one of the sink holes."

Gaz shrugged.

"There's always been loads of sink holes, around there," he said. "It's got nowt to do with us—"

"I don't know about that, Gaz. I really don't know about that."

There was a tone to Mick's voice he'd heard before, and the first stirrings of fear began to take root in his belly.

"How d'you mean?"

"Why would CID turn up to check over a sink hole, Gaz?" Mick asked him, very softly. "Why would they send Ryan?"

Gaz frowned. "DCI Ryan?"

"Aye, you know the one."

Gaz nodded, and took another drag of his cigarette. "I couldn't tell you, Mick. If they're lookin' down there, they're wastin' their time, because as God's my witness, we checked every cave. I'm tellin' you, Mick, we're clear."

"See, you're still not followin' me, Gaz, so let me spell this out for you. Whether they find the woman or not? That isn't my main concern."

Gaz shook his head, struggling to understand.

"If it isn't about the woman—"

"It's about *loyalty*, Gaz," Mick said, and his voice was like a slap. "I want to know how they know another one might be missing, in the first place. I want to know why they thought another one might be down there."

Gaz began to sweat. "I—how, man, Mick, it was pro'ly just them bein' thorough. Coverin' the bases, y'nah?"

Mick turned and walked a few more steps, and Gaz hurried to keep pace.

"I thought about that," he continued, sagely. "I really did think about that, and you might be right."

Gaz let out a long breath.

"On the other hand, this niggle, it just won't go away," Mick said softly, and turned to his friend again.

"Was it you, Gaz, who checked every cave, or was it the boy?"

In the seconds it took for him to formulate a reply, every possible permutation passed through Gaz's brain like lightning. If he replied that he'd been the one to check all the caves personally, then, if anything went wrong, the buck would stop with him. But, if he told Mick that Ollie had been the one to check at least half of the caves, he'd be throwing his son under the bus.

Well, he'd never been much of a father, anyhow.

"Nah, Mick, it was me and the lad, half and half," he said, and it happened to be the truth. "He didn't rush it, mind. Took his time lookin'."

Mick's lips twisted. "Where was he, last night?"

Gaz couldn't say, considering he'd been absent until the early hours.

"At home," he answered, and hoped it was true. "All night, Mick, I'm sure of it. You can check the burners and anythin' else you need to. I swear to you, Mick, he knows what's best for him."

When the other man said nothing, he tried again.

"I'll go and have a word with him now, Mick. I'll go straight home and have it out of him, one way or the other. You can rely on me."

Mick nodded, magnanimously.

"Okay, Gaz. Okay. Don't worry about this, all right, mate? We'll sort this out."

"Th—thanks, Mick. He's a good lad—"

"Course he is, mate."

"I'll go back now—"

Mick put a firm hand on his shoulder.

"Tell you what, I'll come with you," he said, genially. "Been a while, hasn't it? Maybe Keeley can throw a bit of ham and eggs on for us, eh?"

Just like old times, he thought.

CHAPTER 23

At four o'clock, Ryan's team—minus Phillips—reconvened for a briefing at Northumbria Police Headquarters. Although many of Ryan's staff were no longer on shift, or worked regular weekdays rather than antisocial weekend hours, he was amused to note that at least one of them had found the time to take care of important matters on Valentine's Day, such as pinning up a compromising image of DS Phillips on the staff noticeboard, dressed in a tiny pink tutu and little else—taken some time ago on the man's belated stag party following his wedding in Italy. Some of the department had felt it was a sin not to have given Frank Phillips an appropriate send-off prior to him tying the knot, and had made plans accordingly upon his return from honeymoon.

Beneath the image, somebody had circled his face with a large red heart and written the following:

ROSES ARE RED,

VIOLETS ARE BLUE,

PHILLIPS LOVES STOTTIES

AND SO DO YOU!

Chuckling, Ryan let himself into one of the smaller conference rooms to find the others waiting for him.

"Sorry I'm a couple of minutes late," he said. "I stopped off to pick up some sustenance."

He set a tray of fresh coffees on the table.

"Lifesaver," Lowerson muttered, helping himself to a cup and warming his hands around the cardboard holder. "It was cold on the beach, earlier."

"Did you find anything?" Ryan wondered.

But Jack shook his head.

"Nothing we didn't see the first time around," he said. "We did manage to find the cave belonging to that new sink hole, where they found that chocolate wrapper."

"And?"

"It's a pretty narrow entrance," Yates chimed in, once she'd settled herself in the chair beside Lowerson. "You'd have to be a slim adult, or a kid, to get through it."

Ryan considered that.

"Judging by the fact our female victim hadn't eaten in over twelve hours, and had been at the mercy of her captors for approximately six days, it may be safe to assume that any other female victim would have suffered the same treatment," he said. "It's unlikely any of them would fall into an 'overweight' category, so it's possible a woman could have found her way inside that cave."

He took a chug of coffee, and let the liquid warm his cockles.

"On the other hand, it's far more likely to have been kids," he was forced to admit. "Do we have any leads on that anonymous call, from last night?"

"Some good news on that front," MacKenzie replied. "We've traced the call to a phone box in Cowgate."

She reeled off its registration number, and street address.

"I know that area," Yates said, with a note of sadness. "It's been declining for years, and needs more investment. It's overrun with drugs and petty crime."

She'd cut her teeth working the beat around that neighbourhood, which had been an eye-opener.

"Worse than petty," MacKenzie remarked. "It's home to a few people already on our radar—in fact, there's a couple of families I can think of, straight off the bat, who wouldn't blink twice at being involved in something like this."

Ryan nodded, the same thought having crossed his own mind.

"There's the Finnegans, for one," he said. "And the Dobsons. But, neither of those were mentioned by

DCI Chambers, yesterday, as being on their current watch list."

"The Donnellys used to live round there," MacKenzie added. "I'm going back a few years, mind."

"I don't remember them," Ryan said.

"No, it might have been a couple of years before your time," she said. "Frank would know."

Ryan nodded, and made a note to ask Phillips about it, later.

"The area might be a hot bed, but that doesn't help us to narrow things down, unfortunately," he said. "Let's start by seeing if there's any CCTV—I won't hold my breath."

"I'll check it out," Lowerson offered.

"Let's get a list of last known addresses for any 'notable' families within a radius of that phone box, while we're at it, alongside known addresses of any of our informants, if we have that information," Ryan said. "Let's keep in mind that, if anyone affiliated with one or more of these families placed that call, they were putting themselves in danger by doing so. We've got a potential informant, so let's tread carefully and afford them the same protections we would any other covert source."

There were nods around the room.

"Did we get a trace on the call placed to National Heritage?" he asked.

"Not yet," MacKenzie said. "But the similarities are striking."

"Agreed," Ryan said. "If it had only been the one call referencing Spottee's, perhaps we'd have written it off, by now, as the supervisor did in the Control Room. But, two calls, within the same time frame? It's too much of a coincidence for my liking—"

"And there's no such thing," the other three intoned, with broad grins.

Ryan stuck his hands in his pockets.

"I should write you all up for insubordination," he chuckled, before growing serious again. "The fact remains that, if we assume the caller was genuine, they believed there to be a woman trapped inside a cave somewhere along that stretch of coastline. We've searched all of them, and the one we found today seems as likely an option as the next. That being the case, we have to ask ourselves: where did the woman go?"

"If—and I say *if*—she was ever there, and *if* she was affiliated with the wreckage, yesterday, it's possible the same gang who transported her to the UK came back and found her after the anonymous call was made, but before we checked the cave, this afternoon," MacKenzie said.

Ryan considered the timings.

"What time did the tide go out, last night?" he asked, of nobody in particular.

Yates ran a quick search.

"Shortly after three a.m.," she replied.

"Which means that whoever planned to recover the woman had a window from then until daylight to get her out without being seen," Ryan surmised. "The darkness would have been enough cover."

"I'll get onto the pub at the Grotto, and see if they managed to capture anything on their CCTV," MacKenzie said. "We could put a call out for any passing dashcam footage, or see if the cameras on the cliff road picked anything up."

Ryan nodded.

"You do that," he said. "There's no way they could have gone in over the cliffside at that hour, and in those conditions, so it had to have been done via the beach tunnel, if it was done at all."

MacKenzie made a swift note to put those calls through.

"Whilst we're on the subject, has there been any update on the CCTV from yesterday?"

Lowerson shook his head.

"We canvassed all the local businesses and I've been in touch with the Council for any road footage," he said. "The main camera at the junction which covers the car park and the slip road down to the beach has been vandalised, and the Grotto covers its main entrance and the elevator, which came up blank. There's nothing on the beach."

Ryan ran a hand through his hair, keeping a sharp eye on the time.

He had a date to keep, later.

"All right," he said. "That one's always a long shot. Keep digging around the Cowgate connection and see what it throws up, but dig quietly. What about the shipping side? Do we have any details about usual trafficking routes?"

"I had a look into that, and I've spoken with colleagues in SOC," Yates said. "The problem is, because victims of trafficking are brought in globally, there's an infinite number of routes they can take before they reach the UK. That being said, people coming in from West Africa often fly by cheap airline routes, under false identities, whereas people coming from the Far East tend to go overland via Russia or Bolivia. It's cheaper."

"Their business model is based on standard economic principles," Ryan said. "It doesn't surprise me that they'd want to keep their overheads low."

Yates nodded.

"There's general agreement that most who come overland tend to converge in Belgium, or the Netherlands," she said. "That would make sense, when you consider the route that trawler was taking."

"Have we heard from the port authority in Amsterdam?"

"It took a while to get hold of anyone and, when I did, all they could tell me was that every vessel moving in and out of port was accounted for," Lowerson said, with a measure of disbelief. "Nothing to see there, according to the Dutch."

"I'll talk to Morrison about escalating this further up the chain," Ryan told him. "We need to pull strings, if we want to start requesting sight of footage and records."

He turned to MacKenzie.

"What could Faulkner tell you about the trawler?" he asked. "I don't suppose he happened to find a handy wallet with a name and address listed?"

She smiled, but shook her head.

"Chance'd be a fine thing," she said. "He found twenty-odd sets of manacles, most of them still attached to the hold of the boat. There were a few loose shoes, a couple of jackets and other unidentified personal items which he's going through, now. He'll let us know if there's any DNA match, but he says that'd be a stroke of luck, since they were so badly saturated in the water. He doesn't expect much in the way of usable evidence, there. As for the rest, they've gone through the entire boat with a fine-toothed comb but, given the sheer volume of samples, we won't get any swift answers."

Ryan had expected as much, but there'd been no harm in hoping.

"Understood," he said, crisply, and then changed direction. "Mel, Jack? To bring you both up to date, Mac and I attended a meeting with that woman who was formerly the victim of trafficking, but now helps to run a women's refuge."

"How'd it go?" Jack asked.

"It was illuminating," Ryan said, thinking back to the woman who'd called herself Niki. "She suggested we check out a club called Voyeur, down by the station—apparently, they're known to offer 'special' services of the kind usually supplied through trafficked labour or prostitution."

"I've heard of that one," Lowerson said, unthinkingly, and drew a raised eyebrow from the woman seated next to him. "No—no! Not because I've ever…I just mean…I've heard the name before, that's all."

He fell silent, and they watched his neck slowly redden.

"Well, I suggest we check the place out, in a strictly professional capacity," Ryan said. "I want to speak to some of the girls, if we can, and ask a few questions. Our contact said that, if we mentioned her name, we might be met with a bit less resistance."

"I'm happy to go with you," MacKenzie said.

Ryan braced himself for the next part of the conversation.

"Thanks, Denise. You know that, ordinarily, I wouldn't want to draw gender lines in any of the work that we do. That being said, I think this could be a special case," he said, and watched her eyes turn frosty.

God, help him.

"I think it's fairly obvious that these establishments cater largely to a male audience," he said. "I suspect we might look less conspicuous if myself and Jack or Frank go along, posing as punters."

MacKenzie folded her arms, stared at him for a long moment, and then sighed.

"Though it pains me to admit it…you're right. Though some women do go along to these places, I can't say I know many," she said. "And, if we're hoping to find leads on where to find a certain kind of action, I'm the last person your average Pervy McPerverson would talk to. I wouldn't be able to hide my contempt, for one thing."

Mel snorted out a laugh that was pure sisterly solidarity.

"Well," Jack said, clearing his throat. "So long as it's all in the line of duty—"

She gave him a withering look, and decided to have a little fun.

"I don't see any reason why I couldn't pose as a girl looking for a job," she said, innocently. "That might ingratiate me with the other girls, for one thing. I'd play the hapless newbie who's still getting used to wearing seven-inch heels and dancing around a pole without chafing my arse."

"WHAT?" Lowerson almost roared, and spun around in his chair to face her. "You must be mad if you think I'd let my—my—"

"Your what, Jack?" she queried. "In the first place, I don't think it's for you to decide what you *let me do*. I'll be the one making those decisions, thank you very much. In the second place, don't be such a hypocrite. It's all right for you to toddle along there and get an eyeful while I play the little woman back at home, is it?"

Lowerson realised quickly that he'd been backed into a corner.

"No, it's just—well, I wouldn't want—"

"Men leering all over me?" she wondered, sweetly. "Why does that bother you, sweetheart? Because you know me, and love me? I guess it doesn't matter so much, if the woman's a stranger, hmm?"

Lowerson shook his head vigorously.

"I don't know, I never really thought about it…" *And that was half the problem, wasn't it?*

Ryan cleared his throat and judged it the right time to intervene.

"As it happens, if I didn't have serious concerns about placing you in unnecessary danger, Mel, I'd have said that wasn't a bad idea," he remarked. "It would be a great way to get to know some of the girls, and I think you've got the guts to pull it off. However, building up their trust in you would take time we don't have. That's also why it might be easier to do a one-off visit as a group of supposedly lecherous males, to see what information we can elicit."

"Pity," she said, for Jack's benefit.

"There's just one thing," MacKenzie said, in a tone that brooked no argument.

Ryan gulped.

"What's that?"

She pointed a finger squarely at his chest.

"You best have Frank home by midnight, and, so help me, if you so much as let him *near* the stage, you'll have me to answer to."

"Yes, Ma'am."

Later, Ryan reflected that, whilst he had won that particular battle, he certainly hadn't won the war.

After all, he still needed to speak to Anna.

CHAPTER 24

"Run that by me, one more time?"

Ryan and Anna were seated at a cosy table in one of their favourite restaurants, *The Potted Lobster*, enjoying good food, good wine and even better company…

Until he'd opened his big mouth.

"Ah, well, I wanted to let you know I might be a bit late coming home tomorrow night," he repeated, with considerably less bravado the second time around.

"Yes, I heard that part," she said sweetly. "It's funny, I thought you said it was because you'd be going to a notorious strip club with Frank and Jack."

He watched her break a breadstick in half, with deliberate force.

"When you put it like that, I can see how it might sound…" he said, weakly. "But I need you to know, it's purely professional. We got a tip that this was the place to go if we want to find out who's offering kinky services—"

"Are you saying our sex life is too pedestrian for you?" she interrupted, smooth as you like.

"What?" he blustered. "No—no! Not at all, actually, it's—"

"Ryan."

She cast a meaningful eye around the restaurant, to remind him that they could be overheard. "Sorry," he muttered, and made a grab for her hand to hold it in his own. "I haven't explained myself very well…"

He trailed off, having only just noticed the glint in her twinkling brown eyes.

"You're having me on," he realised.

Anna gave a wicked chuckle.

"I've never seen you squirm so much," she said, grinning. "That was priceless."

Ryan felt his shoulders relax again.

"You had me going for a minute, there," he said, and signalled the waiter for another glass of wine.

He needed it.

"Come on," she said. "Don't you think I know the man I married? I know that sort of place isn't your scene."

He gave her a crooked smile and nodded.

"I went along with a bunch of the boys from school when we turned eighteen," he admitted. "Out of curiosity, more than raging hormones, and once was more than enough. The only other times I've been are in connection with an investigation, and that's been surprisingly few and far between."

He hadn't needed to get his jollies in any seedy club, and didn't intend starting now.

"Didn't Frank want to go, for your stag do? Or his, for that matter?"

Ryan only smiled.

"Don't be deceived," he said. "Frank might be a rough diamond, but he's still a diamond. He has far too much respect for women, and for himself. A few of the blokes from work suggested it, but he just said they were free to go at the end of the night, if they wanted. No judgment, no arguments; it was as easy as that. We went our separate ways—Frank and I, and a few others, called it a night, while some of the others went on to gawk at a strange woman's boobs."

"Well, it's as I always say," Anna said, in mock severity. "Why pay to ogle, when you can ogle at home, for free?"

"Words to live by," he said, and wriggled his eyebrows at her cleavage to make her laugh.

"I'd have thought some of the other men from the office would give you some stick for opting out," she said. "What do they call it—conscientious objection?"

Ryan laughed.

"If you hadn't guessed it by now, Anna, I've never been a man to care much about what other people think of me," he said. "No amount of peer pressure would change my views on any subject, least of all this."

And there, she thought, *was the difference.*

"I try not to judge anyone else," he continued. "At least, until I began investigating this case."

"What do you mean?"

Ryan thanked the waiter for their wine, and then clinked his glass with hers before answering.

"Before I started to re-examine human trafficking, and sex trafficking in particular, I don't think I fully appreciated the nature of supply and demand in that industry," he said, softly. "I don't know why that is—possibly because of what I've just told you. Paying for sex or anything related to it isn't a part of my life, as it is for some people, and I don't work in Vice. I'm a murder detective, so I see the consequences of violence against sex workers, and I work hard to bring the perpetrators to justice. That's always my focus. What I haven't really thought about is what drives the demand, in the first place—long before the violence is perpetrated."

Anna nodded thoughtfully.

"A lot of people say it's harmless," she said. "Part of British culture. Certainly, from a historic perspective, prostitution is the oldest profession."

"That may be true," Ryan said. "But there are degrees. For instance, a person choosing to the enter the profession without coercion, in full command of herself and in the full knowledge of its risks and benefits is not the same as a person who's been trafficked by force or coercion, assaulted and abused for profit—a profit they're never likely to see."

He sipped his wine.

"Look, this is hardly dinner conversation—"

"No, I'm enjoying our discussion," she murmured, touching his hand. "It's important."

"I think a lot of people see it as victimless fun," he said. "Harmless, as you say. But, that's because they see the glamorous side, and not the side where women and girls, men and boys, are forced into the sex industry to meet a growing demand. There's a race and ethnic factor, too. It isn't always the British workers who suffer the same degradations; only foreign workers."

Anna shook her head, in sympathy.

"It's like the twenty-somethings who snort cocaine," he said, conversationally. "They think it's mostly a harmless high, their mates at university or in the office are all doing it, so they can work longer hours or be more confident. They think it's a victimless crime. But that's because they don't consider all the links in the chain—all the dealers and distributors, the kids dragged into County Lines, all driven by soaring profits. Every time they buy a few grams, they're adding to the demand. It's the same in the sex industry, as far as I'm concerned. Every time someone buys a lap dance, or more, they're proving that there's a demand. So long as there is that demand, somebody will want to supply."

Anna listened to him and heard the restrained anger, the passion to make the world a better place, and was moved.

"I'm glad our daughter has you as a father," she said softly. "She doesn't know how lucky she is, yet, but one day she will."

Ryan only shook his head, embarrassed.

"She has the best role model in you," he countered, meeting her eyes across the table.

The music playing softly on the restaurant speakers changed to an old track by *U2*, and Ryan smiled.

"A blue-eyed boy and a brown-eyed girl," he whispered.

"The sweetest thing," she said.

CHAPTER 25

"Pull up a chair, lad."

Mick adopted a friendly tone, and Ollie looked between him and his father, who was hovering in the doorway to their sitting room looking restless.

"Is that Mick?" His mother's voice trilled from the kitchen, and a moment later they heard her clumsy footsteps coming down the hallway.

"It is! Long time, no see, Mick…"

He turned to face Gaz's wife, and was struck by how much she'd aged—even in the few months since he'd seen her. Once, Keeley had been every young man's dream; blonde, busty, with big blue eyes and an unenquiring mind, which was the perfect combination, as far as he was concerned.

He'd envied Gaz, and had once tried seducing her, just to have a piece of the pie.

Luckily, she'd been too drunk to remember, and his mate had been none the wiser.

"Lookin' good, Keeley," he lied. "You lost weight, have you?"

She ran a hand over her hip, and preened a bit.

"Maybe…maybe I have! Thanks, Mick. That's more than I ever get from *him*…" she muttered, cocking her chipped thumbnail in the direction of her husband, who lounged against the wall looking bored. "You want a drink, Mick? Fancy a little cocktail, hmm?"

"Not now, love," he said, politely. "I'm here to talk to Ollie about a promotion, as it happens."

"That's grand! That's—" She hiccupped. "That's grand that is, Mick. Aren't y'gonna thank your Uncle Mick, for givin' you a chance?"

She gestured at Ollie to show some gratitude, and he thanked him in a dull voice, knowing fine well their conversation had nothing whatsoever to do with any promotion.

"This def—definitely calls for a celebration," she said. "I'll go an'—an' rustle up somethin' for us."

"Why don't you throw together a few sandwiches, pet?" Mick said, knowing the task would keep her busy for a while. "I'm starvin'."

"Comin' right up," she mumbled, and they heard her humming to herself as she retreated back to the kitchen.

Once she'd gone, Mick's face fell again.

"Have a seat," he repeated, and Ollie lowered himself onto the edge of a grey velvet sofa. "Good. Now, we just want to ask you a couple of questions, lad. Nothin' to worry yourself about, all right?"

Mick gave him a smile, and Ollie might have been fooled, except for the look in the man's eyes.

He knew.

Oh, God. He knew.

His body began to tremble, and he clasped his hands between his knees.

"Let's all have a seat," Mick said, expansively. "Howay, Gaz. Let's all just relax for a minute."

Gaz, who was even more concerned than his son, forced his legs to move towards an armchair which afforded him a good view of both men in the room.

"Right then," Mick said, keeping a tight rein on himself. "I want you to tell me the truth, Ollie. I'll know if you're lying, so don't try and make a mug of me, all right?"

Ollie swallowed with difficulty, and bobbed his head. Fear ran like a torrent through his veins, and he found no comfort in the eyes of his father, who stared through him from his position across the room.

"Yes, Mr Donnelly," he managed.

"Good lad," Mick said, soothingly. "Now, all I want to know is one thing."

He paused, and Ollie felt physically sick.

"Did you find a woman down on the beach, in one of those caves?"

Ollie hesitated, and that was his undoing.

"I—"

"You?"

"Yes, Mr Donnelly," he croaked, and Gaz closed his eyes in defeat.

Mick ran the tip of his tongue over his lips, and linked his hands together.

"All right," he said, softly. "Now, why didn't you tell us about it?"

Ollie should have heard the warning, but he didn't. He thought he was speaking to a family friend, the man he'd seen almost every weekend since he was born, the man who was his godfather, however meaningless that title might have been.

But he was wrong. He was no longer speaking to Michael Donnelly.

He was speaking to The Postman.

"Sh—she was badly injured, Mr Donnelly," he stammered. "I—I knew you wouldn't be able to get her any help, and she couldn't speak any English—"

Mick raised an eyebrow.

"Go on, lad, I'm all ears."

"I—so, I—I called…the ambulance," Ollie lied, having wit enough to know that he could not admit to having sought out the police. In his addled mind, he thought that, perhaps, they might forgive him for trying to seek medical help. It was better than having called in the police.

Unfortunately, he had no way of knowing that Mick had connections spread far and wide, which enabled him to find out exactly what Ollie had said, when he'd said it, and to whom.

But he gave the boy points for improvisation.

"Well, that was a kind thought, wasn't it, Gaz?"

Gaz said nothing—he couldn't.

"Now, you know that isn't how we do business," Mick admonished, in the tone of a favourite uncle. "But, look, now you've explained it to me, I understand you were only tryin' to be kind. The problem is, we can only be so kind, in our line of work. You've got to think of it as a production line, and them as the produce. Sometimes, accidents happen…some of them are defective, or broken. You've got to leave them behind, or put them down. D' you understand?"

Ollie nodded vigorously.

"I'm sorry, Mr Donnelly. I made a mistake."

Mick sighed heavily, then held up his hands, palms outward.

"I understand that, Ollie. No, really, I do," he said, for added effect. "I'm glad you've told me the truth; that's the most important thing."

There was a heavy silence.

"What—what'll my punishment be, Mr Donnelly?"

Mick laughed, as if he'd just told a good joke.

"Don't be daft, lad. I'm not about to punish you for one little mistake, am I? We all make 'em, don't we, Gaz?"

But Gaz had heard this line countless times before, and knew where it would end.

"I don't want you to think any more about it, but, promise me, you don't pick up that phone again—even if you see one of 'em bleeding on the floor. All right?"

Ollie nodded, feeling sick with relief.

"I'm sorry again," he said, quickly. "I should never have—"

"Draw a line under it," Mick said, and crossed the room to give Ollie's hair an affectionate rustle. "I'll be off, now. Thank your Ma for the sandwiches, if they ever come, eh?"

The boy managed a smile at that. "Thank you, Mr Donnelly."

"One last question for you, lad."

Ollie waited.

"Have you ever read The Bible?"

The boy was confused. "N—no, Mr Donnelly. Would you like me to?"

Mick shook his head. "If you ever get the chance, you should read the Book of Job," he said, conversationally. "It's all about proving your loyalty."

"Thanks, Mr Donnelly. I will."

Mick turned, and exchanged a long look with Gaz, who was forced to look away.

"You ever read that one, Gaz?"

His friend raised a hand to cover his mouth, unable to speak.

"I think you'd enjoy it," Mick said, before turning to leave.

Outside, he turned to look back at the house and saw Gaz watching him from the window. He raised a cheerful hand in salute, then stepped behind the wheel of his Range Rover, where Noddy was waiting for him in the passenger seat.

Nothing was said until the car had moved off.

"What should I do, boss?" Noddy asked, once they were clear of the house.

"Blessed is the one whom God reproves..." Mick said. "Do you know the best way to prove your loyalty? By sacrificing something—the most important thing in the world to you."

Noddy frowned.

"D'you want me to give you my X-Box, Mick?"

Donnelly swore, and then let out a long laugh.

"You've never read a bloody book in your life, have you son?"

When the boy only looked blank, he decided to put it in words he could understand.

"Make an example of him," he said, all laughter gone. "Get it done tonight, after the Dragon's been round."

CHAPTER 26

Achara looked at the flimsy scraps of cheap lace she'd been told to wear, and then at the well-used lipsticks and eyeshadows *Caloom* had dumped on the end of her bed.

"Put it on," he'd told her, pointing at the make-up, then at her face.

She hadn't, and she knew there'd be a punishment for that.

The other women had been too frightened not to do as they were told and, as she looked around the room, she saw an assortment of exhausted, incoherent women dressed in lace and polyester, their faces made up like porcelain dolls.

"Right then, ladies!"

Nodi was back, and she pushed herself flat against the wall so he wouldn't notice her.

"Very nice," he said, as he strolled between the beds, tugging and prodding as he went. "What's this, sweetheart? Doesn't it fit?"

He stopped beside one of the women who had struggled into an outfit at least two sizes too small, and was now seated on her bed, her head hanging in defeat.

"Looks better that way, love, trust me," he said, with a laugh.

"He'll be here any minute now," Callum warned. "We better start gettin' them lined up."

"All in good time, Cal," Noddy said, full of confidence ahead of his task later that evening.

The more he thought about it, the more excited he felt.

Just in time to see his favourite girl…

"This one isn't dressed," he said, petulantly. *He'd been looking forward to seeing that one in black lace.*

Achara kept her head bent, long hair hiding her face.

"I left the stuff out for her," Callum said. "Maybe she doesn't understand."

Noddy watched her, then sank onto his haunches so they were eye to eye.

"It isn't that, is it, love? You just don't want to, do you?"

She shivered as he tucked a strand of hair behind her ear.

"Maybe she's shy," he said, and his voice shook with repressed need. "Why don't we give her a helping hand, eh?"

Without further ado, he grabbed her up, and tugged off her sweater with one rough motion.

She cried out, trying to cover herself, trying to run, but he pushed her back and reached for the lace bra he'd liked the look of, so much.

"Wear it," he said, and held it out to her.

Achara wanted to take the material and wrap it around his throat, but she knew there was no chance, and her strength was low.

She took the bra in her limp fingers, shifted away from his prying eyes, and put it on.

"Now the rest," Noddy said, in a low voice.

She shook her head, and he reached for the matching knickers.

"Are you going to put these on, or do I need to help you?"

She needed no translation, and snatched them from his hand, crying softly as she was forced to undress.

Noddy enjoyed the show, and then sat on the edge of the bed beside her, so he could whisper in her ear.

"One day, you know what I'm gonna do?" he said.

She gave an involuntary shudder.

"I'm gonna be even bigger than Mick," he said. "This is just small fry, in comparison with how big I'm gonna be. I'm gonna be a name in this town…maybe even the world."

She tucked her legs up, in a defensive gesture.

"You could be the one who helps to train the girls," he said, in the manner of one who'd just extended a cushy job offer. "You wouldn't have to do more than one trick a night, and that'd just be me."

She didn't understand the words, but they made her skin crawl.

"What d'you think, baby, hmm?"

But, before he could say more, the outer door opened and The Dragon stepped into the room, causing Noddy to spring off the bed as though he'd been burned.

That action alone was enough to warn her that this new man, whoever he was, was more dangerous than any of the others, and she was afraid.

She watched his eyes scan the room, pausing to scrutinize each face until they came to rest on her.

"That one," he said, simply. "The one in black lace."

Her bowels wanted to empty as he began walking towards her, his eyes never leaving her face, and she looked around for a weapon.

But, there was none.

He came to stand beside the bed, and looked down at her.

"What's your name?" he asked, in fluent Thai.

She shook her head, and he asked again.

"Achara," she whispered.

"No," he said. "Your new name is Orchid. Say your new name."

"Orchid," she repeated, like an automaton.

"Good girl," he said, and reached for her hand. "You're coming with me."

Lawana wondered why God had condemned her to a life of darkness.

Why did he not let her die?

Her body was all used up and broken; her legs no longer worked as they should, and she was numb to the rest, having grown accustomed to the pain that seemed never to end.

She thought of the man, and of what a fool she'd been.

Rescuer, she thought, with a harsh sob.

She remembered the time when she'd thought *Pos'man* and his gang were the worst she could have imagined; that surviving the sea and a landslide were all that one person could stand.

How wrong she had been.

This man was different. He moved and spoke quietly, but his eyes…

His eyes were black, and spoke of terrible horror to come.

She looked around the cellar, which was windowless and built solidly of red bricks, accessible only by a single door, which remained locked and bolted from the outside. It had been fully decorated as a bedroom, with a large bed in the middle, covered in a flowery bedspread. In the corner of the room was a plain white toilet and sink, but no mirror. To cover the brickwork, he'd pasted a thousand cuttings on the wall, all of beautiful women, many of whom were naked or semi-nude and cut carefully from the pages of newspapers and magazines. Others were photographs, and she knew the images of those women were real, because she recognised the flowery bedspread upon which they lay. Their eyes were filled with fear and, in some cases, their eyes were no longer open.

She wanted to think they were merely sleeping, but she knew the truth, in her heart.

Those women were dead, just as she would be.

This was his special place, she realised. The place he came to kill, and enjoy the process at his leisure. If he'd wanted to murder her quickly, he could have taken his pleasure in the cave and left her there to rot. Instead, he went to such trouble to remove her, and steal her away for himself, undoubtedly at some great risk to himself.

This was beyond her comprehension.

Gaz, Nodi and the others, she could understand. They were driven by base motivations of sex and money, and power, too. They thrived on it, and enjoyed the acquisition of it, at the expense of women like herself. She'd seen that, in one form or another, since her childhood and, whilst she could never forgive, it was something she understood.

This man...

He was another kind of beast. One that savoured his kills, and guarded them jealously for himself.

Her eyes strayed again to the pictures on the wall, memorising the faces of all the women and girls, wondering if any of them had survived, wondering if their families knew what had happened to them.

But, no. There was no way they could know, for he was still moving freely amongst them, like a tiger amongst a herd of gazelles.

As her eyes focused in the dim light of a single battery-powered light hanging from the ceiling, she saw other details she'd missed before.

Blood.

Some of the pictures were stained with blood.

The scream welled up inside her and broke forth, the long, keening sound of an animal in torment.

But there was nobody to hear.

Minutes and hours ticked by, and Lawana dragged herself from the bed, searching every corner, tugging at the door, crying out for help until her voice broke.

Later, when the world slept, one man crept from his bed and made his way to his special place with a spring in his step and a bulging rucksack slung over his shoulder, full of his favourite toys.

Work hard, play hard.

He'd been careful for a very long time, more than two years, but he was starting to feel the strain, and couldn't wait any longer. He'd begun to look for the next, but then he'd heard about the woman found on the beach.

Death had always held a fascination for him, ever since he'd seen his grandmother lying in her open casket, when he was seven years old. He'd touched her cold, waxy skin with nimble fingers and felt no fear. He was drawn to it, excited by it, and relied on it to help him to remain sane in his 'ordinary' life. Without the fix, every so often, he knew the cracks between his two worlds would begin to show.

And so, he'd made his way to the beach, standing amongst a crowd of others, listening to their inane chatter about how sad it was, and what a tragic loss.

He'd watched them combing the beach, looking for others, and he'd wondered…

And he'd looked, too. Searched, idly at first, without any purpose or hope, until he'd seen her lying there, unconscious, like an offering.

He wished he could have taken her then, but that would have been foolish, and premature. He needed to plan, and to execute that plan with precision.

And so, he'd waited, patiently, as he always did.

He was a very patient man.

CHAPTER 27

Monday, 15th February

Storm Wayne hit the North East coastline just after seven in the morning, sweeping through the cities and villages with merciless fury, whipping the sand from the shore and shaking the very foundations of Northumbria Police Headquarters, whose feeble construction had been designed without reference to its proximity to the sea, or much else, for that matter.

Ryan and MacKenzie made a valiant effort to ignore the rain and wind battering against the windows of the Chief Constable's office, and accepted the cups of coffee she offered them from her own personal machine.

"Times like this, I start wondering whether I should take early retirement and move to Spain," Morrison said.

"You'd miss us, too much," Ryan quipped.

Morrison eyed him over the rim of her mug, and snorted.

"Like a hole in the head," he thought he heard her say.

Then, she set her cup down and folded her hands on top of her desk, and came to the matter at hand.

"Thank you both for finding the time for this meeting," she said. "I know you've got a busy caseload, at the moment."

"Nothing we can't handle," MacKenzie said, automatically.

Morrison smiled.

"And it's precisely that kind of 'can do', capable attitude that's prompted this meeting," she said. "As you know, we've been searching for a new Detective Chief Superintendent to lead the Criminal Investigation Department for quite some time."

They nodded.

"After Gregson and Lucas, you might be forgiven for thinking it's a poisoned chalice," Morrison said, because it needed to be said aloud. "But I'm of the opinion that two rotten apples shouldn't spoil the whole basket. We had a run of bad luck, but that shouldn't tarnish the good reputation of this constabulary."

She paused, and reached inside her desk drawer for a slim folder containing a written proposal, and pushed it across her desk towards Denise.

MacKenzie looked at her, then at Ryan.

"What's this?"

"It's a formal offer," Morrison said. "After much internal discussion, we feel the right person to take up the role of DCS has been sitting under our very noses, for quite some time. We don't have to look any further than you, Denise, if we want somebody with the poise, professionalism and life experience to do the job, and do it well."

MacKenzie was at a loss for words.

"But—surely, Ryan would be better placed?"

Morrison only smiled.

"Who do you think recommended you for this position?"

MacKenzie turned to face her friend, who was already smiling.

"I'd be no good as a DCS," Ryan said, honestly. "Whereas, you have more patience in your little finger than I have in my entire body. You've got the empathy and the backbone to do this, if you want to, Mac. You deserve this opportunity, because you've earned it."

Even hearing the words, she didn't believe it.

"I'm only an inspector," she protested. "I'm not a DCI…I'd be skipping a rung on the ladder."

"You've performed as Acting DCI on several occasions now, and every time in an exemplary manner," Morrison reminded her. "You've put in your time, Denise. There isn't anybody in the department who'd think otherwise."

"I—I don't know what to say. I need to think about it."

"Of course you do," Morrison said. "I don't want to rush you, but I'll need an answer by the end of the week, one way or the other."

"I'll give you my answer by Friday," MacKenzie promised.

When they stepped back out into the corridor, MacKenzie laid a hand on Ryan's arm, when he would have moved off.

"Wait a minute," she said.

He turned to give her his full attention. "Is everything all right? I thought you'd be pleased by the offer, but did I misjudge things?"

She smiled, and shook her head.

"I'm overwhelmed by this," she said. "I would never have dreamed of this kind of promotion, at least not for a few more years. When I think of a natural leader, I think of you."

"Which is funny, because I think of you," he said, and made her smile again.

"I'm not trying to do myself down," she said. "I know that I could do the job, if I set my mind to it."

"You could," he agreed. "So, what's stopping you?"

She blew out a long breath. "Probably all the same things that stopped you," she said. "I'm happy with our team, as it is. I'd miss being out there, in the thick of an investigation, being on the front lines. I can't stand politicians, or career police, who have delusions of grandeur, and I don't know that I'd want to spend more of my time having to pander to them."

"Perhaps you'd shake them up a bit," he said, and could imagine it, very clearly.

"Then, there's the extra hours," she said, thinking of time away from Samantha and Frank. "I need to think about whether I want this enough to let it take me away from home."

Ryan nodded, understanding that particular dilemma only too well.

"On the other hand, it'd be easier on my bad leg," she said, thinking of the long-term nerve damage inflicted by The Hacker. "It's better than it was, and I have regular physiotherapy, but it'll never be the same again. If I've walked too far, or driven for too long, I feel it for days afterwards. Taking up a desk job would certainly alleviate a lot of that."

She paused, and looked off into the distance.

"I can sense a 'but' coming on."

"But I need to think about what I really love best about this job, and ask myself if I'd still be satisfied if I take up the post."

Ryan put a reassuring hand on her arm.

"In some ways, whether or not you decide to take this job is immaterial," he said. "The most important thing is for you to always know that I, and your colleagues, believe you to be more than capable of it, and the decision was yours for the taking. You're a bloody good inspector, Denise, and you'd be a bloody good DCS, too."

"Thanks, Ryan," she said, and gave him a quick, hard hug, uncaring of who should see. "You're a good friend."

"I'm glad to be your friend, but this offer is based entirely on the strength of your work record and personal qualities," he said, because it was important to make the distinction. "I wouldn't have recommended you, if I didn't think you were an outstanding candidate."

She felt a lump rise to her throat.

"After what happened—the injury, I mean," she said, preferring not to reference Keir Edwards by name. "I lost a lot of confidence. I couldn't do the same things I'd always done…or, at least, not with the same degree of competency."

She thought of how she'd loved kickboxing, and realised it had been months since the last time she'd sparred.

"It wasn't noticeable," he said. "You're a fighter."

"I wanted to prove to myself that I could carry on as normal, as if he hadn't torn my life apart, as well as my leg," she said. "Now, I realise that was just burying my feelings. These days, I think of it as a bad episode in my life that would have knocked anybody for six. I'm like you in that respect—I don't like showing any weakness."

"You noticed, eh?"

She laughed.

"Well, anyway, I want to thank you for always keeping faith in me," she said. "You and Frank have always had my best interests at heart. I appreciate it."

Ryan smiled.

"Just remember that, when I'm coming to you asking for more resources, and many more outlandish things," he said.

A reply was on the tip of her tongue, when they were interrupted by one of the constables from Ryan's team.

"Sir? We've just had a report come through," she said, urgently. "Another body has been found at Marsden."

Ryan's face became shuttered.

"Another woman?"

"No, sir, apparently the victim is male."

"We're on our way."

CHAPTER 28

"It's like what happened to John the Jibber."

Ryan waited for Phillips to elaborate and, when he didn't, asked the obvious question.

"Who?"

They stood just inside the opening of a small cave beside the lift shaft at Marsden Grotto, while the storm raged at their backs and the forensics team scurried to protect the scene from the onslaught of wind and rain which swept in from the sea. A large film light had been erected to provide some illumination through the gloom, and its merciless beam was directed upon the sorry sight of a young man's body which had, until a short while earlier, been swinging limply from a rope attached to the ceiling of the cave by means of an old, rusty hook.

"He was a smuggler, back in the day," Phillips explained. "Legend says, he sold information about his comrades to Customs and Excise, and they hung him inside a barrel from the roof of this cave until he starved to death, as a punishment. They say he haunts the place, now."

Ryan looked across at the young man's contorted face, with its network of broken blood vessels, then at an old barrel lying on its side, nearby.

"He can't be more than eighteen," he said, quietly.

Phillips nodded. "Doesn't look like suicide," he said, gruffly. "He couldn't have kicked that heavy barrel over by himself, for one thing."

"No, it's not suicide," Ryan agreed, noting the bruises on the boy's wrists, and thinking of the matching ones they'd found on his ankles.

"Who found the body?" Phillips asked.

"Owner of the pub," Ryan replied shortly. "Lowerson's in there with him now, taking a full statement."

"I ran a check on him and the Grotto—nothing cropped up."

"So did I," Ryan said, with a smile. "Great minds, Frank."

"Can't be too careful—"

"Or suspicious," Ryan put in.

Phillips nodded. "To tell you the truth, I thought they were going to tell me another woman had been found, after all that malarkey, yesterday."

"Me, too, Frank," Ryan said. "But, if you're right, and this is a punishment kill, I think we might have found our anonymous caller…which means there may still be another woman unaccounted for."

"They wouldn't kill anyone for a prank call," Phillips agreed.

"There's no ID on the body," Faulkner put in, emerging from the darkness looking very much like a ghost himself, dressed as he was in white polypropylene overalls. "We'll sweep the whole area, but it's the same story as the day before yesterday. We're fighting a losing battle against the elements, here."

"Just do what you can," Ryan said.

"We found one interesting feature," Faulkner said, and went back to retrieve a small evidence bag which he handed to Ryan. "A Bible, with the page turned back at the Book of Job."

"I haven't exactly been keeping up with my Bible readings," Ryan said, as a self-confessed atheist. "Frank? Does the Book of Job resonate with anything here?"

Phillips cast his mind back to his Catholic schooling, and wished he'd paid more attention.

"It's all about the Problem of Evil, isn't it?" he said, eventually. "This bloke, Job, has got it all—money, a nice big family and all that—and he's God-fearin', n'all. Anyhow, when God's chattin' to Satan, like they do over a scone and a cuppa, Satan says he reckons Job wouldn't be half so pious if he didn't have all those things in his life. To prove the point, God takes it all away from him and Job still stays loyal."

"So, it's a test of faith—and loyalty," Ryan murmured, looking down at the boy's body, which now lay atop a heavy sheet of tarpaulin while the CSIs went about their business. "I wonder who Job is, in this analogy."

"We'll find out, soon enough," Phillips said.

"I might have the answer to that," Yates said, joining their conversation after a brief exchange on the phone. "I've just had an update on that list of names and addresses of 'notable' families in the Cowgate area. The Nicholsons live within the closest range of that phone box, and the father's had a few pops for possession and intent to supply, over the years."

"What's his name?"

"Gavin Nicholson," she said. "The wife's Keeley, and they've got two children. A daughter, Rebecca, who's four or five, and a son, Oliver, who's…"

She glanced over at the young man lying dead on the floor, and swallowed.

"Sixteen, sir."

They followed her line of sight, and agreed it could be possible.

"Thanks, Mel. See if anyone's put in a Missing Persons report, and check the driver's license database," Ryan said. "He might have applied for his provisional licence, in which case we'll have a positive ID before we go and pay Mr Nicholson a visit."

It took her less than five minutes to procure an answer.

"It's a match, sir," Yates said. "Oliver Hayden Nicholson, aged sixteen."

She held out the DVLA record, which showed a beaming, round-faced boy on their provisional database, one who would never pass his test.

"There's no record of any Missing Persons report having been made," she added.

"I'm going to speak to Morrison about setting up some surveillance," Ryan decided. "If the family is involved, I want to know their movements. In the meantime, let's go and break the news, Frank."

Gavin 'Gaz' Nicholson watched the pigs park their car on the kerb at the bottom of his driveway, and decided to finish off the last of his cigarette while he got the measure of who had come to inform him of his son's death. There were two of them, both men, and he recognised the taller one immediately.

DCI Ryan.

So, the man himself had come, had he?

They were honoured.

He watched Ryan unfold himself from the car and walk around to the kerb, eyes scanning the neighbourhood while he waited for his partner to join him. He wore a smart coat and a smart haircut, Gaz thought, but he carried an air of readiness about him, as though he kept himself tightly on a leash.

Not to be underestimated.

As for the other one, he was another thing entirely. Shorter, and older by more than ten years, he looked exactly what he was: tough, with a stocky, boxer's physique and knuckles to match.

Gaz stubbed out his cigarette as they made their way up the path, and took a couple of deep breaths while he waited for them to ring the doorbell.

When he heard the daft, ding-dong chime Keeley had installed a few months ago, he made his way down the hallway.

"Who's that, Gaz?" she called out, from the kitchen.

She was always in the bloody kitchen.

"Dunno," he lied. "I'll go and see."

Ryan's first impression of Oliver's father came as a mild surprise.

Though he preferred not to categorise people, after a certain amount of time it was impossible not to form stereotypes when it came to the various types of criminal they were faced with, on a daily basis—and there were many. When it came to drug dealing, they tended to meet men and women who bore the physical effects of having sampled their own product, or having taken or received physical assaults as a matter of course.

However, the man who greeted them at the door was smartly dressed, with a light tan. He wore chinos and a fitted polo shirt, such as they might have found at their local golf course, and, aside from the shadows beneath his eyes, there was no evidence of any recent trauma. From what they could see, his home appeared well-kept, and had been recently decorated.

"Can I help you?"

"Are you Gavin Nicholson?"

"Aye, who's askin'?"

"DCI Ryan and DS Phillips, Northumbria CID," Ryan said, and they held out their warrant cards for his inspection.

Gaz didn't bother to look. "What d' you want?"

"May we come inside, please, Mr Nicholson?"

It was still raining heavily.

"Not until you tell me what this is all about," he repeated, folding his arms across his chest.

"Gaz? Who is it?" Keeley asked again, from over his shoulder.

A moment later, she appeared, squinting at the first light she'd seen that day. When she caught sight of Ryan, she dragged the ties of her dressing gown together and patted a self-conscious hand to her hair.

"These two are from the police," he said.

She looked them up and down. "Well, howay, let them in, it's pourin' out there!"

"Thanks, Missus," Phillips said, injecting some warmth into his voice for her benefit. "We need to speak to the both of you, as it happens."

She led them through to the sitting room, and waved towards an enormous L-shaped sofa, which they politely declined in favour of standing on the far side of the room, by the window.

"Well?" Gaz repeated.

Ryan straightened his shoulders, looked him in the eye, and said the words he'd said to so many other parents—this time, without the same open-minded sympathy he might otherwise have felt.

"I regret to inform you that your son, Oliver, was found dead this morning," he said, watching closely for the man's reaction. "We're very sorry for your loss."

"What?" Keeley whispered. "What did he just say, Gaz?"

Her husband looked down at the floor, then across to her, belatedly remembering he ought to be consoling her, as any normal husband would.

"They said they've found Oliver dead," he said, and moved across to put an awkward arm around her shoulders.

She might have been surprised by the unusual display of affection, if she wasn't trying to compute what had just been said.

"That's—that's just nonsense," she argued, and her voice began to rise as hysteria took hold. "Ollie's at school. Tell them, Gaz."

"You've got it wrong," he said, and tried to sound like he believed it.

"I'm afraid there's no mistake," Ryan said. "However, we will need one of you to come down and make a formal identification."

Keeley began to wail, and tears spilled from her bloodshot eyes, running in tracks down her face.

"Gaz—I—I—"

She sank onto the nearest chair and, when Gaz looked down at her with the expression of a man who didn't know what to do, Phillips stepped into the breach.

"Have you got any tissues, Mr Nicholson?" he asked. "With your permission, I could make your wife a cup of tea?"

Gaz hardly wanted them nosing around his house.

"I'll get it," he said, and sent a warning glance towards his wife, before leaving the room.

Ryan moved to sit on a chair beside her, taking full opportunity of the man's brief absence.

"We're very sorry, Mrs Nicholson," he said again.

It seemed she hadn't heard him, but then she looked up and sought out his eyes. "Is it true?"

Ryan nodded. "Yes. I'm sorry."

Her face crumpled again, her body heaving.

"Mrs Nicholson? I'm sorry to have to ask you any questions at a time like this," Ryan said, keeping an eye on the door. "But, could you tell me when you last saw Oliver—Ollie?"

She hiccupped, and opened her mouth to speak.

"Last night," Gaz interrupted, from the doorway. "He went to bed around ten, as usual."

"You didn't see him for breakfast this morning, before school?" Phillips queried.

Gaz set a cup of tea on the table beside his wife, who looked at it as though it might be poisoned. "I left for work before eight," he said, and Ryan glanced meaningfully at the clock on the mantle, which read ten-thirty.

"You're home early," he observed.

Gaz thought quickly.

"I'd left something at home," he explained. "I was planning to head back, when you arrived."

"What line of business are you in?" Ryan asked.

"Scrap metal and salvage," he said, after an infinitesimal pause. That was their legitimate front, at least.

This time, it was Phillips who sent a meaningful glance around the room, and over Gaz's attire.

"Business must be boomin'," he remarked. "Back in my day, workin' the scrap was a messy job."

Gaz said nothing.

"Been on holiday, lately?" Phillips prodded, eyeing up the man's tan.

Again, Gaz remained silent, and so Ryan turned his focus back to Keeley. "Mrs Nicholson? When was the last time you saw Ollie?"

"I've already told you, it was last night," Gaz said.

Ryan gave him a long look. "I'd like to ask Mrs Nicholson, please."

"I don't want her upset," Gaz said. "If you have any questions, you can ask me."

"Oh, I will," Ryan said. "Don't worry, Mr Nicholson."

When any further questioning was met with stony silence, they knew their time was up.

"One final thing, Mrs Nicholson," Ryan said, as they prepared to leave.

She raised her head, and tried to focus.

"Your son was found hanged," he said, looking across to her husband. "With a Bible tucked inside his jacket, marked at the Book of Job. We're treating his death as murder, not suicide."

She dissolved into fresh tears and, this time, when Gaz laid a reluctant hand on her shoulder, she shrugged it away.

"We'll see ourselves out," Phillips said.

Outside, Ryan stood for a moment beside his car, letting the rain wash against his face.

"He never asked, Frank," he said. "He never asked how his son died."

Phillips nodded, and looked back towards the house.

"Neither did she," he said.

Ryan ran his hands over his hair, slicking back the water, and got behind the wheel again.

"They'll close ranks," he said. "If we could only get her alone—"

"He'll not let her out of his sight," Phillips said. "She's a liability to him."

Ryan sat there for a minute, thinking of the boy who'd risked his life to save another, even though it went against every principle he'd been taught and every instinct of self-preservation.

"They're not all lost causes, are they, Frank? Sometimes, we're the ones who fail."

Phillips thought of his own upbringing, with all its hardships and imperfections, and nodded.

"Sometimes the apple rolls away from the tree," he agreed. "If we'd only had another day, we might've found the lad and been able to take him somewhere safe. But there isn't anything we failed to do, lad. It's what his own kin failed to do that matters."

Ryan started the engine.

"Let's make his sacrifice worth something, and find those other women, Frank."

CHAPTER 29

Lawana awakened to another day, and to the familiar, shaking feeling of drugs withdrawal.

She didn't know what the man had injected her with, the night before, but it had made her sleepy afterwards, for which she was grateful.

When memories snapped at the corners of her mind, they were violently thrust away.

There were some things she would never choose to remember.

But she recalled the blinking light of the camcorder, sitting on its tripod, and the flash of an old-fashioned polaroid camera, again and again. She wanted to flay her own skin as she remembered the feel of his hands washing her body with pungent soap, every crevice and corner, every intimate place, until he was satisfied that she was clean enough for him to despoil.

After that, her mind closed the door.

She'd wished for death, all the way through the night, and yet it hadn't come. She'd waited for it, waited for him to choose his implement and strike, and had made her peace with God long before the first blow.

Yet, it seemed she had pleased him, because he'd spoken tenderly to her at the end, mopping up the blood and dabbing at her wounds, before leaving her there to wait and wonder how long it would take him to come back for seconds.

Slowly, she came around, and saw things clearly again.

She had not survived this long to die such a death, at the hands of such a man.

She refused.

Lawana pushed herself up onto her elbows to survey the room again, ignoring the headache raging at the base of her skull and the dull, painful ache between her legs.

The door was locked, there were no windows or air vents, no telephones or other means of contacting the outside world, and she had no use of her legs. These were the basic facts; therefore, the chances of her escaping were almost zero, and any remote chance was entirely dependent on her actions. She'd considered the possibility of trying to befriend him, or otherwise build some sort of rapport, such that he might keep her alive long enough for her to formulate a better plan.

But she saw nothing behind his eyes she could appeal to; no spark of human kindliness she could hope to ignite.

She'd spent much of the previous day shouting and screaming, banging on the door with all her might, but nobody had come. She had to assume, then, that the place where she was being held was somewhere remote, or otherwise sound-proofed.

He was no fool, that one.

Except, perhaps, in one regard.

Twice, now, he'd given her a dose of some narcotic, and twice she'd wakened from it sooner than he might have expected. That was the effect of having been fed heroin for the week prior to his abduction—her body had developed a degree of tolerance that would not have been the case in other women.

She could use that to her advantage.

Lawana lay back down on the bed and began to meditate, taking herself away from the confines of that awful place, with its rancid odour of dried blood, far away to the land of her birth. She imagined clear blue seas—though, she'd never seen them, herself—and swaying palm trees. She saw a small house with a beautiful garden, where vegetables could grow. She saw Achara, her beautiful Achara, as a mother with a kind, well-mannered husband by her side, and herself as a grandmother.

It was a good life, she thought. Too good to give up dreaming of, just yet.

Achara woke up in a new bed, in a room with another locked door.

It was better than the last, insofar as she had the room to herself, and it was reasonably clean, with fresh linens on the bed and even a small en-suite bathroom she was allowed to use. There was soap and clean towels, and she'd enjoyed her first bath in over a week.

The man they called 'Dragon' had brought her to her new home, in the back seat of his car, which smelled of expensive leather. He'd driven through the night, watching her in the rear-view mirror, passing rows of houses which all looked alike, until he came to one in particular.

He'd even walked around to open the door for her, and had given her his coat, for warmth.

"I'll buy you new clothes," he said, as he'd taken her arm and led her towards the front door. "Until then, you'll be safe here."

All the while, he'd spoken in a language she could understand.

Inside the house, there was another woman who looked like her, who smiled warmly and ushered her inside.

"I'll be back tomorrow night," he'd told her, and the woman nodded.

"She'll be ready."

Achara was so tired, and so hungry, she hadn't really been listening. As she entered the house, she could smell the familiar scent of homemade curry, like her mother used to make.

Her mother.

She'd begun to cry again, and the woman held her close, murmuring, soothing, rubbing slow circles around her back.

It would be better now, she'd said.

You're very lucky to have been chosen, she'd said.

Do as you're told, and everything will be fine.

Then, she'd ladled big spoonfuls of curry and rice into a dish and watched her eat every morsel, before leading her upstairs, to her room.

This is your room, she'd said. *Keep it tidy and clean.*

To Achara, it seemed like a palace.

"Where has he gone?" she'd asked, peering behind the other door to see if he was waiting for her.

The woman laughed.

Take your chance, she advised. *You won't get another night like this, so make the most of it.*

Achara hadn't understood.

Nothing is free, she'd said. *You have to earn your keep, like everyone else.*

"I thought I'd be working in a nail bar," she said.

The woman only shook her head, and pulled a fresh syringe and a small brown cube from the pocket of her colourful kimono.

You'll learn, she said.

Now, Achara stared at the locked door and wondered when her first 'lesson' would be. During the night, she'd heard a stream of knocks at the door, and the tread of footsteps back and forth on the stairs. She'd heard banging from the room next door, and a woman's cries, until she could hear no more and had shut herself away in the bathroom to escape the sound.

Her mother had wanted an education for her, she'd always said.

But, not this.

Never this.

CHAPTER 30

Lawana's eyes flew open at the first sound of his key entering the outer lock.

By the time he entered, she was rolling back and forth on the bed, moaning softly, as if in pain. She instructed her body to tremble, and it obeyed, so that he truly believed she was in the throes of withdrawal.

"I'm sorry I have to do this to you," he said, not meaning a word of it.

She heard his rucksack thud against the floor, and the turn of his key in the lock. Afterwards, he placed the key on the edge of the sink, and began to remove his clothes.

"I have a sandwich for you," he said. "But let's have that later."

She didn't understand the words, but she didn't need to. She had already calculated what she would do, and how she would do it.

So long as he stayed true to form.

She'd read somewhere, once, that killers stalked their victims and learned their routines. The more predictable a person, the easier it was for them to fall prey.

It worked the other way around, too.

If she was right about him, and she hoped she was, this man was a creature of habit. He liked to collect women, and images of women he would eventually hurt. But he liked the anticipation of it, most of all. She'd felt his hand tremble as he'd washed her body, and his need had escalated until he'd been unable to contain himself, any longer.

Like an animal—though, in truth, no animal she'd ever known had been so cruel.

They hunted for food, or killed in defence; they rarely inflicted pain for sport. That was an entirely human trait.

She listened to him setting up the tripod for his camcorder, and heard the *click click* as the metal legs snapped into place, just as he'd done the day before. She heard him whistle the same tune—something she didn't recognise—while he filled a small bucket of water. To her disgust, it was a child's bucket, the kind they used to build sandcastles, with a little black handle.

He added a squirt or two of soap, the same one he'd used the day before, and set it on the floor beside her bed.

Then, he rummaged inside his rucksack for his implements of choice, which he laid out at the end of the bed, beside her feet.

"All right, let's get you all cleaned up," he said.

She remained perfectly still, trembling now and then, as she might have done if she hadn't been fully lucid.

She endured his hands rubbing her body with the soapy water, training herself not to react, not to vomit or claw at him, too soon.

There was time for that.

Then, came the photographs of her glistening body, still wet from the water. He seemed to like taking plenty of those, perhaps as a counterpoint to the end product he planned to create.

He snapped pictures from every angle, the strap of the camera dangling low as he shifted her body this way and that. She suffered the abuse, waiting…waiting…

When he moved to straddle her, so he could take a picture of her confused, disorientated face, he didn't capture the image he was expecting.

Instead, he saw a woman, wide-eyed and full of hatred, teeth bared and ready to fight.

There was no time to react.

She reached low and grasped his erect member punishingly hard and twisted it, until he screamed and fell back against her dead legs. He dropped the camera but, when it would have slid from the bed to the floor, she made a grab for the strap and swung it, hard, rearing up with all the strength she had to aim for his head.

She didn't miss.

Howling from the pain in his groin, surprised by the blow to his head, the man fell to the floor.

But he would not stay down for long, and she acted like lightning.

Forcing herself upward, she grabbed the first thing she found from his crude assortment at the bottom of the bed, which happened to be a wire coat hanger.

She had the jagged edge ready between her fingers when he reared up, eyes wild with anger and outrage.

She aimed for those black eyes, scoring a line across the left one.

He howled, clutching both hands to his bleeding eye, and stumbled backwards, half blind for the crucial moments it took her to take aim once again with the blunt end of the camera.

The sound she made as it swung back was guttural, like an ancient war cry, and she could have wept with happiness when she heard it crack against the side of his skull.

He went down again, but she knew it was not the time to stop.

She needed to finish the job.

Still armed with the camera, she rolled off the bed and onto the floor beside him, and he made a blind grab for her legs, ready to bite her flesh.

She raised herself up and drove the camera back down upon his head...

Again...

And again.

Until he lay still, a thin line of blood trickling from his temple and onto the dusty floor.

Shaking, sobbing, she discarded the hateful device and looked for a way to move around him, but there was none. The only way to get past his body was to climb across it.

Terrified he should suddenly wake up again, she placed her hands on the other side of his torso, then lowered onto her elbows to begin commando crawling towards the sink, where she knew he'd left the key. Her legs trailed after her, dragging across his body, and she made small, whimpering sounds of fear, expecting him to grasp her feet and pull her back.

But he didn't and soon enough she heard the thud of her feet hitting the floor, once she was clear of him.

She glanced back over her shoulder, sweating from the effort, and thought she saw him twitch.

Galvanised again, she crawled over to the pedestal and reached up to curl her fingers around the rim of the sink, pulling her body up with all her might so she could determine where he'd left the key.

Beside the right tap.

Exhaustion forced her back down again, and she panted for endless seconds, watching his body for any further signs of movement, before she had recovered enough to try again. This time, the strain was worse, for it required her to support her own body weight with one hand, leaving the other free to reach for the key, without knocking it down the drain.

It took three attempts before she was able to grasp the small silver key in her sweaty palm and, by the time she did, his fingers had begun to move.

She held the key between her teeth and crawled across to the door, but found the lock too high for her to reach. Adrenaline riding high, she looked around for a means to propel herself upward, and her eye fell on the tripod.

She made a grab for it, wincing as the camcorder fell from its perch with a crash, and she froze for a moment, waiting for him to come around and fall upon her with all his fury.

Still, he didn't.

She grasped the legs of the tripod in both hands, her teeth clenched hard around the key, and used it as a support until she was in a kneeling position, her floppy legs held at a right-angle for just long enough to allow her to push the key inside the lock.

When she heard it click open, she sobbed.

The cellar was at the back of a much larger, long-abandoned stone outbuilding, in the middle of open fields. It took Lawana another fifteen minutes to make it outside, dragging herself over sharp pebbles and crusted earth, over the droppings of rabbits and sheep, until she emerged into the open air.

It was raining, and bitterly cold, but she didn't care.

She was free.

But, only so long as he remained unconscious—and he might come stumbling out of the cellar at any moment to drag her back again, snatching away this small moment of triumph before it had really begun.

She saw his car parked nearby, but knew he would not have left keys in the ignition.

Where were all the houses, and other people?

Where was the road?

She heard the distant sound of a car's engine and knew it could not be far away, if she headed in the right direction, but it was so hard to see from the ground, and her body was almost done.

She began to crawl, placing one arm in front of the other, counting each movement until she reached one thousand, before starting again.

CHAPTER 31

Ryan and Phillips were on their way back to Police Headquarters when the call came through, and the former performed a swift, illegal U-turn to begin making the journey to the Royal Victoria Infirmary, with all possible speed.

"Gan canny, lad," Phillips told him, as he was thrown against the side of the passenger door. "I fancy makin' it to m' next birthday, if it's all the same t' you."

Ryan responded by leaning on his horn to usher another car out of the way.

"The woman was picked up just past Slingley Hill, not far from Houghton-le-Spring," he said. "The driver took her to the local walk-in clinic, but they've transferred her to the RVI, given the extent of her injuries."

He paused to overtake a speeding Porsche.

"I want a team down there, right away," he continued. "I want a statement from the driver who picked her up, with full details of the exact location. Tell Jack he needs to take a full support team, once he has the precise location," he said. "Whoever transported the woman to that location should be considered armed and dangerous."

Phillips nodded, and put a call through to Lowerson, who was still managing the scene in Marsden.

"Jack says he'll get onto it straight away."

Ryan nodded. "If this woman is still alive, and can talk to us, we might have found the missing piece of the puzzle, Frank."

The two men made their way directly to the Accident and Emergency Department, and were informed that their witness had been transferred to the ICU, where she was being treated for multiple injuries.

"I'm sorry, Chief Inspector, but she isn't in any condition to talk to you, at the moment," her consultant told them. "She's in a critical condition, and requires urgent surgery to repair the vertebrae at the base of her spinal cord, in addition to having suffered multiple breakages to her ribs and fracturing her wrist. She's in severe shock, aside from anything else, and is suffering from pneumonia."

"Will she recover?"

"Mentally, or physically?" the physician asked. "Hopefully, we can repair the broken bones, although we're awaiting the results of a further MRI scan to assess the extent of the damage to her spinal cord. Her legs are unresponsive at the moment, which is a very worrying sign. I can't imagine what she's been through to sustain injuries like these and, unfortunately, she speaks very little English."

"We'll source a translator," Ryan said. "This woman may be a key witness to a murder investigation, so her safety is paramount. We'd like her moved to a private room, if possible, where there'll be an armed guard on the door, around the clock. I want a total media ban, which includes all the staff in your department. Can I rely on your cooperation?"

The consultant looked between their serious faces, and nodded.

"Of course," she said, briskly.

Ryan watched a nurse enter the ICU with a small bowl of warm water and a sponge, making directly for their witness.

"Stop that nurse!" he said, and the consultant spun around in confusion.

"She's only going to clean up the patient's hands and feet," she explained. "The poor woman is covered in cuts and bruises—"

"You don't understand," Ryan said, urgently. "We need to take swabs from her hands and feet, for forensic analysis."

The consultant understood immediately, and hurried inside to intercept the nurse, who was on the cusp of lathering up the woman's feet.

"Good thinking," Phillips murmured, approvingly. "You never miss a trick."

Ryan wished that were true.

When the consultant returned, she confirmed that the woman remained largely in the same condition as when she'd arrived—albeit, more comfortable, with the necessary pain relief and fluids to flush out some of the impurities in her system.

"We've taken various blood samples for our own analysis," she said. "We'll be glad to procure more, for toxicology purposes."

Ryan nodded.

"Thank you," he said. "We have reason to believe this woman may have been exposed to heroin, and possibly other narcotics."

The consultant made a swift note on the pad she held in her hand.

"That's very helpful," she murmured, and altered the dosage of opioid-based pain medication she'd planned to give her patient. "Do you know anything else about her?"

"Only that she's been through hell and back," Phillips said, sadly. "We think she may be a victim of trafficking, so it's worth checking her for sexual assault."

The consultant nodded.

"We already noted some trauma in that area," she said, looking down at her chart so they wouldn't see the grief in her eyes. "She'll be treated accordingly. We have specialist counsellors who would normally help, but, with the language barrier—"

"Leave it with us," Ryan said. "We'll find someone."

He thought immediately of Niki, and wondered if she had any contacts through her refuge who might be able to help the poor woman.

He'd pay another visit to the bookshop café, as soon as he could.

"Has she said anything?" Phillips wondered.

"Just one word," the consultant said. "*Achara*. She's repeated it several times."

They looked back through the long window overlooking the ward and watched the woman sleep, wondering what secrets lay inside her troubled mind.

"We'll take the first watch," Ryan said. "Until a member of the firearms team arrives."

The consultant looked between the two men and was glad the woman had somebody to watch over her, in her most critical hour.

Once she'd moved off, Phillips spied a vending machine down the hall and sent his friend and enquiring look.

"Fancy a cup of sludge?" he asked.

"Tempting, but I think I'll opt for an Irn-Bru, this time."

"Drink of champions," Phillips proclaimed, before trundling off in search of sugar.

CHAPTER 32

While Detective Constable Jack Lowerson pulled together a team of firearms specialists to accompany him to the last known location where their star witness had been found collapsed by the roadside, the man who had been her captor slowly returned to consciousness.

His left eye burned, there was a dreadful ache in his groin, and the side of his head had swollen to the size of a golf ball.

Reality came flooding back, and he sat up slowly, looking around at the spattered blood that was, for once, his own.

Stupid bitch!

He struggled to his feet, clutching a hand to his eye, and searched the floor. When he found no sign of her, he noticed the door hanging open on its hinge, and let out a raw sound of anguish.

No.

No!

Still half naked, he hurried out of the cellar and into the main outbuilding, which was empty, too. An inspection of the floor showed a twin trail of drag marks through the damp earth, which he followed until they disappeared. He spent useless minutes scouring the immediate area, roaring like a wounded tiger, until he was forced to admit that he'd been remiss. It could only have been the dosage, he realised. He hadn't given the woman enough to keep her sedated.

He stood there, in the middle of a nearby field, and let out another long roar, blood still streaming from his eye and down his chest.

When he had expended himself, he acted quickly.

If she'd been picked up, they would have taken her straight to the police, who could be making their way to his special place at that very moment.

He ran back across the field to his car, where he fumbled for the key to open the boot.

When it popped open, he made a grab for the small can of petrol and matches he kept for emergencies such as these.

He ran back into the outbuilding and across to the cellar, where he stuffed his personal items back into his rucksack and selected one or two of his favourite images from his collection on the wall. It angered him to have to leave this place; he'd used it for the past ten years without fear of discovery and yet, thanks to the actions of one woman, he was now forced to abandon his one sanctuary from the drudgery of his ordinary life.

Furious, enraged, he began swilling the petrol around the cellar, then around the edges of the outbuilding, until the can was empty. Then, he began striking matches, watching the flames lick and crawl along the bodies of the women covering the walls, until the paper curled and turned to ash and he could no longer bear the heat.

He waited until the outbuilding had begun to burn, its walls charring as the fire took hold, then got into his car and left his special place for the last time.

He'd have to find a new one, now.

"The place was incinerated," Lowerson said, when he took his place at the team briefing, an hour later. "Whoever had been there beat us to it, maybe only by a few minutes."

"Did you manage to salvage anything?" Ryan asked.

"The fire was too strong," Jack replied. "By the time the Fire Service arrived, the place was burned out."

"The Fire Investigator will go over it with Faulkner," Ryan said. "There might be something left."

It never hurt to remain optimistic.

"How about the witness?" Jack asked them. "Could she tell you anything?"

"She was in no fit state," Phillips said, placing a can of Lilt in front of him. "Go on, wrap your laughin' gear around that—it's got a totally tropical taste."

"Bring, bring," Yates said, pretending to hold a telephone to her ear. "Hey, Frank, 1990 just called. It wants its drinks advert back."

They all laughed.

"I can't help it, if I don't like all this modern muck," he said. "I've tried all the smoothies and the juices and the soya-whatsits, but it just isn't the same."

"I could be converted," Lowerson said, after a satisfying gulp. "I can tell you one thing about the place, though. There was no sign of any other occupancy, or of there being any other women. The main outbuilding was mostly a ruin, and wouldn't have been suitable to house anyone. As for the back room, it looked pretty small. I don't think you could have kept more than ten people in there, at one time."

"I don't understand this," Ryan muttered, half to himself. "If it wasn't the same gang of traffickers we've been looking for, then who the hell was it who took the woman there?"

"If we assume the anonymous caller was Oliver Nicholson," Yates said, "and we also assume he *did* see a woman trapped in that cave beneath the sink hole at the bottom of The Leas, which is the information that ultimately got him killed, it may be safe to assume this woman was the same one that was once inside that cave."

"A lot of assumptions, not a lot of hard evidence, but I'm still with you," Ryan said. "Go on."

"Why did it have to be the same gang who removed her from the cave?" she finished. "Couldn't it have been some other unknown party who is responsible for abducting her to the location at Slingley Hill?"

It felt like a shot in the dark.

"Seems fantastic," he said. "The probability of some other third party having taken her before either we or the gang recovered her is incredibly low. How would they happen to be looking in the right place?"

"It's not impossible," Phillips said.

"No, not impossible," Ryan conceded, and let the idea roll around his mind. "It's not too much of a stretch to imagine that the type of person capable of abducting a woman is also the type of person who would turn up to have a snoop around the crime scene at Marsden. We won't know until our witness comes around and talks to us."

"I've been looking into local translators," Yates said, and handed him a list of names and contact numbers. "Any of the first three on that list are available to attend the hospital tomorrow."

"Excellent," Ryan said, and folded the paper into his back pocket. "Morrison has given her approval for twenty-four-hour security on the ICU ward, with access granted to authorised personnel only. She's also given the go-ahead for three days' surveillance of the Nicholson property. Have there been any developments on that score?"

Lowerson and Yates had been left jointly in charge of the crime scene.

"Faulkner's due to go in and sweep the boy's home," Yates said. "But, given this recent turn of events, we may have to prioritise the site at Slingley Hill, unless he has the capacity to do both."

"They're very stretched," Ryan said. "Prioritise, if you have to."

She nodded. "According to the owner of the pub in the Grotto, he found the body while he was heading out for a few supplies, this morning," she said. "He lifted the body down, to check if he was still alive."

And compromised any trace evidence, Ryan thought.

"It's a natural reaction, to want to help," he said. "But it doesn't make our job any easier. I take it the camera beside the car park is still not working?"

Yates nodded, miserably. "Yes, I'm afraid so. The Grotto doesn't have CCTV coverage on that side of the building, either. They say it's usually a very safe place."

"Okay, so we don't have any shortcuts on this one," Ryan said, and paced around the room, to ease out the kinks in his shoulders. "Oliver Nicholson was the only son of Gavin Nicholson, a known drug dealer, albeit one who dresses like he's off to the races."

Phillips chuckled.

"Dig out known associates—starting with Michael Donnelly, who runs 'Donnelly's Scrap Yard'."

"We'll pay him a visit," Lowerson said.

Ryan nodded. "If Oliver's death was a message, or a punishment for disloyalty, I have to ask myself how they knew he'd put the call through," he said.

Lowerson leaned forward. "My mate at the Control Room—Robbie—rang me because he thought it was wrong it had been labelled a prank call," he said. "I suppose anyone with access to the system could have checked for particular calls coming through, but that seems pretty labour intensive. It's more likely Robbie, his supervisor, or someone eavesdropping decided to leak the details."

Ryan moved across to the window and thought about the sequence of events.

"Oliver made the call at nine-forty-five on Saturday night," he said quietly. "He made another call to National Heritage fifteen minutes later, reporting the sink hole. The next morning, you got a message from your friend, Robbie, to say he thought the caller was genuine and worth checking out—this was around lunchtime on Sunday."

Then, a thought struck him.

"There were television cameras," he remembered. "On the clifftop, while we were checking out the sink hole. There were cameras filming for the afternoon news."

"Aye, and they'd be keeping an eye on things, since they're probably holed up somewhere," Phillips said. "They'll have seen the police presence."

Ryan swore beneath his breath.

"One of them clocked us, and began to be suspicious about why we were so interested in that sink hole," he said. "They flushed the poor kid out, so it might not have been anybody on the inside who leaked information about the call. We might have been the hapless morons to arouse their suspicions."

"We couldn't have known," Phillips argued, knowing that his friend would berate himself, more than anyone else. "Our first duty was to preserve life, and that's what you were trying to do by checking out the cave. You had to be sure she wasn't still down there—dying, or in pain."

Ryan knew it was true, but it didn't make the rest any easier to bear.

"We know they're without mercy, and that they have a strict code," he said. "What we need to do is find out where these women and girls go, once they arrive on our shores, and who profits from them." He checked the time.

"Jack? Frank? I'll meet you outside *Voyeur* just before ten," he said. "We need to arrive suited and booted, to give the right impression."

"I suggest you invest in some fake moustaches," Yates said, and three heads turned to her in surprise.

"Why?" Jack wondered.

"I dunno," she said. "Whenever I see a man with a moustache, I automatically think, 'perve'."

There was a short silence, before they erupted into laughter.

CHAPTER 33

"Frank, what the hell are you wearing?"

Ryan stared at his sergeant's chosen ensemble, and struggled to keep a straight face. His friend had opted for a snazzy pinstripe suit and a black tie embroidered with tiny red hearts, to go with the red silk square he'd stuffed into his breast pocket and the shiny black patent shoes which hadn't seen the light of day in at least thirty years. To top it off, he'd adorned his upper lip with what Ryan could only describe as the rear end of a dead animal.

"You look like Lucky Luciano," he declared. "The only thing missing is a cigar and a bowler hat."

Phillips scowled.

"You said we had to jazz it up a bit," he argued. "And, with us sort of being under cover, I thought—"

"You'd take your style inspiration from *Some Like it Hot*?" Ryan finished for him. "We're not looking to find ourselves a gangster's moll, you know."

He grinned, and reached across to rip off the fake moustache.

"I'm pretty sure Mel was only joking about that," he said. "And besides, it looks like you picked it up from the joke shop."

Phillips couldn't argue with that, since the receipt was still burning a hole in his pocket.

"Well, I just don't want anyone to recognise me, that's all," he said, casting a nervous glance around the street corner where they were awaiting Lowerson's arrival.

Ryan gave him a lopsided grin. "Are you embarrassed, by any chance?"

"Eh?" Phillips waved that away with one knobbly hand. "Nowt embarrasses me, lad…I've seen more pairs of…well, I've seen plenty of…plenty in my time, don't you worry."

Ryan chuckled, and raised a hand to Jack, whose shiny grey suit reflected the light from the streetlamps overhead.

"Very dapper," he said, as the younger man approached.

Lowerson smoothed a hand over his hair, which had been gelled to within an inch of its life.

"If we're supposed to look like a certain kind of punter, I thought I'd get into the guise of a local bachelor with money to burn," he said. "What's your persona, Frank?"

"I'll be Dirty Old Git Number Two," Phillips said.

"Who's Number One?" Ryan enquired.

"Look in the mirror, son," Phillips said, and let out a booming guffaw.

"I had that one coming."

"Aye, you did. What's the game plan, once we're inside?"

"Let's get the lay of the land, first," Ryan said. "Check out the layout of the club, watch where they take people for private dances or anything else. Chat to anyone who's open to it, ask the right questions. We want to know where to go if you want fresh blood, straight off the boat."

They nodded.

"What about the girls?"

"Let them approach you and see if you can engage them in conversation. You'll need to buy them a drink, otherwise they won't be allowed to sit and talk to you. This might be the only time in your lives that buying a half-naked woman a drink will be acceptable to our other halves, so make the most of it and see what they can tell you. The name to mention is 'Fuchsia,'" he reminded them. "We don't want to stay any longer than necessary, so let's see what we can find out and try to be out of there by midnight."

They were ushered inside *Voyeur* by two tall, stony-eyed bouncers in dark suits, who frisked them all for weapons and issued a warning about taking any photographs or videos on their mobile phones. Their eyes might have lingered on Phillips' eccentric get-up, but they said nothing, and he shuffled in behind Ryan and Jack.

The walls of the club had been painted a deep, burgundy red, and dark red and black voile was draped from the ceiling of the main space, gathering in the middle around the edges of an enormous gold chandelier, whose lights were dimmed. The room itself was large, with one main stage lit by professional spotlighting and several smaller stages dotted around. Rather than one bar area, there were at least three, each of which boasted its own array of topless waitresses ready to serve up whatever was required. Tables seating two, four and six were arranged around the space in between, with larger 'VIP' booths being reserved for those willing to pay extra for the relative privacy afforded in the shadows.

"Let's get one of those," Phillips said, but Ryan shook his head.

"We're trying to elicit information, not hide ourselves away," he said. "Don't worry, they won't bite you."

Phillips wasn't so sure.

"Welcome to *Voyeur*! My name's Candy. You fellas lookin' for a table?"

As if she'd read his mind, a woman in an itsy-bitsy neon pink bikini and skyscraper heels approached them, armed with a menu.

"Ooh, do you do food, love?"

"Er, just nibbles," she said, with a degree of confusion. Food wasn't usually the first thing her regular punters ordered. "This your first time here, sweetie?"

She ran a delicate hand over Phillips' arm, and he had to stop himself from snatching it away.

"He's just shy," Lowerson said, with a wink.

"*Oh*! That's so cute. Well, let me explain how it works," she said. "There's a minimum spend: if you want to sit at one of these tables, you need to spend more than a hundred quid. If you want to sit at one of the V.I.P. booths, you need to spend more than five hundred. You can sit at the bar for fifty, each."

She waited for them to make their choice, batting a set of enormous false eyelashes.

"We'll take a table in the main space," Ryan said, and cast his eyes around for one which would afford the best view—of the punters, rather than the dancers. "Is that one free?"

He pointed to one in the middle.

"Sure! Follow me," she said, and all three men averted their eyes as she led the way, bare butt-cheeks sashaying as she went.

She set the menu down on the table, and leaned across Ryan to light the candles in the middle of the table. To avoid suffocation, he turned his face away, but had an easy smile in place once she stepped back again.

"I'll have a rum and co—" he started to say, before remembering he was supposed to be playing a part. "Make that a bottle of champagne. Four glasses—have one yourself."

Obviously pleased with his choice, and the mark-up on the bottle of Laurent Perrier he'd ordered, she gave him a slow smile.

"Don't go anywhere," she said.

"Champagne?" Phillips squeaked, once she'd moved off. "I thought I'd have a swift half and be done with it—"

"My treat, and we don't have to drink it," Ryan said, keeping his voice down as he looked at the faces of the men around the room. "It's for show. They inflate the prices by a few hundred per cent, and the girl gets to meet her quota for the evening. That puts us in her good books, and she'll be more likely to feel chatty."

Phillips relaxed again. "Oh, aye, I forgot. How d' you know about all this, anyhow?"

"I had a word with a friend," he said, thinking of one of the women in the office he happened to know had funded her university degree stripping on the side. "She gave me a few pointers about what to expect, from the inside track."

Their conversation was forestalled by the arrival of two other women, who stalked towards them in similarly scanty outfits.

"You boys look lonely," one of them said. "Why don't we keep you company. I'm Honey, and this is Sugar."

Both were blonde, perma-tanned, and wore heavy make-up which made it hard to judge their ages, at first. However, upon closer inspection, Ryan wouldn't have put either of them at more than nineteen or twenty, whereas the average age of the punters in the room looked to be forty plus.

They pulled up a couple of spare chairs, and pouted at the menu.

"I'm thirsty," Honey said, meaningfully.

"You must be parched, after all the dancin' and walkin' round in those heels," Phillips sympathised. "Let me get you a glass of water, pet."

She stared at him, and then broke into a smile.

"That isn't…quite what I meant," she said, and glanced again at the menu.

"Oh, aye! Listen, love, why don't you tell us how much you need to make on the bar tab, tonight, and we'll see what we can do, so you can just relax a bit?"

Honey and Sugar looked at each other, then at Frank.

"Well, we have to hit a thousand each," she confessed. "I've managed seven hundred, and Sugar's at five-fifty—"

"*How* much?" Phillips burst out.

"We'll make up the difference," Ryan said quickly, and handed over his credit card again.

"Do you want a private dance? You could get a few, for that—"

"Thanks," Ryan said. "But, why don't we just chat?"

Both women visibly relaxed.

"My feet are killin' me," Sugar confessed.

"You girls worked here long?" Lowerson asked, keeping his eyes firmly above chest-height.

"I've been here for a year," Honey said. "Sugar's only been here for a month, haven't you?"

The other woman nodded.

"I haven't seen any of you in here, before," Honey said, and would have remembered the tall, dark-haired one, for sure. She'd have given that one a private dance, for free.

"Yeah, this is our first time," Lowerson said. "We heard it's the place to come to."

While they talked, Ryan kept an eye on the door, watching the faces of those who came in and out. He saw men getting handsy, and being thrown out; he watched the girls' faces when they thought nobody was looking, and saw the cracks in their armour. He watched some of them leading men—and the occasional woman—by the hand to one of a series of numbered doors, before returning again five or ten minutes later.

"—love?"

Ryan realised Candy had returned with their champagne, and accepted a glass from her, which he sipped and then put back on the table.

"Thanks."

"You looked miles away, then," she said, while her eyes catalogued and assessed. "You need somebody to talk to, tonight?"

She touched a long nail to his hand, and trailed it across.

"I've heard I'm a good listener," she purred.

Ryan had seldom felt more uncomfortable in his life, but he couldn't blame her for that. She was only doing her job, and so was he.

He pulled his hand away and was about to reply, when he caught sight of Phillips, whose face had turned the same shade as the walls since Honey had decided that she was feeling too hot in her string bikini top.

"Here! You'll catch your death—have my jacket," he blustered, and before she could protest, he'd draped the pinstripe blazer over her shoulders.

She didn't know what to say.

"Er...thanks?"

"Don't mention it," Phillips said, in a fatherly tone.

Lowerson and Sugar were chatting amiably enough, with the latter telling him all about how she was studying for her qualification in Social Sciences, whilst Candy seemed irritated at having backed a horse who seemed less interested in her than in their surroundings.

"Can I get you anything else?" she asked, sharply.

Ryan shook his head, frowned as he watched a man stumble behind a dark curtain, and then gave her his full attention again.

"What's behind that curtain?" he asked.

She glanced over at it, then at the bouncer who stood guarding all who entered and left.

"Um, that's a private area," she said.

"For dances?"

She looked uncomfortable.

"Yeah, listen, if you're not lookin' for anythin' else, I've gotta speak to some of the other customers," she said quickly, catching the eye of her manager, who tapped the watch on his wrist.

Ryan raised a lazy eyebrow, and tried a bit of charm, instead.

"I haven't been very good company, have I?" he said, apologetically. "To tell you the truth, I was looking around to see if I could find a girl I used to know. She went by the name, 'Fuchsia.'"

Something flickered in the girl's eyes, before her mask fell into place again.

"I don't know her," she lied. "Now, if you'll excuse me—"

She moved off quickly to speak with one of the other girls, and dipped back inside the dressing room soon after.

Interesting.

"Now—stop that—I don't need any head massages," Phillips was saying, as Honey trailed her fingers over his balding head.

"Spoilsport," she chuckled. "What's wrong, handsome? Worried your wife will find out?"

She already knew, and that was bad enough, Phillips thought.

"Now, here, you were about to tell me all about your plans to train as a vet," he reminded her, a bit desperately.

"Who do we ask, if we want to liven the party up?" Ryan said, suddenly.

"What d'you mean?" Sugar asked. "Shots?"

"I was thinkin' a bit more along the lines of…" He passed a finger beneath his nose.

"Oh," she said, and found herself surprised. She hadn't thought he was the type, but it turned out you could never tell. "Yeah, look, we're not supposed to encourage that. It's illegal, isn't it?"

She didn't sound sure.

"Yeah, but we won't tell," Lowerson said, playing along.

"See over there?" Honey said, leaning across the table to point a discreet fingernail in the direction of a youngish man in a well-cut suit who had stationed himself at one end of the main bar. "He's the one to talk to about that."

"Thanks," Ryan said, and signalled the other two that it was time to move on.

There were the obligatory expressions of disappointment but, by the time the three men had made their way over to the bar, Honey and Sugar had moved on to the next table.

Rather than approaching the dealer directly, they slid onto some free stools at the bar, all of which provided a good view of the man at the other end, as well as the dark voile curtain tucked against the wall behind him, where a steady stream of inebriated or intoxicated men were slipping behind its veil. Unlike the other, more obvious private spaces, Ryan hadn't seen a single one of them return since they'd been in the club.

They ordered a round of beers, and Phillips took a grateful chug.

"I needed that," he said.

"Dutch courage?" Lowerson joked.

"You can say that, again. My blood pressure can't take all this excitement."

Jack grinned, and gave him a manly slap on the back.

"You'll survive," he said, before turning to Ryan. "I thought we were going to have a word with the dealer?"

"No, I want to watch him," Ryan said. "There's another room—maybe a network of rooms—behind that curtain. The men who go in there go in alone, and its entry is guarded, whereas the other private rooms aren't. What does that tell you?"

"That's the bit they keep off the books," Phillips said, and took another sip of his beer. "You wouldn't get anythin' out of him, anyway. His lips look tighter than a fish's backside, if y'ask me."

Ryan almost choked on his beer.

"Frank, you've got a wonderful way with words," he said, when he was able.

"I tell it like it is."

"One thing I notice about this place," Lowerson said, glancing around. "All the girls are mostly white."

Ryan nodded.

"In this part of the club, at least."

His eyes sharpened as a man of around his own age lurched towards the dealer at the other end of the bar, already fumbling for the wad of cash he planned to exchange for a bag of cocaine.

He might have been clumsy, but the dealer was slick, Ryan noted. If he hadn't been looking out for it, he'd have hardly noticed the exchange.

A moment later, the man made his way towards the dark curtain, where he was stopped by the bouncer.

Another quick exchange, and he was shown inside.

"We're in the wrong part of the club," Ryan said. "What we need to do is get behind that curtain."

"I draw the line at that," Phillips said, swiping a hand through the air.

Ryan shook his head.

"Nobody's talking, out here, and they're not likely to. Anyone after the kind of private, specialist service catered to by non-British girls won't be sitting out here with the mainstream crowd. They're through there… and I think I've found someone who might talk. Come on."

But, when they reached the bouncer, they found the way barred to them.

"Where's your ticket?" he asked. "You need a special ticket to come into this area."

"Where do we get a ticket?" Ryan asked.

"Speak to the boss," he advised them, and pointed out a man of around sixty, who was working his way around the room, checking everyone was having a good time.

"Or, we could speak to you," Ryan said, and took out a wad of notes.

The bouncer eyed up the cash, checked nobody was watching, and then palmed a hundred.

"Alreet, get yourselves inside," he said.

"Which room did that last bloke go into?" Ryan asked.

"Can't tell you that," the bouncer said. "Now, piss off."

"Can you tell me for another hundred?"

He could, and it was door number four.

Behind the curtain, they found themselves in a long corridor, each marked with a brass number on it, and they made directly for the fourth on the left.

"Why don't we try a different persona?" he said to the others. "Let's be three murder detectives, on the hunt for a band of ruthless killers, eh?"

"I like that one," Phillips said.

"Let's start by making a drugs bust," Ryan said, putting his ear to the door of Room Four. "Lowerson? Watch the corridor. Frank? You're with me. On three…"

Two…

One…

Ryan gave the door one good shove and it flew open to reveal a boudoir, of sorts, with a large round bed in the middle and mirrors on every wall.

And there, in the centre of it all, was the man he'd recently seen purchasing cocaine—only, now, he was in the middle of snorting it off the rounded backside of a nude woman.

She screamed…he screamed…and promptly fell off the bed in a cloud of white smoke.

"Northumbria CID," Ryan said, holding out his warrant card. "Stay exactly where you are."

He reached across to pluck a robe from a peg on the wall, which he threw across to the woman who was presently trying to cover herself in black satin sheets.

"You can go," he told her, and she hurried from the room before he could change his mind. "As for you—"

He walked around the edge of the bed to find the man hiding on all fours, his trousers around his ankles.

"Get up," Ryan told him, firmly. "We'll be arresting you for possession…maybe with intent to supply—"

"No! Oh, God, please, no…you don't understand, my wife…this will kill my wife, if she finds out."

"Perhaps you should have thought of that sooner, Mr—?"

"Smith?" the other tried, hopefully.

Phillips reached inside the man's pocket and pulled out his wallet.

"David Sean Hopper," he read. "There's a business card here, too… well, look at this. He's the headteacher of a local primary school."

"Tut, tut, Mr Hopper," Ryan said. "Caught with your pants down. This won't look good at the next Governors' meeting."

"Please! I'll lose my job, if this gets out…"

His bottom lip began to tremble, at which point Ryan decided to make him and offer he couldn't refuse.

"Tell us a bit of information, and perhaps we'll rethink whether it's in the public interest to charge you for possession of Class A drugs."

"That's up to seven years in prison," Phillips put in, helpfully.

The man began to sweat.

"What—what do you want to know?"

"For starters, I want to know why you still haven't pulled your trousers up," he snapped. "For God's sake!"

Hopper tugged his trousers back up his legs, apologising profusely.

"That's better," Ryan said. "Now, I want to know where people go for the hard stuff. The really specialist girls, you know what I mean? Not the mainstream stuff. Younger girls—Thai and Oriental, mostly."

"You're thinkin' of The Dragon," Hopper said, slowly.

"The Dragon? Who's that?"

"I've never met him," Hopper said, quickly. "A couple of months ago, I got chatting to one of the other regulars in here, and he said The Dragon runs the best girls out of the Golden Triangle. He brings them over, fresh, like—every couple of months."

Ryan and Phillips said nothing, so he carried on talking.

"He told me to ring a number and they'd give me the address—"

"What number?" Ryan asked.

"I can't remember—it was a mobile number, and I threw it away, after."

"You threw it away?" Phillips said. "Why would you do that, son? Didn't the idea appeal to you, after all?"

Hopper swallowed, and shook his head.

"I rang the number, and they gave me an address in Killingsworth," he said. "I—I went, but, when I got there, I just—"

He trailed off, and ran nervous fingers through his hair.

"Look, please, does my wife have to find out about this?"

"That all depends on you, Mr Hopper," Ryan said. "You were telling us you went to the address."

"Yes…yeah, I did."

"What was the address?" Ryan demanded.

"I can't—"

"Don't bother tellin' us you can't remember, lad. It's written all over your face," Phillips warned him.

"All right. Okay. Um, maybe I can remember."

He told them a house number and street name, which Phillips made a note of.

"What happened, when you went?" Ryan asked him. "Did you meet The Dragon there?"

"No, like I say, I never met him…there was a woman running the place."

He could picture himself now, knocking at the front door.

"She asked me what I liked, I had a drink, and then she brought out this line of girls…"

He scrubbed a hand across his eyes, feeling suddenly tired, and dirty.

"They—they were too young," he confessed, and couldn't meet their eyes. "I swear to you, I decided to leave. I never went through with anything. They were just too young."

They'd reminded him of his nieces, who lived three doors down, and who often babysat for his own children.

"I have some standards," he said, and realised how that must sound, for a man in his position.

He looked between them.

"Is that all you need to know? Can I go now?"

Ryan looked at Phillips, who nodded at his unspoken question.

"Thank you, Mr Hopper, that's been very helpful," Phillips said, and then drew in a deep breath. "I am arresting you on suspicion of possessing Class A drugs. You do not have to say anything—"

"What? But—you said, you said—"

"That we'd consider whether it was in the public interest to charge you. After due consideration, Mr Hopper, I can tell you it's definitely in the public interest. On your feet."

They finished reading him his rights, then Phillips took him by the arm.

"Time to go, bonny lad."

CHAPTER 34

By the time the clock struck midnight, Ryan, Phillips and Lowerson had made a total of twelve drugs arrests, including booking the dealer for intent to supply and the owner of the club for causing or inciting prostitution, as well as running an illegal brothel.

That was all they could manage, before the remainder of the club's clientele scarpered like rats.

"Not bad for a night's work," Phillips said, with a yawn. "Makes me wonder whether it wouldn't be better to just make these brothels legal, then you wouldn't have folk like Hopper slippin' behind closed curtains, hoppin' from one arse to the next."

The image of that was more than Ryan could stomach, at that time of night.

"There's an argument on both sides," he said, and left it at that.

"At least we got an address out of him."

Ryan nodded.

"We'll go there, first thing tomorrow," he said, and turned his collar up against the wind. "Tonight was…an experience. How are you holding up, Jack?"

Lowerson pulled a face.

"Knowing what we know about how some of the women are trafficked into the industry…it takes the edge off, doesn't it? When I was chattin' to that girl, you could almost start to believe she was enjoying my company…but I could tell she didn't really want to be there. Who wants to have to pay for company, like that?"

"There are a lot of lonely people in the world," Ryan said. "Not everyone is as lucky as we are."

"And on that note, I'm off home before the boss gives me my marchin' orders," Phillips said, roundly. "Night, all."

Ryan waved them both off, then began to make his own way home through the dark streets, the pitter-patter of the rain and the sound of the windscreen wipers keeping him company on the journey while his mind was far away, thinking of all they'd seen and heard that evening, and, perhaps more importantly, of all the things they hadn't. He wanted to pretend that was all there was to it; to wash his hands of the whole, seedy world and go back to his own happy home.

Then he thought of the woman on the beach, and of the woman lying in hospital, fighting for her life.

He could not turn his back on the darker parts of the world, no more than he could turn his back on them. He would continue to peel back the layers, to lift each new veil, until he found the people responsible, no matter how uncomfortable it made him and no matter how ashamed.

For, that's what he felt.

Shame.

The same shame he'd seen on Hopper's face as he'd knelt on the sticky floor of that private room, with his trousers around his ankles and several grams of coke spilling out of his nose. The look he'd seen in the man's eyes as he'd confessed that the girls supplied by The Dragon had seemed too young, even for him, had turned his stomach.

Ryan thought of his wife and daughter, and his hands tightened on the wheel.

If anyone—*anyone*—ever hurt them, they'd have him to answer to. It was a promise he'd made, on the day Emma had been born. To think there may be other families out there, other mothers and fathers, who were missing their sons and daughters but were unable to seek help made him deeply ashamed.

He could not save them all—nobody could.

But, if he could even save one, that would make it all worthwhile.

"Tell me the truth."

Gaz looked up from the telly as his wife stumbled into the sitting room, smelling of liquor.

"Go to bed," he said, and turned the television up louder.

"I said…tell…me…the…*truth*!"

On the last word, Keeley picked up the remote control and flung it at the television, where the cheap plastic cracked and fell to the floor in a heap.

Gaz could feel anger rising up, but he'd promised Mick there'd be no more trouble. They were moving the women that night, and needed no police drama or reports of domestic disturbance, on top of…

On top of what they'd found in Marsden.

He couldn't bring himself to say his son's name, and wasn't sure he'd ever speak it aloud again. He'd made his decision, and now he had to live with it.

What choice did he have, really?

He knew what Mick was capable of, and when he said it was either him or the boy, he'd meant it. Friendship or no friendship, it could have been him swinging from a rope, and he'd worked too long and too hard to see it all end there.

Besides, the boy had been warned about the consequences, hadn't he?

It wasn't personal, it was business.

"I don't know what you're goin' on about, Kelz."

He called her by the old nickname they'd used in high school, to butter her up a bit.

"We've both had bad news today," he continued, thinking of the pay cut he'd been forced to take, thanks to his son's efforts. "It doesn't help for you to keep on."

"Keep on?" she repeated, in disbelief. "Gaz, he was our son! They said he was hanged—"

"Aye, and loads of youngsters kill themselves over nowt, these days," he told her. "It's sad, but it's true."

She shook her head.

"No. No, I don't believe that," she said. "It's to do with you, and with Mick. When he came over the other day—"

"To visit, and say 'hello'?" Gaz said, in a tone that suggested she'd lost her mind. "Look, I know me and Mick have had our fingers in a few pies, over the years, but it comes to somethin' when you start throwin' accusations round, like that. He was my son, too, Kelz."

He injected just the right amount of hurt into his voice, she might have believed him.

"Ollie—he'd—he'd been doin' that apprenticeship with Mick," she argued. "What if he ended up mixin' with some other lads—"

"We don't know what could have happened," Gaz said, realising she wasn't about to let the matter drop. "Leave it with me, and I'll ask around, all right? Let me ask around."

"The police—"

"You know we don't talk to the police," he said, flatly.

She folded her lips, and brushed tears from her eyes.

"Good girl," he said, rubbing his knuckles against her cheek. "You know they're not there to help us, they're there to trap us. Do you want to see me put away? How would you live?"

Keeley remembered once, a long time ago, she'd wanted to work as a nursery nurse.

But that was a long time ago.

"And then there's Becki to think of, isn't there? D'you want her growin' up in care? Is that what you want for her? The same start that you had?"

Keeley thought back to her own miserable childhood, and of how the drink made her forgetful and neglectful, and knew that, if someone were to make a report, there was a good chance her daughter might be taken from them.

"A—all right," she mumbled, and walked from the room with her head bent, defeated once more by the weight of her own fear.

They moved the women in the dead of night, while the city slept.

The van left the scrapyard shortly before two in the morning and made its steady journey west of Newcastle towards Cumbria and The Lakes, before veering north, taking the scenic route towards Scotland. There might have been an All-Ports Warning in place, but there were ways around that, if you knew the right people, in the right places.

Noddy and Callum drove along the winding road to Scotland through the dense forests of the Northumberland National Park, up and over the hills until they reached the border, which was unmanned—little more than a pretty stone with a placard carved into it, which bade them welcome.

Onward they drove with their cargo, further and further away from the Northumbria Constabulary's Command Division. The storm followed them all the way, its angry wind pushing and shoving the van from all directions, as though Mother Nature herself knew that what they were doing was wrong.

Twice, the van skidded against black ice, and twice it recovered, continuing its unwavering journey through the eye of the storm until its twin headlights disappeared into the all-consuming fog, lost in the folds of the valley as if it had never existed at all.

CHAPTER 35

Tuesday 16th February

The semi-detached house in the little cul-de-sac known as 'Garth Two' was wholly unremarkable.

Located on the western outskirts of Killingworth, it had been built during the sixties, and had fared better than many of that era but significantly worse than others, taking into account its sagging roof and generally tired appearance. Killingworth, which lay to the north of the city of Newcastle, had been built as a 'new' town during that swinging decade, replacing the old colliery land that had lain derelict for some years before the town planners took charge of it, and creating what some had called a 'revolutionary, avant-garde' architectural landscape of concrete high-rises and angular walkways. The area was largely a commuter suburb, safe for young families and older people, and as Ryan and his team drove through its quiet streets, they were struck once again with the realisation that crime hid in plain sight and, in this case, with a good view of the boating lake.

It was barely seven-thirty when the police van turned into the cul-de-sac, transporting Ryan and Phillips alongside a team of specialist firearms officers, whilst another van carrying more police personnel covered the rear of the property by closing off access to the back alley running along its northern edge, where a number of private garages were located.

Both teams spilled out of their vans, some to guard the safety of neighbouring properties, whilst others made directly for the front and back entrances to Number 15.

"Doesn't look occupied," Phillips murmured, as he peered through his field binoculars. "Blinds are all closed."

"It's still early," Ryan said, and gave the order for armed police to enter.

ARMED POLICE! ARMED POLICE!

They heard the warning shouts, followed by the splintering of doors, but there were no answering shouts or cries, as they might have expected.

They watched the live footage as their colleagues cleared every room in the house with military precision, until they could be sure that Phillips was right.

Nobody was home.

"They've cleared out," Ryan said, and ran a frustrated hand through his hair.

"Aye, but the question is *when*," Phillips replied.

"No way they could have done this overnight," Ryan said. "They had no way of knowing we'd bust Hopper, or that he'd give us the address."

"There's always a chance of discovery," Phillips said.

"They screen their clients before giving it out," Ryan said. "But, even so, I agree—the business model carries a large degree of risk. Perhaps they mitigate that by shifting address, every so often."

Though it was an unpalatable line of thought, Ryan had to admit that's what he would do, if he was criminally inclined.

"I've been thinkin'," Phillips said. "Why do they call him The Dragon?"

"The Far Eastern connection?" Ryan offered. "I don't know, Frank. Maybe he watched one too many episodes of *Game of Thrones*."

"Aye, you never can tell with these crackpots," Phillips agreed. "What do we do, now?"

"I want the whole place swept for forensics," Ryan told him. "I know Faulkner is run off his feet, at the moment, so pull in a team from a neighbouring command, if you have to. I want every room checked for DNA, especially the bedrooms, and I want an express service—no more than twenty-four hours."

Phillips nodded. "It's frustrating, always playin' catch up with these bastards," he said.

But Ryan shook his head. "I can smell them, now, Frank. It was a mistake, killing that boy," he said. "By doing that, they told us who's involved."

"Any word from the surveillance team at the Nicholson house?"

Ryan nodded. "They've had eyes on the house since yesterday evening," he said. "Nobody's come in or out, except the little girl, who was picked up and taken to school by a neighbour."

"Not the parents?"

Ryan shook his head. "They're bedding down."

"If we could only get Keeley on her own," Phillips muttered.

"We could bring her in for questioning," Ryan said. "I would, if I didn't think she'd be in the same danger as her son. We need to be careful, with that one."

"You never know," Phillips said. "Maybe her mother's instinct will shine through."

"Stranger things have happened."

Lawana opened her eyes to blazing white light.

Was this Heaven?

She blinked, her eyes watering as they tried to adjust, and her mind slowly registered other things.

A persistent beeping noise, in time with her heart…
The distant murmur of voices.

She tried to move her head, but found she couldn't, for it was strapped securely in a neck brace to protect her spinal cord from any further trauma.

She panicked, and must have alerted one of the nurses, who came running to her bedside.

"Hey, there, hey! It's okay. It's okay," she said, soothingly, and laid gentle, firm hands on her shoulders to steady her.

Lawana tried to speak, but found her voice croaky and sore.

The nurse must have understood, for she reached for a cup of water with a long, bendy straw and placed it on her lips.

"Here," she said. "Have some water, it might help."

Lawana drank thirstily, then tried again.

"Achara," she said.

"You keep saying that," the nurse said, worriedly. "I wish I knew who or what you meant. I'm going to call someone who can help."

Lawana recognised the single, important word in that sentence, and was satisfied.

Help.

"Hel'," she repeated, and gave the nurse a smile.

While Phillips supervised the scene at Garth Two, and Lowerson and Yates took themselves off to Bolam Lake to honour Gemma Yates' memory, Ryan and MacKenzie made their way to the hospital with a Thai translator in tow.

When they arrived on the ICU, they were pleased to find an armed officer standing guard, and even more pleased when he insisted upon seeing their warrant cards, despite the fact he knew them both by sight.

Process was all-important, and could mean the difference between life and death.

"How's she doing?" Ryan asked, when they were met by the consultant outside one of the private rooms.

"Better," she replied, with a measure of relief. "I was worried about her, yesterday, but her vitals have improved overnight and her MRI scan hasn't thrown up any further problems—other than those we're already aware of. She'll be going in for surgery this afternoon, but we thought you would want to speak to her, first."

"Thank you," MacKenzie said. "We've brought a translator with us."

She introduced the young man standing beside them, whose name was Kamnan.

"That'll be a big help to us, too," the consultant said. "Follow me."

She tapped on the door behind her, and then led them inside.

Ryan and MacKenzie were not often shocked. They had seen too much, borne the weight of too much waste and human destruction, to be surprised.

And yet, as they looked upon the bruised and battered body of the woman, whose frame was scarcely bigger than that of an adolescent, they were forced to bear down upon the wave of human empathy which rose up and threatened to choke them.

"You have two visitors," the consultant said, and appealed to Kamnan for help with translation.

He repeated the words in his own language, and the woman replied.

"She wants to know who they are."

"Detective Chief Inspector Ryan, and Detective Inspector MacKenzie, from the police," Ryan said, and stepped forward so that she could see his warrant card. "Can she tell us her name?"

There was a short pause, then her quiet voice echoed around the room.

"Lawana."

"Lawana," the translator repeated, and they all laughed.

"May we sit down?" MacKenzie asked, gesturing to one of the chairs near the bed.

Lawana nodded, with difficulty.

"I'll leave you to it," the consultant said, after she'd asked a few pertinent medical questions.

Once the door clicked shut, MacKenzie began again.

"Can you tell us what happened to you, Lawana?"

The translator repeated the question, and Lawana closed her eyes for a long moment, wondering where to begin.

She told them about *Pos'man,* and *Nodi*…about *Gaz* and the arduous journey overland to the sea, and then of the terrifying journey in the hold. She spoke slowly, softly, eloquently, about her fear, about the other women and how many there had been. She spoke of what happened on the beach, of her fall into the cave and of the boy who had come to help.

"This boy," Ryan said. "What did he look like?"

She described him as best she could, and told them he'd given her a chocolate bar. They listened, without interruption, as she told them of the man who'd come to save her…or, so she'd thought. They exchanged a sharp glance as she described what he had done, and how he had done it. She paused only once to take a sip of water, before continuing to describe her ordeal in the cellar attached to the side of the abandoned outbuilding, detailing what it looked like, and how many others she feared had come before her. Her voice faltered, as she came to describe the first night, and she pressed her lips together.

MacKenzie leaned forward to place a hand over hers, a gesture that meant more than any trite words she could have said.

Lawana drew herself together again, and continued, describing it as best she could, although she struggled to remember it all. Her mind had closed itself off from the worst of it, to protect her from the memories.

Still, it was enough.

When she fell silent, Ryan stood up and moved quietly to the window, unwilling to allow himself the indulgence of tears, though they threatened to fall. Never, in all his career, had he met a survivor who had endured so much pain, without ever giving up or giving in.

He turned back to face her, and said as much.

"I'm more sorry than I can say, for the pain you've suffered. You have my deepest respect," he said, quietly. "Thank you for giving us your testimony. We'll do all we can to find the people responsible."

She said something to the translator.

"She says you'll never find Postman, and his gang," he told them. "They've done it many times before."

Ryan acknowledged that.

"Everything must end," he told her, with simple conviction.

Lawana said something else, and became agitated.

"Her daughter, Achara, was also part of the group," Kamnan told them. "She's very worried about her, and hasn't seen her since the night of the shipwreck."

MacKenzie exchanged a glance with Ryan, then brought up a picture of the female they'd found dead on the beach, that first morning.

"This will be difficult," she said, gently. "Is this woman your daughter?"

Lawana's lips trembled, but she forced herself to look.

And, God forgive her, felt nothing but relief.

"It's not her," the translator told them. "It's a woman called Chantara."

They made a note of all she could tell them about the dead woman, and hoped it would be enough to trace her next of kin. Then, they took down a full description of all the other women they were looking for, including Lawana's daughter.

"Can you remember the gang saying anything about where they were headed?" Ryan asked her. "Anything at all?"

Lawana thought hard, trying to remember all their broken conversations in an alien language, but the effort was too great and the pain in her back had started to return.

"That's all for today," MacKenzie murmured, and gave the woman's hand another squeeze. "Please let us know the details of anyone you'd like us to contact, Lawana, or let us know if we can bring you anything."

She reached down to grasp the handles of the carrier bag she'd brought, with a few things inside it.

"I don't know if these will fit," she said. "But, I thought you might like to have them."

Lawana looked at the woman with the flaming red hair, and reached for her hand again.

"Than' yoo," she said.

CHAPTER 36

Keeley Nicholson spent some considerable time getting ready, that morning.

She chose her outfit with care, discarding anything that seemed too gawdy in favour of a plain black dress and low heels. She dipped her finger into a bottle of beige foundation and spread it over the clusters of broken veins beneath her eyes, dabbing it over the deep lines that had gathered around her mouth, and then brushed false colour against the apples of her cheeks, remembering a time when they'd had a natural bloom. She reached for the small keepsake box she'd forgotten she had, and selected a pair of cheap silver ear-rings Oliver had given her, one Mother's Day, when he'd been too young to realise his mother wasn't worth celebrating.

She dabbed at the fluid which leaked from the corners of her eyes, then added a line of deep pink lipstick to her mouth.

Then, she looked at the woman who stared back at her in the bathroom mirror, and wondered when it had all gone wrong.

You killed him, she thought.

You killed him.

She walked unsteadily to the door, and made her way downstairs, where Gaz was prowling the hallway waiting for her.

"About time," he muttered, and then looked again at his wife. "You look good," he conceded.

"It isn't for you," she said, dully. "It's for him."

Gaz said nothing, and propelled her out of the house and into the car, so they could make their way to the mortuary.

She listened to his warnings on the journey across town, and his voice sounded like flies buzzing in her ears. She looked across at him, at her co-conspirator, and wondered if it would be easier to pull the handbrake while they were on the dual carriageway.

"What?" he barked, not liking the strange look in her eye.

She said nothing, and looked away.

Soon enough, the hospital came into view—the same place where she'd brought Ollie and Becki into the world. She'd been different, then—or she hoped she had. She hoped her son and daughter might have at least some decent memories of their mother.

As for their father…

She watched him from the corner of her eye, and thought how funny it was that her one wish for Ollie had come true.

He'd been nothing like his father.

"The Nicholsons have arrived at the mortuary," Ryan said, as he and MacKenzie were about to head back to Police Headquarters. "You carry on, Denise. I'll head back, once they're done, but I want to see his reaction, if I can."

"He might be the 'Gaz' Lawana was talking about," MacKenzie said. "Do you want to pull him in, now?"

Ryan thought about it.

"We've already got him under full surveillance," he said. "Let's show her a picture of him, once she comes around again, and bring them in after that. We can only hold him for so long without charging him, so we need something more solid."

MacKenzie nodded, and Ryan left her to make his way down to the mortuary to meet the Nicholsons, who had been taken to a specialist viewing area.

He found them with Pinter, who spoke to them in calm, well-rounded tones about what they were about to see on the monitor, explaining the procedure.

They looked across when he entered the room, but said nothing.

"All right," Pinter said. "I'm going to instruct one of my team to lift the shroud now. Please prepare yourselves."

He spoke through an intercom, and one of the mortuary technicians lifted a paper shroud to reveal their son's mottled body. Ryan watched them from the edge of the viewing room and saw the woman's head drop to her chest with a single sob, but it was the man's reaction he found most interesting of all.

He didn't look.

Not once.

Pinter spoke into the intercom again, and the shroud was replaced, following which the screen went blank.

"I want to see him properly," Keeley whispered. "I want to see my baby."

"That's your right, Mrs Nicholson, but I must warn you that you may find it very traumatic," Pinter said.

"It doesn't matter," she said, and followed him towards the side door leading into the clinical area. "Gaz? Aren't you going to come?"

He shook his head and turned away.

Keeley paused at the door, looking down at the clipboard Pinter had left on the table.

"Do I need to sign those?" she asked.

Pinter nodded.

"I'm afraid so," he said. "They're to confirm your son's identity."

"Bring them with you," she said, and stepped through the doorway.

After they'd left, Gavin said not a single word to Ryan, and the two men stood at opposite ends of the room, observing one another.

"Must have been hard," Ryan said, eventually. "Having to make that kind of choice."

Gaz looked up quickly, then away again, keeping his mouth firmly shut.

"Where've they taken the women?" Ryan asked him. "Come on, Gaz. They killed your son, and we'll prove it, soon enough. Why protect them?"

Still, he was met with silence, and a moment later, Keeley returned.

"Time to go," Gaz said, and led her out, without further discussion.

Ryan had almost reached the exit when he heard the sound of running footsteps approaching.

He turned to find Pinter chasing after him, waving a clipboard in his hand.

"Ryan! Wait a minute!"

He couldn't recall ever having seen Jeffrey Pinter move so quickly, and he wondered what could have possessed him.

"Jeff? What's wrong?"

"Look at this," he panted, thrusting the clipboard beneath Ryan's nose. "The signature page."

Ryan flipped the pages until he found the official form whereby a person's next of kin signed their affirmation that the deceased was the person whom they'd identified.

Except, instead of signing 'Keeley Nicholson', the boy's mother had written a single word:

STRANRAER

Stranraer was a town on the shores of Dumfries and Galloway, in Scotland. It was also the closest town to the ferry line which ran from there to Belfast, in Northern Ireland.

Ryan thrust the clipboard back into Pinter's waiting arms.

"Thanks, Jeff!"

He broke into a run, bursting out of the staff entrance to sprint across the tarmac back to his car, setting his mobile to hands-free.

"Frank? Get onto HM Customs and police in Stranraer, and the same in Belfast," he said, as soon as Phillips picked up his call. "That's where they'll be, unless we've missed them."

"Aye, lad. Who gave us the tip?"

"Keeley Nicholson," he said. "It turns out she had something left in her, after all."

With that, he ended the call and flipped the switch on his emergency siren, flooring it all the way back to Police Headquarters.

CHAPTER 37

Mick Donnelly decided that, next time, he was writing in a new clause to his contracts, one which covered unforeseen natural disasters, including—but not limited to—Arctic storms.

He'd spoken to the lads first thing that morning, having expected to find them well on their way to Belfast, by now, but the weather had not been kind to them.

Well, there was nowt he could do about that, and he certainly wasn't procuring another bloody fishing trawler.

He listened to the man at the other end of the phone line and tried to placate him.

"Look, I'm not happy about this, either," he said. "They're ready and waitin' to get across, just as soon as the ferry reopens, all right? It's the best we can do."

More complaints, this time about killing the boy.

"You look after your business, and I'll look after mine," he growled. "I've got a reputation to look after, and if you let any of them take a lend, the whole bloody house falls down."

They'd found the missing woman, and she was talking to the police.

Mick was silent, while he thought about what she could possibly know.

"She has no idea about what route we're takin'," he said. "The plans changed, remember? She wasn't here to overhear anythin' important. Don't worry about it."

But he did worry, he worried a lot.

"You concentrate on makin' sure the buyers pay on time," Mick advised him. "How's that lass you picked up, yesterday?"

He'd let him know, tomorrow.

Mick laughed, which turned into a hacking smoker's cough.

"Aye, you do that. I'll let you know when we're home and dry."

Donnelly ended the phone call and immediately took out the battery on the burner phone, adding it to a pile of others he intended to destroy.

They'd have nothing on him, he thought, and so what if the woman talked? A message would be sent to her, soon enough, reminding her she still had a daughter to think of.

Loose lips sunk ships, so they said.

Phillips was waiting for Ryan in the foyer of Police Headquarters, when he returned.

"What have you got for me?"

"I've been onto the authorities on both sides of the channel," he said. "The ferries didn't run last night or this morning, because of Storm Wayne. It's moved over that way and stopped all the transit." "Let's hope they didn't manage to catch an earlier ferry," Ryan muttered, as they speed-walked back to the office. "What's the plan?"

"There's a bunch of cars and lorries already in the holding zone, checked in and waiting to board the next one. I've told them to delay it and search every one of them. Morrison's given the go-ahead for all of it."

Ryan made a note to thank her, later.

"We've got an All-Ports Warning in place," he said. "Why weren't enhanced checks taking place, anyway?"

"Your guess is as good as mine," Phillips said, darkly. "What now?"

"Now, we wait."

When they returned to the office, they found MacKenzie and Morrison in deep discussion.

"Ryan," Denise said, moving forward quickly. "I know you're waiting to hear from Stranraer, but there's something else you might want to see. It's about that house you raided, this morning."

"What about it?"

He followed her across to her desk, where several printed reports were laid out.

"Faulkner started running the swabs, room by room, since you requested a rush-job," she said. "The first bedroom has come back with a match to someone we know, whose details were already on file."

"Who? Is it Nicholson?"

"No," she said, catching Morrison's eye. "It's DCI Chambers, from Serious and Organised Crime."

Ryan laid his hands on the desk.

"Have we checked to see if they'd performed their own search of those premises? We don't want to jump to conclusions, over the sake of skin particles—"

"It was semen," she said.

Ryan swore, and then apologised.

"No need to be sorry," Morrison said. "I already called him every kind of arsehole, before you arrived."

"Where is he now?"

"I've been in touch with his DCS," Morrison said. "Apparently, he's working from home, today."

"There's more," MacKenzie told him. "When this came through, I had a quick look back over some of the busts Chambers has been responsible for, over the past couple of years. At least four came to nothing, thanks to minor errors in procedure that could only have come from him, or one of his team. On the face of it, they could be explained away, but—"

"Once might be explained away, even twice," Ryan said. "But, four errors of the same kind? Call in the Ghost Squad."

He referred to their colloquial name for their anti-corruption unit.

"Already done," Morrison said. "I've referred that side of things to them, for internal review, but I thought you and MacKenzie might want to bring Chambers in and see what you can get out of him, before they take over?"

"Thank you, ma'am—and for your support, throughout this investigation."

Morrison put a hand on his shoulder, then left him to do what he did best.

CHAPTER 38

Unaware of the dramatic events unfolding back at Police Headquarters that morning, Lowerson and Yates made their way west of the city towards Bolam Lake Country Park. It was situated in the heart of the Northumbrian countryside, and had been a favourite place of Melanie and her sister, Gemma, when they were children.

"We used to like trying to spot the red squirrels," she said, as Jack parked the car. "I don't suppose we'll see many, today. Look at the weather."

He'd seen it, and had come prepared with gloves, which he presented with a flourish, to make her laugh.

"We can handle a bit of cold weather, he said. We're made of strong stuff, us northerners."

She smiled, and rested her forehead against his.

"Thank you for coming with me," she said.

"Any time."

They stepped out into the blustery wind, and began making their way towards the lake, their feet crunching against the icy earth underfoot.

"Gemma and I used to bring our bikes here," she murmured, remembering two little girls pedalling as fast as they could through the autumn leaves. "Mum used to bring a bag of cheap bread, to feed the ducks."

He reached for her hand, and they made their way along the circular lakeside walk until they came to a particular tree. Its trunk was old and hollowed out, and had been the hiding place of many a small child over the years in which it had stood overlooking the water. Mel let go of his hand and walked over to it, resting her gloved palms against its old bark, as though she were giving it a hug.

And he realised, this is where they'd scattered Gemma's ashes.

He followed behind slowly, careful not to startle her.

"Is she here?" he asked softly.

Mel nodded, wiping tears from her eyes.

We scattered her ashes at the base of the tree, then covered them with a layer of soil, so they'd be a part of the earth and the old roots of this tree.

"It's a beautiful spot," he said.

He left her there for a while, stepping back to give her the privacy she needed, and was grateful the day was so inclement they had the place to themselves.

Eventually, she stepped back again, and said her 'goodbye', until the following year.

"I told her about you," she said, with a smile. "I know it's stupid, talking to a tree—"

"It's a living thing," he said. "And it's not stupid."

She took his hand again.

"Do you want to go back, now?"

"If you can stand the cold a little while longer, why don't we carry on around the rest of the lake?" she suggested.

"What cold?" he joked, and slung his arm around her shoulders.

"Jack?"

"What?"

"I might change my mind, one day."

"About what?"

"About getting married."

His heart caught in his throat. "You don't need to say that, for my benefit—"

"I'm not," she assured him. "I'm saying it because I feel it."

He turned to kiss the tip of her nose. "In that case, I'll keep it in mind," he said.

While Melanie reminisced about her sister's life, Ryan received news that would alter the lives of seventeen other women.

"*Bingo!*" he said, turning to MacKenzie and Phillips, who were gathered around the desk while he spoke to the Scottish authorities. "They've got the bastards. They found seventeen women stuffed into the back of a transit van, without food, water, toilet facilities or much else. They've arrested two men—Nathan "Noddy" Palmer and Callum Shepton, both of Newcastle upon Tyne."

"Thank God," MacKenzie said, sinking back against her chair.

Then, she thought of Lawana and her daughter.

"I thought Lawana said there were twenty women, in total," she said, leaning forward again. "Discounting Lawana and Chantara, that should leave eighteen, but the authorities have only counted seventeen. There's one missing."

Ryan thought quickly, and rang his contact back.

"It's Ryan, again," he said, without preamble. "Look, we've got a possible discrepancy. Can you take some pictures of the women and send them through to us, urgently? They don't have to be professional, just phone pictures will do. Okay, thanks."

"They're going to send those through as soon as possible," he said, but felt the same niggling worry that MacKenzie did.

"If one's missing, they could have dumped a body anywhere," Phillips was forced to say. "They have no scruples."

Ryan nodded, and checked the time, which was a little after four o'clock.

"Bring Chambers in, now," he said. "I don't want any cosy chats at home, away from the office. I want him transported in the back of a squad car, cuffed, in full view of his colleagues."

"Thought you'd never ask," Phillips said, rubbing his hands together. "Anything else, while I'm at it?"

"Yes, you can bring Gavin Nicholson in, and hold him overnight," he said.

"And the wife?" Phillips queried.

Ryan thought about it for all of three seconds.

"She's a potential accessory to murder," he said flatly. "Bring her in, as well."

Ryan left DCI Kieron Chambers to stew for twenty minutes in one of the holding cells in the basement of Police Headquarters, before he and MacKenzie made their way down to the Interview Suite to ask a few pertinent questions of a man supposedly tasked with fighting serious and organised crime.

"DCI Ryan and DI MacKenzie, entering Interview Room B, at sixteen-thirty-seven," he said, and reeled off the date. "Also present are DCI Kieron Chambers and his legal representative, Diana Hepple, of Hepple and Co. Solicitors."

He ran through the formalities, and linked his fingers on top of the desk.

"Well, Kieron," he said. "I'm disappointed to find you here."

"Detective Inspector, my client hasn't been formally charged with any offence," his solicitor began.

"No, but he will be," Ryan said, cheerfully. "Presently, he is arrested on suspicion of perverting the course of justice, but we'll add to the charge sheet, wherever necessary, don't you worry."

He turned to Chambers.

"You're finished," he said, succinctly, so there could be no misunderstanding. "Your semen was found at an address we understand to have been formerly used as a brothel, run by a man or woman known by the street name, 'The Dragon'. Are you The Dragon, Kieron?"

"No comment."

"Ah, my favourite type of interview," Ryan said, folding his arms across his chest. "We could go on all day with a 'no comment' interview, couldn't we, DI MacKenzie?"

"I've got nowhere else to be," she said, and it was true—Phillips was taking care of the school run.

"Can you tell us how your semen came to be found at that address, Kieron?"

"No comment."

"It isn't your registered home address, is it?"

"No comment."

"In fact, the address was formerly registered to a man and woman by the name of Polly and Yannis Theodopoulos, both registered disabled. Do you know how their address came to be used for these nefarious purposes?"

"No comment," Chambers said, defiantly.

"It's funny, isn't it DI MacKenzie, that, when we looked back over DCI Chambers' work record, we found numerous instances of missed opportunities and avoidable errors," Ryan said, rattling off names and dates. "Can you account for this unusual pattern, DCI Chambers?"

"Circumstantial," he said. "All of those examples have entirely innocent explanations. This is a stitch-up."

"What do any of these allegations have to do with the reason you're holding my client?" Hepple demanded.

"I'll tell you," MacKenzie said, licking the tip of her thumb to turn a page. "In each of these cases, the target address was a suspected 'cuckoo' house, by which I mean a house registered to a vulnerable person or persons which has been taken over by criminals in order to conduct their business. In each case, the investigating team found the target house abandoned or otherwise cleared out, by the time they arrived. We have a list of these addresses, DCI Chambers, and will be instructing our Forensics team to re-examine them to the fullest. Is there anything you wish to tell us, before that examination takes place?"

He looked slightly less confident now, Ryan thought. Slightly less cocky.

"I ordered a full forensics sweep of those houses and flats, at the time," he argued.

"Which is very strange, because we can't find any record whatsoever of a report having been filed," MacKenzie shot back. "Can you explain this?"

"N—no comment."

"It's all caving in around you," Ryan said softly, and leaned forward to reinforce the point. "You know me, Kieron. You know I won't let this drop until I've found everything there is to find."

Chambers knew it, but told himself they'd never find the missing women. They were already across the sea to Ireland, by now.

"We found the women," Ryan added, as though he'd read the man's mind. "They're safe, now, and the men who were transporting them to Belfast are also safe—behind bars, that is."

Noddy and Callum would never talk, Chambers thought. They knew the consequences, if they did.

"We've got Gavin Nicholson, now," Ryan said. "And we'll be looking at his old school pal, Michael Donnelly. How long do you think they'll hold their tongues, Kieron?"

The other man turned back and linked his hands behind his head.

"No comment," he said, with finality.

Ryan looked at him, past the bravado and the lies, to the heart of the man, and realised something important.

He was frightened.

That could only mean one thing.

"You're not The Dragon," he said aloud, and pushed back from his chair to hurry back to the office.

CHAPTER 39

MacKenzie hurried to catch up with Ryan as he stormed back down the corridor towards his desk.

"Wh—what are you looking for?"

"It struck me last night, when we were at that club," he muttered. "When I mentioned the name 'Fuchsia', the girl I was speaking to didn't relax or grow more talkative—she ran off."

MacKenzie tried to follow the dots.

"So—?"

Ryan looked up from the computer screen.

"She was frightened," he explained. "That woman we met, Niki, wasn't trying to help us out, she was using us to send a warning to those girls, and to anybody else thinking of talking to us."

He picked up the phone, preparing to call their Digital Forensics department.

"I still don't follow—"

"She was a decoy, Mac, nothing more. Who put us onto her?"

"Wentworth."

"Yes," he said, and paused to rap out some urgent instructions to his colleagues down the hall.

"What are you going to do?"

"If I'm right, then he's behind this," Ryan muttered, tapping a finger against the edge of his desk. "He has to be. Wentworth has the connections, and you said yourself, there haven't been any major busts in Vice, lately, except the one we executed last night—which might have been one of his competitors, for all we know, so we helped the bastard out."

Ryan's jaw hardened.

"Digital Forensics are accessing his computer remotely, now. I want to know which files he's brought up lately, especially regarding vulnerable persons," he said. "I want to know whether Chambers has been feeding him that information."

"You're thinking he uses their addresses to set up mobile brothels?" MacKenzie said.

Ryan nodded.

"He gets the inside track on new addresses which register on the vulnerable list, then orchestrates the cuckoo operation himself, with a little help from his friends," he said, with disgust. "The question is, where's their current habitation?"

At that moment, a call came through from their colleagues in Scotland, which made Ryan smile from ear to ear.

"Call off the search," he said. "One of the ones they picked up at Stranraer has caved, already. We've got three addresses."

MacKenzie grinned.

"I've always liked the Scots," she said. "Let's move."

Achara stared at herself, and then at the woman with the bright pink hair, who stood behind her.

"Very pretty," the woman said, approvingly. "You'll make him very happy."

"I don't like it," she said softly, and tried to scrub away the garish make-up.

Fuchsia's hand whipped out to grab her wrist in a hard grip.

"Now, you listen to me," she snarled. "This can be a good life, if you don't mess things up. Do as I tell you, and you'll have a roof over your head and food in your belly. There are worse things, and worse places."

She'd seen it, and lived it.

"You have no idea," she said, bitterly. "You should be grateful."

She snatched the mirror away from the girl's hand and stuffed it back into her make-up bag. Then, she reached for several small, square packets, which she left on the bedside table.

"Use these, if he lets you," she told her.

"What are they?" Achara asked.

Fuchsia muttered something unintelligible, and checked the time.

"Never mind," she said. "He'll be here any minute."

She walked back to the girl and took her chin in a hard grip.

"If you play this right, you could be like me, one day," she said. "I have a good life now, with nice clothes and more freedom. But you have to give them what they want—you understand? It'll go easier for you, that way."

Achara pushed her hand away and moved back against the wall, crossing her arms across her breasts.

Fuchsia only shook her head, and told herself she'd done all she could with the girl.

"Don't say I didn't warn you," she said, before slamming out of the room.

A moment later, the key turned in the lock.

Ryan and MacKenzie tried the first two addresses they'd been given, taking a full complement of armed police with them, but to no avail. At each one, they found a flat or a house which had been recently evacuated, bearing the remnants of foodstuff and even milk in the fridge, which was still in date.

"Lawana says none of those women are Achara," MacKenzie told him, having received a message back from the consultant at the hospital. "She's our missing number eighteen."

Ryan nodded, and looked up at the moon, which shone an eerie white light over the quiet streets.

"There's one more address to try," he said. "Wentworth isn't at his home address, or at the office, either."

"Oh, God."

They hurried back to the car, and sped towards their last hope.

Achara heard his footsteps on the stairs, and the sound of Fuchsia's tinkling voice, welcoming him back, as if he were a king, or a lord, and she little more than his chattel. She waited in the far corner of the room armed with the heel of her shoe, which was the only sharp thing she could find, and listened for the turn of the key in the lock.

When he appeared in the doorway, she gripped the shoe and held it out.

"There, now, Orchid," he said in Thai, closing the door and locking it behind him. "I didn't realise there was so much fight in you. You must get it from your mother."

She frowned, wondering how he knew her mother.

"She's dead now—or didn't you know?" he said, lowering himself onto the edge of the bed, to remove his shoes and socks.

"*What?*" she whispered.

"I'm sorry to be the bearer of bad news," he said, and began to undo his tie. "You need to look out for yourself, now."

Dan Wentworth turned to look at the woman, who was little more than a girl, really, and smiled. "I can help you with that," he said. "Like I've helped a lot of other girls."

Her hands began to shake as he rose up and moved towards her.

"What are you going to do with that, hmm?"

In a flash, he snatched it from her, and threw it across the room. When Achara made a small sound of panic, his smile grew wider.

"Didn't Fuchsia tell you?" he whispered. "I like it best when my girls put up a fight."

There were lights in the windows of the small, terraced house in North Shields, and, to the outside world, it might have been any other family home in a respectable area of the city.

"You're sure this is the address?" MacKenzie wondered, eyeing the other houses with their family cars and cosy lights.

"Positive," Ryan said, and spoke swiftly into his radio. "The other car's going around the back, to cover the rear exit."

MacKenzie nodded.

"What'll you do, if you find him here?" she asked suddenly.

Ryan turned to her with eyes that were flat and hard.

"*When* I find him there, you mean," he said, and raised a finger towards a car parked further along the street. "That's Wentworth's BMW."

She looked back at him, waiting for a response.

"The answer is, I'll do whatever it takes," Ryan told her.

"Good," she replied. "Because I don't have the strength to do what needs to be done, myself. Lowerson and Yates are making their way down, by the way."

"More the merrier," Ryan said, and slammed out of the car.

Their footsteps echoed across the cobbled Victorian street as they made their way to the front door, sounding a death knell to the man who was inside.

Ryan raised a hand to bang on the door and, a moment later, Fuchsia opened it, her smile already fixed in place to welcome her next visitor.

When she saw who it was, she tried to slam the door shut.

"Excuse us," Ryan growled, barging his way inside.

The woman they'd known as Niki began to cry crocodile tears, trilling out a fast stream of Thai, telling tales of her own trauma, her own coercion.

"We'll get to that, later," Ryan said, and something in his voice must have warned her that now was, most definitely, not the time. "Where is she? Where is Achara?"

She raised a shaking finger towards the ceiling.

"Second door on the right," she said, and sank back against the wall.

"You go," MacKenzie told him. "I'll watch her."

Ryan nodded, and took the stairs two at a time, still believing that every second mattered.

He came to the door and didn't hesitate, but planted his boot against the flimsy wood and kicked it wide open.

When he stepped into the room, a red mist descended.

Ryan saw a grown man, older than himself, pinning down a young woman half his size with one strong hand, while he struggled to divest himself of his remaining clothes. He saw nothing remotely bordering on consent; only fear, loathing, and desperate cries for help. He saw his wife, his daughter, his sister, his mother, his friends, and every other woman he'd never met nor was ever likely to.

Ryan made a low sound, deep in his throat, and grabbed Wentworth by the scruff of his neck, propelling the man off the bed with enough force to send him sprawling against the back of the wall, where he crashed into a chest of drawers.

"Up," Ryan ground out, and came for him again, this time taking a fistful of hair and dragging him towards the door. "Your time is *up*."

Wentworth swung out wildly, catching a glancing blow against Ryan's arm, which bought him only seconds of time.

"You're a disgrace to the uniform," Ryan told him, as the man tried to crawl away along the landing. "The way out is this way."

He grabbed the waistband of the man's trousers in one hand, and his collar in another, and heaved him towards the stairs, sending him crashing halfway down.

MacKenzie watched from the hallway, and made no move to intervene.

"Show DCI Wentworth the door," she said, and held it open for them.

"Thanks," Ryan said, and planted his foot against the man's backside so that he went crashing through the front door.

Lowerson and Yates were crossing the street when they saw Wentworth spill out of the doorway, and began rushing forward to prevent his escape, before realising that things were very much in hand.

"Should we—?" Yates wondered.

But Lowerson shook his head, knowing that Ryan was still in command of himself.

"He knows when to stop," he said. "He's teaching the bastard a lesson that's long overdue."

CHAPTER 40

All staff who were present on site at Northumbria Police Headquarters received word of an impending arrival, and promptly shut down their computers to turn out en masse. They lined the entrance foyer all the way down to the custody suite, waiting silently to greet the man who had sullied all that they worked to uphold each day. Then, as Ryan strongarmed him across the tarmac and inside the building, they turned their backs on Daniel Wentworth; one by one, he saw their heads turn away from him, their silent dismissal more painful than he could ever have imagined. If they saw his bloodied face, they thought it a small price to pay for all he had inflicted upon others, and all they had yet to discover.

After Ryan deposited him in a holding cell and made his way back, each of those people turned around again and began to clap, until the sound was a roar throughout the corridors. He didn't stop to talk, but carried on walking, eager to reunite a mother with her daughter.

As he rounded the corridor, he was intercepted by the Chief Constable.

Ryan came to attention, clasping his hands behind his back.

"Ma'am."

"A word, please, Ryan."

He stepped into her office, where he found Lowerson and Yates already waiting for him, MacKenzie having excused herself to look after Achara and ensure she was taken directly to see her mother, at the hospital.

"I heard you brought in DCI Wentworth," she said, leaning back against her desk. "Can you explain how he came by his injuries?"

Ryan opened his mouth, but Lowerson was quicker.

"I can, ma'am. When we arrived at the scene, we observed DCI Wentworth attempting to escape the target address via the front door," he said. "Unfortunately, Wentworth seemed to trip down the stairs in his haste. DCI Ryan was on hand to intercept, and used reasonable force to prevent any flight risk."

"Is that also your recollection, Yates?"

"Yes, ma'am," she said, without hesitation.

She pushed back from the desk to approach Ryan, who hadn't said a single word.

"It looks as though congratulations are in order," she said, and held out her hand to shake his. When he took it, she turned it over and glanced pointedly at his torn knuckles, then back at his face.

"Good work," she said. "Dismissed."

Lawana thought it was a dream.

She saw Achara in the doorway and wondered if it was a mirage, but then the vision moved, running towards her with arms outstretched, crying tears of joy.

My baby, she thought. *My baby girl.*

She took the girl's face in her hands and saw the bruising at her neck, saw the hurt hidden behind her eyes, and knew there would be a reckoning.

But she was alive.

They were both alive, and that was all that mattered. Wounds could mend, scars could heal, and so could hearts.

She looked across to the other woman who remained in the doorway, and smiled.

"Thank you," she said, in careful English.

"Mai pen rai," MacKenzie replied, in broken Thai. There was no need to thank her.

It was all part of the service.

"You're tellin' me I missed a good fight?"

Phillips was incensed, but eager for more details of who'd thrown what punch, and when.

"Did he go for the body, or give the bloke a few jabs to the head?"

MacKenzie added a splash of milk to their tea, and rolled her eyes heavenward.

"Frank, I'm not a sports commentator," she said. "How should I know where he hit him? All I can say is, he did a thorough job, and you'd have been proud."

Phillips leaned back against the sofa and nodded, like a proud uncle.

"Aye, well, I taught the lad all he knows, o' course," he said, modestly.

"Mm hmm," she said, settling herself beside him.

"You might not be able to look the other way, when you take that DCS job," Phillips said, suddenly. "Would you dish out a disciplinary?"

MacKenzie took a sip of her tea, then cupped it in her hands.

"Perhaps, if I took the job," she said. "But I'm not going to."

He looked at her, his face a comical mask of surprise.

"Eh? Why ever not? There's nobody who could do that job better than you."

She smiled, and gave him a peck on the cheek, for that.

"Thanks, love, but it's not that. Working on this case the past few days, I realised something Ryan must have realised a long time ago," she said. "I don't want to sit behind a desk. I don't want to miss moments like that, tonight—"

"Oh, go on, rub it in," he grumbled.

"You know what I mean," she said. "I'd have to be satisfied with reading a report, or hearing the news second hand. I'd never be the one to witness the busts, or to see a mother's joy at being reunited with her daughter."

That was a memory she knew would remain with her, for many years to come.

"I'm not ready to give up those moments, Frank. Not for any amount of money or prestige."

Phillips took her hand in his, and raised it to his lips.

"You know that, if you'd wanted it, I'd have done everything I could to help," he said. "I'd have been cheering you on, every step of the way."

"I know, Frank, and I love you for it."

"And, in the interests of full disclosure, you know a little part of me would've got a thrill out of being with the boss lady."

MacKenzie jabbed a finger against his chest.

"I've got news for you, Frank Phillips. You're already with the boss lady."

The smile he gave her was pure mischief. "Fancy some hot chocolate?"

She gave him a long-suffering look.

"I may be many things, but I'm not bloody superwoman. I'm gonna need a bacon sarnie and a foot rub, before I'm ready for any hot chocolate."

Jack and Mel were curled up on the sofa with the cat at their feet, unwinding after a long day, when there came a knock at the front door.

"Wonder who that is?" Jack said, noting the time was almost nine o'clock.

When he opened the door, he found Ryan standing there.

"Ryan! Come on in," he said, stepping back to allow his friend to enter. "Did I forget something at the office?"

Ryan shook his head, and wondered whether he should have called ahead. He thought the news he had to impart was best given in person but, now it came to it, he hoped he'd made the right call.

"Jack, something important's come up—"

There was no time to issue a warning before Mel stuck her head around the living room door, and smiled.

"Hello! D'you fancy a cuppa?"

"No, thanks Mel. I won't stay long."

"Anything wrong?" she asked, growing concerned at the odd expression on his face.

It was…

It was the kind of expression he used when he was speaking to the families of victims, she realised.

A chill ran up her spine, and she wrapped her arms around herself.

"What's this all about?" Jack said.

But, it was to Mel that Ryan addressed himself.

"I received an e-mail alert, as I was on my way home," he said quietly. "I didn't think this was something that could wait until the morning, so I turned around and came here. I hope I've done the right thing."

"You're scaring us now, mate," Lowerson said, with a forced laugh. "What did the e-mail say?"

Ryan cleared his throat.

"When Lawana was brought into the hospital, I asked the hospital not to clean her hands or feet, because I wanted her body swabbed for DNA," he said. "The results of those swabs came back, along with a single match to another DNA record we already have on file."

A dull ringing began in her ears, and Mel put a hand on the wall, to brace herself.

"Tell me."

"The DNA we extracted from the blood sample recovered from Lawana's body is a 98.6% match to the DNA sample found in the hair follicle recovered from your sister's body."

She'd waited so long, Mel thought. So long.

"Do you have a name?"

Ryan shook his head.

"I'm sorry," he said. "The sample is unidentified. But, Mel, this time, we have a witness. She's cooperative, and she might be able to help us."

He was right, she thought. It was more than they'd ever had before.

"I hope I did the right thing, in telling you."

Mel's eyes glistened, and she simply nodded.

"You don't—you couldn't understand what this means to me."

"I think I do," Ryan said softly, remembering his own sibling. "You've waited a long time to bring your sister's killer to justice, and now, you might be one step closer."

"It may lead to nothing," she said.

Ryan shook his head.

"Never give up, Mel. There's always hope, in everything."

With that, he left them to it, and made his way back to his own family, a more humble man than when he'd left them, that morning.

AUTHOR'S NOTE

The Rock is my eighteenth DCI Ryan novel and, though my books have covered difficult subject matter in the past, I found this was one of the hardest to write and release upon the world—not least because we suffered a bereavement on the cusp of the book's original publication date. Nonetheless, trafficking of women is something I have wanted to incorporate into one of my storylines for a long time, and it was merely a case of waiting for the right inspiration to come along. It is a complex subject matter to distil into a single novel but, ultimately, the purpose of my story is to celebrate the tenacity of the human spirit; as in all my books, there is darkness and light. As we all know, happy endings do not always happen in real life, but there are people working hard every day to be good people and good neighbours. It is to them that this book is dedicated, because they are the glue that holds all else together, and inspire the rest of us.

LJ ROSS
February 2021

DCI Ryan will return in

BAMBURGH

A DCI RYAN MYSTERY

Turn the page for an exclusive sneak peek...

BAMBURGH – PROLOGUE

June, 2007

Newcastle upon Tyne

Gemma heard raucous laughter coming from the direction of her sister's bedroom.

She looked up from where she'd been studying a textbook covering advanced mathematics for A-Level students, mildly irritated. Technically, she wasn't due to start the course until the new term began in September, but she liked to be prepared.

Goody-Goody Gemma, her sister called her…amongst other things.

More laughter filtered across the hall and, if she'd been more confident, she'd have set aside her book and gone to find out what was so funny, but she knew Melanie wouldn't welcome the intrusion. It wasn't that she and her sister didn't love one another, they were just polar opposites—despite having been born only a minute apart, with identical features. Where she was quiet and studious, Mel was vivacious and worked just hard enough to get by without their parents having to cut off her allowance. Where she kept her hair long and wore minimal make-up, Mel had recently cut hers into a shorter style she knew their mother hated. Mel never lacked friends, or boyfriends, whereas she…

Gemma sighed.

Between sports practice, schoolwork and helping at the local animal shelter, there never seemed to be any time left for boys or make-up or…well, fun.

She heard the bedroom door open across the hall and, a moment later, hers swung open without so much as a cursory knock.

"I'm going out," Mel declared, leaning her slim body against the doorframe. "Mum and Dad aren't back until tomorrow, but I need to know you won't rat me out when they get home—okay?"

Gemma looked down at her book, to hide sudden tears.

"I've never told them about any of the other times, have I?"

Melanie heard the note in her sister's voice and felt a stab of guilt. It was true that Gem never squealed, but there was always the possibility her innate honesty would lead her to do the worst of all things when it came to dealing with their overbearing parents: tell the truth.

"Okay, cool," she said, in bored tones.

Gemma looked up again, and her eyes were drawn to Melanie's risqué attire, which consisted of a black miniskirt barely larger than a belt, fishnet tights with knee-high boots, and a red 'boob tube' style top that left her midriff bare to the summer winds. To complete the look, she'd applied a liberal layer of make-up and any number of bangles and rings that jangled every time she moved.

"Dad would never let you go out in that," she said, with the ghost of a smile.

Mel grinned.

"Why d'you think I'm wearing it?" she said, with a flick of her new fringe, and then cast her eyes over Gemma's simple jeans and t-shirt combo. "You should try getting your legs out, some time. They could probably use the vitamin D."

Gemma thought of the contents of her wardrobe and wondered whether she even owned a skirt or a pair of shorts that still fit. She should probably go shopping for some new clothes, but she wouldn't know where to start.

Her eyes slid over to where her sister still hovered in the doorway. "What is it?" she asked.

Mel shrugged. "I'm down to my last tenner," she admitted. "I need to borrow a few quid—I'll pay you back."

It wasn't the first time Gemma had subbed her sister's lifestyle; in fact, it was an almost weekly occurrence. Yet, this time, she hesitated.

"It isn't as if you need it," Mel pressed. "You never go out."

Gemma looked up sharply.

No, she thought. She didn't.

She came to a sudden decision. "I'll lend you the money," she said slowly. "But, this time, I'm coming with you."

Melanie laughed harshly. "You must be kidding. Goody-Goody Gemma underage drinking? Going clubbing? You'd be breaking the law, you know…"

There was a challenge in her voice, and Gemma heard it. "Don't call me that," she snapped. "I might not like the same things as you, but that doesn't mean I don't know how to have a good time. You aren't the only one who can wear a miniskirt—or maybe you're worried I'll look better in one?"

Melanie's eyes widened—not in offence, but in newfound respect.

"All right," she said. "You're on. What are you going to wear? You can't go out clubbing looking like that."

Gemma tipped up her chin. "I'm lending you beer money," she said. "You can lend me one of your skirts."

Melanie laughed, and folded her arms across her chest. "You won't like it," she decided.

"I'll be the judge of that," Gemma argued, and went off to raid her sister's wardrobe.

As it happened, Melanie was right.

Gemma didn't like the skirt.

More accurately, the dress, which was a skin-tight electric-blue sheath that clung to her body in all the right places. Paired with long, curled hair and heels she could scarcely walk in, let alone dance in, she felt like a Barbie doll—all stiff limbs and frozen features.

"It isn't too late to go back," Melanie told her, as they made their way from the train station towards the bright lights of the city centre. Her friends trailed behind them, already half-cut after a session drinking the cheap corner-shop booze they'd bought and consumed in her room.

"I'm fine," Gemma lied.

Some sense of common decency compelled Melanie to convey a simple truth. "You look...really good," she said.

Gemma shot her a surprised glance. "Thanks...so do you."

And Melanie did, in her own way. Not everybody could pull off charcoal eyeshadow without looking like they'd suffered a black eye.

"Where are we going, anyway?"

"The Boat," Mel replied.

Gemma gave her a blank look.

"It's a party boat called the Tuxedo Princess, moored on the Tyne," she explained, with a roll of her eyes. "Most people call it 'The Boat'. It has a revolving dance floor and a few different rooms playing all kinds of music, but mostly dance stuff or R 'n' B. Best of all, a tenner gets you inside with free drinks all night."

"A tenner?" Gemma queried. "That seems...cheap."

"Yeah! Great, isn't it?"

Gemma thought privately that there must be a catch somewhere...perhaps they watered down the drinks—which wouldn't be such a bad thing, in her case.

"The options are pretty limited," Melanie admitted. "A few of the bouncers at the other clubs know we're not eighteen, so they won't let us in."

"I thought everywhere had to check ID?"

Mel's smile held a touch of condescension.

"Yeah, maybe they're supposed to, but they don't," she said. "They're always a lot more lenient with the girls, anyway. All you have to do is spin some sob story about forgetting your provisional licence at home, and they wave you inside."

"What if they don't believe me?" Gemma wondered aloud, and could only hope they turned her away so that she could go home and rest her weary feet.

Fate was not kind to Gemma that night, nor any other night that followed.

The two overweight, pigeon-chested men who stood like sentries at either side of The Boat's entrance cast an appreciative glance over the young woman in the bright blue cocktail dress and evidently decided she would be a decorative asset to its interior, so didn't bother with trifling things like identity checks. The other young woman who, upon closer inspection, bore a strong resemblance to her fine-boned sister, was also granted admittance since she had a nice pair of legs too.

As for the rest of their cohort, they flashed a set of fake ID cards and avoided eye contact, which did the trick, no questions asked.

The small party made their way along the gangplank and onto the boat, which had probably seen better days as far as marine vessels went, but for a sixteen-year-old girl who'd never stepped inside a club before, it was a floating palace of colour and sound. The air was hot and carried a heavy scent of body odour and methane, offset by a layer of cigarette smoke. A nationwide smoking ban was due to come into effect but, until then, clubbers continued to puff on their little white sticks and shoved all thoughts of cancer or passive smoking out of their minds for a few short hours.

"What d'you think?" Mel asked, raising her voice to a shout, so that she could be heard above the thumping notes of Voodoo Child.

Gemma looked around at the gyrating bodies of men and women. "It's…loud," she decided.

Melanie slung an arm around her sister's shoulders, feeling a rare moment of kinship.

"Your ears'll be ringing in the morning!" She laughed, and then tugged her in the direction of the bar to claim their first 'free' drink.

Dancing in a circle with Melanie and her friends, laughing with them while sipping an over-sweet alcopop in a dubious, radioactive shade of bright green, Gemma felt she was part of a tribe for the first time in her young life. Finally, a barrier had been breached; a wall between her and Melanie had fallen away, and the two girls were almost giddy with delight.

Gemma couldn't have known she had only a few, precious hours left to enjoy it.

Melanie couldn't have known it, either; and, in the long years that followed, would berate herself for not telling her sister the words she longed to say above all else…

That she loved her.

Available to buy now!

LOVE READING?

JOIN THE CLUB...

Join the LJ Ross Book Club to connect with a thriving community of fellow book lovers! To receive a free monthly newsletter with exclusive author interviews and giveaways, sign up at www.ljrossauthor.com or follow the LJ Ross Book Club on social media:

f @LJRossAuthor

◎ @ljross_author

ABOUT THE AUTHOR

LJ Ross is an international bestselling author known for her atmospheric mystery and thriller novels, including the DCI Ryan series which has sold over 12 million copies worldwide. Her debut novel *Holy Island* published in 2015 and reached number one in the Amazon UK and Australian digital charts. Louise has since released over thirty novels, most of which have been UK number one digital bestsellers. She is also the creator of the bestselling Dr Alexander Gregory series and the Summer Suspense series. Louise is a keen philanthropist and proud to support numerous non-profit programmes in addition to founding the Lindisfarne Prize for Crime Fiction, the Northern Photography Prize and the Northern Film Prize.

Born in Northumberland, England, she studied Law at King's College, University of London, then abroad in Florence and Paris, and worked as a lawyer before pursuing her dream to write. She lives with her family in Northumberland.

If you would like to get in touch with LJ Ross on social media, please scan the QR code below – she would love to hear from you!

Discover the 24th novel in the DCI Ryan series...

New for 2026

If you enjoyed this book, why not try the bestselling Alexander Gregory Thrillers by LJ Ross?

Atmospheric thrillers featuring forensic psychiatrist and criminal profiler Dr Alexander Gregory. Loved by readers for the fast-moving and page-turning plots, international locations and shocking twists, with psychology adding fascinating depth to the stories.

**Discover now the bestselling
Summer Suspense series from LJ Ross**

Suspense and mystery are peppered with romance and humour in these fast-paced thrillers set amidst the beautiful landscapes of Cornwall